J. Kenner (aka Julie Kenner) is the *New York Times*, *USA Today*, *Publishers Weekly*, *Wall Street Journal*, and No. 1 internationally bestselling author of over seventy novels, novellas, and short stories in a variety of genres.

Though known primarily for her award-winning and internationally bestselling erotic romances (including the Stark and Most Wanted series) that have reached as high as No. 2 on the *New York Times* bestseller list, Kenner has been writing full-time for over a decade in a variety of genres, including paranormal and contemporary romance, 'chicklit' suspense, urban fantasy, and paranormal mommy lit.

Kenner has been praised by *Publishers Weekly* as an author with a 'flair for dialogue and eccentric characterizations' and by *Romantic Times* for having 'cornered the market on sinfully attractive, dominant antiheroes and the women who swoon for them.' A four-time finalist for Romance Writers of America's prestigious RITA award, Kenner took home the first RITA trophy awarded in the category of erotic romance in 2014 for her novel, *Claim Me* (book two of her Stark Trilogy). Her books have sold well over a million copies and are published in over twenty countries.

Visit her online at www.juliekenner.com to learn more about her and her other pen names, and to get a peek at what she's working on. Or connect with her through www.facebook.com/JKennerBooks or via Twitter @juliekenner.

By J. Kenner

The Stark Series
Release Me
Claim Me
Complete Me

The Stark Ever After Novellas
Take Me (e-novella)
Have Me (e-novella)
Play My Game (e-novella)
Seduce Me (e-novella)
Unwrap Me (e-novella)
Deepest Kiss (e-novella)

The Stark International Series
Say My Name
On My Knees
Under My Skin

The S.I.N. Series
Dirtiest Secret
Hottest Mess
Sweetest Taboo

The Most Wanted Series
Wanted
Heated
Ignited

JKENNER

DIRTIEST *Secret*

headline
ETERNAL

Published by arrangement with Bantam Books,
an imprint of Random House,
a division of Penguin Random House LLC, New York.

This book contains an excerpt from the forthcoming book
Hottest Mess by J. Kenner. This excerpt has been set for this edition
only and may not reflect the final content of the forthcoming edition.

First published in Great Britain in 2016
by HEADLINE ETERNAL
An imprint of HEADLINE PUBLISHING GROUP

1

Cataloguing in Publication Data is available from the British Library

ISBN 978 1 4722 3898 6

Offset in 11.44/14.62 pt Minion Pro by Jouve (UK)

Printed and bound in Great Britain by CPI Group (UK) Ltd, Croydon, CR0 4YY

Headline's policy is to use papers that are natural, renewable and recyclable
products and made from wood grown in well-managed forests and other
controlled sources. The logging and manufacturing processes are expected
to conform to the environmental regulations of the country of origin.

HEADLINE PUBLISHING GROUP
An Hachette UK Company
Carmelite House
50 Victoria Embankment
London EC4Y 0DZ

www.headlineeternal.com
www.headline.co.uk
www.hachette.co.uk

acknowledgments

Writing a book is a solitary business. Sure, an author can call up a friend to bounce an idea or ask a spouse to read over a paragraph. He or she can trade pages, brainstorm with other authors, or participate in writing sprints. And, yes, s/he can pop over to social media for the necessary water cooler moments. Ultimately, though, writing a book is about sitting in a chair with fingers on a keyboard, getting lost in an imaginary world, hanging out with imaginary people, and trying to convince those sometimes obstinate made-up folks to let you spill their souls onto the page.

Contrary to the writing side, the publishing part of getting a book to readers is not solitary at all. And I'm so grateful for the wonderful group of folks that I work with to get my books out into the world. Amazing and talented folks such as Shauna Summers, Gina Wachtel, Sarah Murphy, Matt Schwartz, Jess Bonet, Alex Coumbis, Kelly Chian, Scott Shannon, and Sue Grimshaw, not to mention the copy editors, proofreaders, sales and marketing folks, the brilliant team in the art department, and everyone else at Bantam. And, of course, the amazing people I work with outside of my publisher, including my agent Kevan Lyon, KP and Dani at Inkslinger, the Kenner Krew, my fabulous assistant Melissa, and my husband and partner, Don. Hugs, kisses, and chocolate chip cookies to you all!

DIRTIEST *Secret*

If I could change it, I would. The wanting him. The craving him.

I close my eyes at night and touch myself, imagining it is him. His hands stroking me. His fingers penetrating me.

I do this, and I hate myself. Because my desire isn't warm and soft, but twisted and wild and wrong.

We destroyed each other, he and I. Even now, after so many years, we're still cracked and broken.

And broken we'll remain, because without the other, we can never be whole. And yet we can never be together. Not again. Not like that.

Our desire has teeth, after all. We survived once, just barely.

But push our luck, and it just might swallow us whole. . . .

The King of Fuck

Even by Southampton standards, the party at the nine-thousand-square-foot mansion on Meadow Lane reeked of extravagance.

Grammy Award–winning artists performed on an outdoor stage that had been set up on the lush lawn that flowed from the main house to the tennis courts. Celebrities hobnobbed with models who flirted with Wall Street tycoons who discussed stock prices with tech gurus and old-money academics, all while sampling fine scotch and the season's chicest gin. Colored lights illuminated the grotto-style pool, upon which nude models floated lazily on air mattresses, their bodies used by artisan sushi chefs as presentation platters for epicurean delights.

Each female guest received a Hermès Birkin bag and each male received a limited edition Hublot watch, and the exclamations of delight—from both the men and the women—rivaled the boom of the fireworks that exploded over Shinnecock Bay at precisely ten P.M., perfectly timed to distract the guests from the bustle of the staff switching out the dinner buffet for the spread of desserts, coffee, and liqueurs.

No expense had been spared, no desire or craving or indulgence overlooked. Nothing had been left to chance, and every person in attendance agreed that the party was the Must Attend event of the season, if not of the year. Hell, if not of the decade.

Everyone who was anyone was there, under the stars on the four acre lot on Billionaires' Row.

Everyone, that is, except the billionaire who was actually hosting the party. And speculation as to where he was, what he was doing, and who he was doing it with ripped through the well-liquored and gossip-hungry crowd like wildfire in a windstorm.

"No idea where he could have disappeared off to, but I'd bet good money he's not pining away in solitude," said a reed-thin man with salt-and-pepper hair and an expression that suggested disapproval but was most likely envy.

"I swear I came five times," a perky blonde announced to her best friend in the kind of stage whisper designed to attract attention. "The man's a master in bed."

"He's got a shrewd head for business, that one," said a Wall Street trader, "but no sense of propriety where his cock is concerned."

"Oh, honey, no. He's not relationship material." A brunette celebrating a recently inked modeling contract shivered as if reliving a moment of ecstasy. "He's like fine chocolate. Meant to be savored in very limited quantities. But so damn good when you have it."

"More power to him if he can grab that much pussy." A hipster with beard stubble and a man-bun wiped his wire-rimmed glasses clean with his shirttail. "But why the fuck does he have to be so blatant about it?"

"All of my friends have had him." The petite redhead who

pulled in a six figure wife bonus smiled slowly, and the flash of her green eyes suggested that she was the cat and he was the delicious cream. "But I'm the only one of us to enjoy a second helping."

"All your friends?"

"How much pussy?"

"At least half the women here tonight. Maybe more."

"Man, don't even ask that. Just trust me. Dallas Sykes is the King of Fuck. You and me? Mere mortals like us can't even compare."

Three floors above the partygoers, in a room with a window overlooking the Atlantic Ocean, Dallas Sykes sucked hard on the clit of the lithe blonde who sat on his face and writhed with pre-orgasmic pleasure. The blonde's cries of "yes, yes!" mingled with the throaty moans of delight coming from the curvaceous redhead who straddled his waist while he finger-fucked her hard and deep.

They'd surrendered to him, these women, and the knowledge that they were his tonight—for tenderness, for torment—cut through him. A wicked aphrodisiac with an edge as sharp as steel, and at least as savage.

He was drunk—on sex, on scotch, on submission. And right then, all he wanted was to get lost in pleasure. To let all the rest of the shit just melt away.

"Please." The redhead's muscles clenched tight around his fingers, and a tremor ran through his body, his need for release now so potent that it crossed the line into pain. "I'm so close, Dallas. I want you inside me. Now. Oh, god, please. Now."

He could barely understand her words, lost as they were in the wet sounds of his mouth on the blonde's sweet pussy. But he heard enough, and in one wild, rough movement, he rolled the girl above him to the side, so that she stretched and trembled on the bed, her nipples hard and her pussy slick and open and inviting.

Dallas felt his body tighten with need. With desire. But only for release. He didn't want either of these women. Not really. Their company, yes. The escape they offered, sure. But them?

Neither was the woman he craved. Neither was the girl who had both saved and destroyed him. The woman he wanted.

The woman he could never have.

And so instead he sought pleasure and passion in the violent rapture of hard, hot sex.

"Sit back," he said to the blonde as he pushed away his dark thoughts and regrets. He reached for the crystal highball glass and downed the last of the Glenmorangie, relishing the way it burned his throat and buzzed his head. "Back against the headboard. Legs spread wide."

She nodded, moving eagerly to obey as he urged the redhead off his waist. "Fuck me," the redhead begged. Her green eyes flashed, her expression pleading. Her lips were swollen, her skin flushed. She smelled of sex, and the scent—so familiar, so dangerous, so goddamned compelling—made him even harder. "I want you to fuck me." Her words were a pout—a plea—and Dallas almost smiled in response.

Almost, but not quite.

Instead he lifted a brow. "Want? Baby, this isn't about what you want. This is about what you need."

"Then I need you to fuck me."

His lips twitched. He liked a woman who knew her own mind, that was for damn sure. And the redhead truly amused him. He'd plucked her from the crowd downstairs because he'd liked the way she'd filled out the flirty black dress that was now crumpled in a heap on his bedroom floor. That, and the fact he happened to know that she had a cousin who worked for a government official in Bogotá, and that connection might prove handy one day.

As for the blonde, Dallas had no particular agenda with her. But he appreciated her limber little body and quiet obedience. Right now, she was sitting exactly as he'd told her, her legs wide apart and wonderfully vulnerable. She wasn't moving a muscle, but the beat of her pulse in her throat telegraphed her excitement at least as much as her tight nipples and hot, wet pussy.

He met the redhead's flashing green eyes, then nodded toward the blonde. "You want to get fucked. I want to watch. And I promise you, she wants to do whatever I say. Sounds like a perfect recipe, don't you think?"

The redhead dragged her polished white teeth over her lower lip. "I've never—"

"But you will. Tonight." He met her eyes. "For me."

She licked her lips as he slid off the bed and stood. She was still sitting, her knees pressed into the mattress as she sat back on her heels. He leaned forward, then took her in a long, slow kiss. She tasted of strawberries and innocence. He wanted to devour the first; he wanted to erase the second. "Hook your legs around her waist and kiss her deep. Suck her tits. Touch her however you want to. But she's going to fuck you with her fingers while you and I both imagine it's my cock. And, baby? You're going to come harder for me than you've ever come for anyone."

"And you?"

He could hear the tremor of excitement in her voice and knew that he had her. "I'll be right here," he said as he took her hand and urged her toward the blonde, who was flushed pink with anticipation. He moved behind the redhead, cupping her breasts as she put her legs around the blonde's waist, then he squeezed her nipples hard as the blonde's fingers slid into her core.

Pressed against her back, he could feel every tremor of pleasure, every quickening in her pulse. And as she started to shake with a series of little convulsions, he slid his hand between her legs from behind, dipping his fingers into her wet pussy. As he did, his hand brushed up against the blonde's, whose sensual moan shot straight to his cock.

Next, he slid his now-slick finger up to tease the redhead's ass as she bucked against him, her body clearly on fire from this dual assault. "Dallas," she moaned as her body shook with release. "Oh, god, Dallas, this is so fucked up."

"That's the way I like it, baby," he said. "That's the only way I play."

It was true. He liked his sex dirty. Wild. He wanted to be reminded of who he was. What he'd become.

The King of Fuck. He'd heard what they all called him, and he had to appreciate how apt—and ironic—the moniker was. Because god knew he was fucked up. His whole goddamn life was an act. A facade.

He was damaged goods. As broken as a man could be. But he'd turned that shit around. Claimed it. Made it his own.

Maybe he would never again have the woman he craved in his arms, but if that was his reality, he was going to damn sure make the most of it.

With his free hand he reached down to stroke his cock. The sensation of his sex-slicked palm moving rhythmically over the steel of his erection mingled with the wild, almost feral sounds of the two women. He closed his eyes, imagining another place. Another woman.

He thought of her. He thought of Jane.

But not like this. Not fucked up. Not like a goddamn evening's entertainment, as fungible as a night at the movies and at least as unimportant.

Except everything was fucked up. Him, most of all.

Goddammit. He needed to shut it down. These thoughts. These wishes.

All these damn regrets.

The sharp trill of his cellphone startled him from his

thoughts, and he slid back away from the redhead who cried out in protest.

"Sorry, baby." His voice was tense, his chest tight. "That's the one ringtone I always answer." He grabbed his phone off the bedside table, lightly brushing both women's skin before turning his back to them and taking the call.

"Tell me," he demanded, expecting the worst. His best friend, Liam Foster, wasn't due to report in until the next morning. If he was calling now, it meant something had happened.

"It's all good, man," Liam said, his voice as close to excited as his military training would allow.

"The child?" Dallas had sent his team to Shanghai to recover the eight-year-old son of a Chinese diplomat who'd been kidnapped ten days prior.

"Fine," Liam assured him. "Dehydrated. Malnourished. Scared. But he's back with his family, and physically, he should make a full recovery."

Physically, Dallas thought, the word sounding vile in his head. Because that wasn't all of it, was it? Not even close.

He shoved the thoughts aside, forcing himself to focus. "Then why are you—"

"Because the German asshole who grabbed him tried to trade freedom for intel. He knows, Dallas. This dickwad Mueller knows who the sixth kidnapper was."

The words were simple. The impact on Dallas wasn't. His blood turned to fire. The room turned hot and red. He wanted to beat the shit out of the sixth man. He wanted to curl up into a ball and cry.

He wanted to finally know the truth.

There had been two in charge of the six fucks who had snatched them—and surely this sixth man could identify his employers. First, there'd been the main guy who sat back, keeping his hands clean, but who was dirtier than all of them. That man lived in Dallas's memory only as hints and impressions.

He'd been smart. He'd kept his distance. But he'd been the puppeteer, the one who'd hired the six and pulled all the strings.

Dallas and Jane had come to think of him as the Jailer, and he'd spoken directly to Dallas only twice. He'd told Dallas that he deserved it all—every moment of agony, every pang of fear, every prick of humiliation.

And then there was the Woman. She was supposed to feed and tend to Dallas and Jane, but instead she brought pain and fear along with a twisted darkness and a bone-deep shame that hadn't faded even after Dallas was free of the confinement of those mildewed walls.

But he wasn't fifteen anymore. He wasn't locked in the dark, tortured and hungry and helpless.

He might be damaged goods, but he had money and power and he knew how to wield both like a goddamn medieval mace.

"We're getting close to ending this thing," Liam said. "We use this douchebag's intel to grab the sixth. We interrogate him. Get him to tell us who hired him. It's the last puzzle piece, Dallas. We get that, and you can finally say that it's over."

Dallas closed his eyes and drew in a breath, soaking in the words. Liam was wrong, of course. It would never really be over. But he couldn't deny the anticipation that was building in him. The fantasy that he really could end this.

For himself.

For his sanity.

But most of all, for Jane.

2

Once Upon a Time

Seventeen Years Ago

"You're a bloody git, you know that right?" Quince Radcliffe leaned casually against the doorframe as Dallas hurried to shove his feet into his sneakers. He'd already pulled on a pair of threadbare jeans, having stripped out of the sweatpants he'd been wearing as he laid in bed reading Nietzsche instead of working on tomorrow's calculus assignment. He'd tackle the five problems in the morning; tonight, he was too engrossed in *Thus Spake Zarathustra*. Or he had been until he'd gotten her call.

"Dean Phelps is going to have your head on a pike."

"I'm pretty sure that would violate at least a dozen school rules." Dallas turned in a circle as he spoke, scowling at the room in general as he searched for a clean shirt. He was fifteen years old and knew how to do his own laundry, but that didn't mean he bothered very often.

He found a faded black T-shirt under the small, book-covered desk. He yanked it up, sniffed it, then pulled it over his head. He took another sniff, then hoisted it up so that he could reach his underarms with the deodorant. No time now for a shower, and he regretted not bothering earlier.

"Fine," Quince said. "Whatever. But if you get caught . . ."

Dallas pressed his hand to his heart as his suitemate trailed off. "Oh, Quince, I didn't know you cared."

Quince narrowed his eyes, then slowly turned his hand until his middle finger was displayed. Dallas barked out a laugh. "Quit worrying. We're just going to hang out for a few hours. I'll be careful. You'll cover for me. And no one will know I'm gone."

They better not, because although Dallas wouldn't admit it out loud, Quince was right. He was taking a hell of a risk. His dad had pulled serious strings and forked over serious dough to get him into St. Anthony's, one of the most prestigious boarding schools in Europe, if not the world. At the time, Dallas had been royally pissed—and he sure as hell hadn't wanted to be shipped off from the States to the UK—but now, after a year, he had to admit he liked it here.

Or, he had to admit it to himself—he wasn't about to tell Eli and Lisa the truth. Not yet. Maybe not ever. He loved his parents. He did. But there was always that thing between them. That distance. Maybe because he knew too much about who he was and where he came from. Maybe kids weren't meant to know the truth about themselves. Maybe they just couldn't handle it.

He thought of Nietzsche's favorite motto: *Become what you are.* And he thought of his own corollary: Figure out what the fuck you are before you start to become it. Not to mention who you are.

Well, he was trying, wasn't he?

He'd been working hard, playing by the rules. More or less,

anyway. Doing all the shit he was supposed to. He couldn't take back the months of drugs and stealing cars and sneaking out at night and generally acting like a fucking asshole, but he could stay here, do the work, and become the man he wanted to be. The man he knew he could be.

Any other night, he would have stayed in and studied.

Or, more accurately, he would have stayed in, amused himself with books or videogames, then spent ten or fifteen minutes before class finishing his homework or studying for a test.

Not tonight.

Tonight, she was here.

Tonight, Jane had called from the station. "I took the train from London. Everyone thinks I'm spending the night at my friend Donna's, the one who moved to London last year when her dad took the job at the embassy." Her words spilled from her, fast and furious, as if she had to get them out before she lost her nerve. "But I'm not with Donna. I'm here. And I really want to see you tonight. You know. Before it gets crazy. Before it's more than just us. So I'm coming. Right now. And I don't care if you think I shouldn't. I'm coming, and you can't say no."

She was coming; she was really coming.

And, of course, he couldn't say no.

"Don't go," Quince said as he peered out the window toward the canopy of a nearby willow tree and the common area below. "I've got a bad feeling."

Dallas patted his back pocket to make sure his wallet was there. "Give it up, man. I'm going. I mean, come on. What's the worst that can happen?"

Quince turned to face Dallas, and as he did the moonlight through the willow's fronds cast shadows on his face. "Oh, gee, let's think. Expulsion?"

"As much money as my dad pumps into this place? I don't think so." The words came easily, but he didn't really believe them. Despite the family fortune, Eli Sykes had to fight to get Dallas admitted to the Academy. Apparently Dallas wasn't the model of decorum that the school usually accepted. And it wouldn't take much for Phelps and the administrative board to decide they should never have caved in the first place.

Didn't matter. Even if it meant living at home and getting his damn GED, he'd do it. He'd sneak out.

He had to see her.

"You'll cover for me?"

The shadows moved over Quince's face. "I still don't like it. It's going to get all fucked up."

"Q, come on, man. Back me up here."

Quince sighed. "Fuck. You know I will."

Dallas flashed a wide grin—the one that would put him on the cover of *GQ* and *Esquire* in later years. A decadent, knowing smile that promised sin and redemption all wrapped up together.

"I owe you big-time," Dallas said.

"Hell, yeah, you do." Quince cocked his head toward the window again. "She's down there. Go. And for god's sake do it quietly."

He'd had plenty of practice sneaking down the back stairs of Lancaster Hall, and Dallas was out of the room, down the corridor, and through the fire escape door in less than three minutes. He hesitated just long enough to make sure none of the guys with too-tight neckties and sticks up their asses had reattached the alarm trigger, but all stayed quiet.

He crept through the moon-dappled dark, through the shadows casting patterns on the damp ground. A small tributary of the Thames ran through the school property, dividing the common area between Lancaster and Wellington Halls. Jane had never been here, but he knew where she would be.

Hadn't he written her enough emails describing the campus and where he liked to go to sit, to think?

And, yes, to curse the fact that the girl he wanted—the girl he loved—was the one girl he couldn't have.

The path curved to reveal the bench. It was plain enough, the paint faded from years of exposure to the elements despite the limited shelter provided by a majestic oak that was undoubtedly older than the school that had been founded three centuries ago.

He hurried toward it, his chest tight. *She wasn't there.* Had she changed her mind? Surely she hadn't changed her mind.

Then the shadows near the bank of the river shifted, and there she was, just standing there looking out at the ghostly reflection of the moon on the water. Her back was to him, and he stood perfectly still. But she must have heard him. Or maybe she just sensed him.

She turned. And when she smiled it was like the rest of the world just fell away.

He took a step toward her, and then another and another until they were standing only a breath apart.

He reached for her, and she did the same, but both pulled back the second their fingers touched.

Her mouth quirked into an embarrassed smile, and she dropped her gaze.

The moment turned awkward, and he didn't know how to erase the thick unease that seemed to fill the air between them. All he knew was her. All he wanted was to touch her, hold her.

He wanted to kiss her, wild and hot, and so much deeper than the one gentle kiss they'd shared over a year ago. And, dammit, he didn't care if it was wrong. He wanted it. Wanted her.

He always had.

But there were promises between them. And so he held his arms firm to his sides, forcing himself not to move. Not to reach out. Not to touch despite the need that curled through him, a longing so intense and pure and strong that he didn't understand how it could be wrong. More, he didn't understand how he was able to resist.

"Jane."

She looked up, but still didn't quite meet his eyes. "I know. But—" She cut herself off and her shoulders rose and fell. He held his breath, hoping she was less strong than he was, because if she capitulated, then he would, too.

He should have known better, and when she lifted her head and finally met his eyes, the awkwardness was gone. There was no uncertainty. No embarrassment. He saw only resolution. And regret.

"I had to see you," she said. What she meant was, "The most we can have is to see each other."

"I know," he said. "Before everyone gets here. I get it." One more day of classes and then it was spring break. His parents were in London, his father accompanied by his key staff members and their families. The plan was that Dallas and his mom, Lisa, would travel to Oxford. Dallas might only be fifteen, but his grades and test scores were such that he had a good chance of being admitted, and the various appointments his parents had lined up all but filled his short vacation.

While Lisa and Dallas did Oxford, Eli, his father, would stay in London and visit the new Sykes department store that had opened last year. And since Jane was doing an afterschool internship in the marketing department through her private school back in the States, she'd be in London with Eli while Dallas was in Oxford.

If they were going to see each other alone, now was the time.

Thank god she'd called. He wished to hell he'd had the nerve to call her first.

"I'm glad you came," he said. "I'm so damn glad you came."

Her smile reached her eyes, making her already beautiful face radiant. She'd always been a pretty girl, but she was fifteen now, too, just a few months younger than him, and she was growing into a stunning woman. She wore her dark hair long and parted simply in the middle so that it cascaded to her shoulders, so lustrous that it shone in the moonlight. Her brown eyes were wide, and her eyebrows angled slightly, giving her an expression of permanent amusement, as if she saw how much the world was askew even if no one else did. Her pale skin was luminous and though her face was round, her stunning cheekbones added an air of runway model elegance to an otherwise girl-next-door visage.

All in all, she was perfection. But it was her mouth that caught and held his attention. Her lips that he dreamed about. That he wanted to touch. That he wanted to taste. He imagined the heat of her mouth pressed against his, the softness—and he felt himself get hard in response.

He dropped his eyes, hoping she couldn't see the evidence of how much he wanted her. He was still a virgin and pretty damn inexperienced, too. But he could fantasize well enough, and right then his mind was churning with the scent of her, the feel of her, warm and naked against him, and—

Shit. Stop.

He drew in a breath and forced himself to think of non-sexual things. Calculus would be good. Or statistics.

He shuffled his feet, then looked back up at her. "So, um, did you walk from the train station?"

She shook her head, her gaze mostly on the ground, too. God, weren't they a pair? "I took a cab. I—I wanted to get here as fast as I could."

The words lit a fire inside him. "Yeah? I'm glad." He exhaled loudly. "Right. Um, what do you want to do?"

He was looking at her as he asked the question, and even in

the darkness, he could see the blush rise on her cheeks. His insides twisted, and his cock that had calmed down at the thought of differential equations stiffened again.

Man, they were so screwed. They were both so damn screwed.

"I saw a flier in the common room about a midnight concert in the park," he said quickly. "It's probably totally lame, but that'll just make it more fun. Some guys doing covers of Beatles songs to celebrate the somethingth anniversary of some album or other."

She laughed. "Music is so not your thing."

"But it's yours."

Her sweet smile just about gutted him. "Yeah. It is." She dragged her teeth over her lower lip and his pants were suddenly way, way too small. "And it does sound lame." She took a step toward him, then nudged his foot gently with her toe. "And I think it'll be a blast."

"Yeah?"

She nodded, looking excited and happy, as if they were about to set out on a grand adventure.

He started to lead the way toward the park, and she fell in step beside him. The silence was comfortable, and right then there was nothing he'd rather be doing, and no one he'd rather be doing it with. So naturally, he had to go and toss cold water all over their good time. "Eli's going to shit a brick if he finds out you're here."

"He's the one who decided to bring an intern to London with him," she said lightly. But then she grimaced as she shot him a quick glance. "I don't think I've ever heard you call him Dad."

He cocked his head as he looked at her. "Do you think I should? Never mind," he said before she could answer. "It's not important. I shouldn't have even said anything."

She studied him as if trying to figure out what he wasn't saying. "Are you still pissed he sent you over here? I mean, boarding school is one thing, but he shipped you halfway around the world."

He shook his head. "If you tell him this, I'll deny it, but no. I was fucked up back home. All that shit I was into. And—"

He cut himself off, then shoved his hands in his pockets. He'd been about to say, "You." And he really didn't want to go there.

She came to a stop, taking his hand and making him halt beside her. "Am I making it worse? Should I not have come?"

"God no." The words came out too fast, revealed too much. He looked down at their joined hands, then back up at her. "Maybe," he whispered.

Their eyes met, and even though it was a cliché, he *felt* it. The power. The heat. Right there between them, and so much stronger than them both.

"Dallas." That was all she said, and he didn't know if she spoke in protest or invitation.

He wasn't about to wait to find out.

In one motion, he leaned in, his palm cupping the back of her neck as his mouth closed over hers. She tasted like honey. She tasted like home. And when she gasped, the sound opening her mouth just a bit more, he took advantage, exploring with his tongue. Tasting, *taking,* deepening the kiss until there was nothing separating them. Not air, not skin, not the goddamn world that said they shouldn't be doing this. That it was crazy.

That it was wrong.

Breathless, he drew away, suddenly afraid that he'd taken too much. That he'd pushed too hard.

Terrified that when she opened her eyes he'd see fear. Or, worse, regret.

But her face was soft, her pale skin almost angelic in the

moonlight, and when she opened her eyes and looked at him, he saw his own desire reflected right back at him in her wide, brown eyes.

"We shouldn't," he whispered.

"I know."

Neither one of them moved. They stood there, only inches apart, and he could feel her breath on his face, minty and tantalizing. He thought he could hear her heart beat; he was certain she must be able to hear his.

And then, as if pulled together by the weight of their connection, they stepped forward at the exact same time. Mouths came together, hard and fast. Hands grappled, fingers stroked. He'd never been so hard in his life, even in all the times he'd laid in bed, his hand down his briefs as he imagined her. For a moment, mortification washed over him, but then she made the softest noise, and he realized that it was his name. And it was so full of need and desire, that it was a wonder he didn't come right then.

"Jane, I—" He didn't know what he'd intended to say, but it didn't matter. His words were cut short by her scream, sharp as a knife and brutally short.

Someone had her. Two black-clad men stood on either side of Jane, their faces hidden by ski masks, their grips locked tight on her arms as they dragged her away from him, her head lolling to one side.

"No!" It seemed like forever before he bellowed the word, before he tried to lunge forward to help her. But he realized in the moment that not even seconds had passed. And that he couldn't help her—he couldn't even help himself. He was caught, too.

He struggled, managing to break the hold on his left arm, and he spun to the right, trying to get free—trying to see whatever he could before they grabbed him again and held him fast.

Four men. Two holding him. Two standing beside them, one with a cloth in his hand.

And then the two who had Jane.

That made six men altogether. Six attackers.

Six kidnappers.

Six, he repeated to himself as he fought fear, battling it down and forcing himself to listen to their voices. To judge height and weight. To study their eyes and fight the terror and *think* even as the man with the cloth came toward him and pressed the chloroform-soaked rag over his mouth and nose.

And as the world faded from beneath Dallas, he held fast to his mental image of those six dead men. Because that's what they were. *Dead.* No matter how long it took for him to make them that way.

3

Deliverance

"Dallas? Shit, man, you still there?"

He realized with a start he'd been clutching his phone as if it was the sixth kidnapper's neck, so tight it was a wonder the damn thing didn't shatter in his hand. Irritated, he pushed his memories aside and focused.

"Where are you calling from?"

"The jet," Liam said. "In transit from Berlin to the safe house in Mendoza."

Dallas frowned, wondering how Argentina played into the mix as he walked naked onto the balcony so that he could speak freely. Below, at the party, a few women nudged each other as they looked up and pointed. He barely noticed them. "I'm listening."

"Mueller pulled the kid from his private school in Shanghai and managed to smuggle him to Europe. We finally caught up to the bastard in Germany. Quince did a fine job getting him talking," he added. Dallas's boarding school roommate was now officially an MI6 operative and unofficially one of the core members of Deliverance, the handpicked covert team that Dallas had put together over a decade ago.

He'd started the organization as a way to find—and destroy—his tormentors, but it had evolved into so much more than that. Deliverance had become a powerful force, doing whatever was necessary to rescue kidnapped children, and its select, discreet clientele found their way to the organization through word of mouth and referrals. And no client could point the way back to Dallas or any of the other men.

Deliverance pushed the envelope, it bent the law. Most of all, it got the job done.

Dallas took a breath, just to ensure that his voice was steady. "So you're saying that Mueller told you about the sixth?"

"In the course of the interrogation, yes. We went through the standard questions to determine if he knew anything about your kidnapping."

"And he did."

"The son of a bitch is a goddamn rabid dog in service to anyone with a tasty enough bone."

"Any reason to believe that Mueller was actually involved?" It was a stretch, but maybe Mueller was the sixth, now trying to obfuscate the facts. Hell, maybe he was the goddamn Jailer.

"Negative," Liam said. "He was serving time in a German prison for six months before and eighteen months after you two were snatched. He wasn't involved—I'd bet my reputation on it. But he's still a source, and potentially a key one. He knew about your kidnapping and a shit ton of others."

Dallas clenched his fists as he drew a breath, forcing down the fury that threatened to overwhelm him. "How'd he know about mine? Word on the street?"

If so, that was interesting in and of itself. Eli Sykes had kept the kidnapping secret—he hadn't told anyone except his closest circle. Not the press, not the FBI, not Scotland Yard. Nobody. He'd taken matters into his own hands, hiring mercenaries, arranging to pay ransom. And above all, keeping it very, very quiet.

To this day, Dallas wasn't sure if his father had done too much or too little. Yes, he and Jane had gotten free. But the price they'd paid was brutal.

Even now, almost two decades later, the world believed that Dallas Sykes, the screwup son of billionaire retailer Eli Sykes, had left his posh boarding school for a stint in a private hospital. As for Jane, the press hadn't noted her disappearance at all, and she'd kept it a closely held secret.

When he'd recruited for Deliverance, Dallas had told his team the truth. They needed to understand the purpose, after all. Besides, each man had his own reason for being dedicated to Deliverance and its mission. More important, Dallas knew he could trust them.

But even they knew only about the kidnapping. They didn't know the worst of what happened inside those dank, locked rooms. Hell, not even Jane knew the worst of it, and she'd been in the dark with him.

"Not street gossip," Liam confirmed. "Our target's name is Silas Ortega. He was the sixth, and he's got a rep for doing pretty much anything if the pay is right. He's also got a rep for keeping his mouth shut, but I guess the thrill of bragging about how he screwed over the great Eli Sykes was just too much even for him. He told someone, and Mueller got wind."

"And he traded that intel to us."

"You could say that," Liam said.

A thin smile touched his lips, but Dallas didn't press. He didn't need to hear what Quince had done to Mueller in order to extract the intel. Every member of Deliverance did what they had to do. Hell, the group was named for its mission to fuck the bad guys in the ass.

"And check this out," Liam added, a hint of excitement coloring his businesslike presentation. "Mueller said Ortega would have known who he was working for. Said he isn't the kind of asshole who works for a voice with a bank account. He's loyal and he's brutal and he's damn effective, but he only works for people he knows."

Hope curled in Dallas's gut. Not soft, but as hard and as harsh as the bastard he was chasing. The bastard who Ortega could identify. "And Ortega's in Argentina?"

"He owns a vineyard there. Security's intense, but Quince is on it, and Noah's providing support from the States."

"And Antonio?" Dallas asked, referring to the fifth and final member of Deliverance.

"Wrapping things up in China."

Dallas nodded as he considered the options. "Move in at the first opportunity. Grab Ortega and get Quince working him. Eventually, we'll want to get him across the border to Valparaiso. We can smuggle him out on a cargo ship." Deliverance had solid connections in the Chilean port city.

"Already on it. Looks like the Minerva's scheduled to arrive soon," he said, referring to a freighter they'd hired before. "I'll let you know when—oh, hell. Hang on."

"What?"

"Give me a second," Liam said with unmistakable irritation.

He clicked the call to mute, leaving Dallas frustrated but not concerned. Most likely Antonio was reporting in. Or maybe Noah and Quince had learned something about Ortega's compound. Whatever it was, Liam would handle it. Quickly. Efficiently.

Dallas stepped back inside, paying no attention to the women still on the bed. Instead, he moved the other direction, crossing to the polished mahogany bookcase, one shelf of which doubled as a bar. He put down the phone as he poured himself a fresh glass of scotch, then forced himself to not give in to the voice in his head that was telling him that this was it. That the chase was almost over.

He closed his eyes and let the scattered memories of the last seventeen years roll over him.

They'd been close to finding the Jailer before. Five times, actually. It had taken years, but they'd managed to track the other five kidnappers, and each time, Dallas had hoped that he would get a solid lead on the son of a bitch who'd masterminded his kidnapping.

But each lead had proved useless. Two had died before the team even identified them, one of cancer and the other during a prison fight. Another shot himself in the head rather than let himself get captured. The other two had been hired by the cancer victim, and neither one knew a damn thing about the Jailer or the Woman. They'd provided a few tidbits of intel about their three dead co-conspirators, but so far that intel had led nowhere. And they'd known nothing about the sixth.

Now it looked like Deliverance had a real shot at finding number six. But Dallas knew only too well that it could all go wrong. And if this lead crapped out, too, then the odds of finding out who had taken him and Jane dwindled to almost zero.

Fuck.

Dallas slammed back the scotch, then pressed his palms against the warm wood as he leaned forward, his head down as he let the whiskey burn through him. But there wasn't enough alcohol in the world to burn out his memories. Or his regrets.

He sighed as he straightened, his gaze going automatically to one of the books on the shelf, just at eye level. Its white dust jacket was scuffed at the top and bottom of the spine, the result of being taken from and returned to the shelf almost daily.

He pulled it out now and looked at the cover. A yellow school bus. Crime scene tape. The title spray-painted like graffiti across the bus—*The Price of Ransom*.

And the author's name larger than life along the bottom: Jane Martin.

He and Jane rarely saw each other alone anymore. For the last four months, she'd been living in LA, so their lack of contact made sense. But even when they were both in the same city, there were no dinners, no quick jaunts to lunch, and very few calls and texts. They still had a common circle, sure, but their encounters weren't frequent—or satisfying.

Ever since the kidnapping, they'd kept their distance from each other. Emotionally and physically. He missed her—he missed her so damn much—but he also knew this was the best way. The only way.

Apart, they were safe.

Together, they were combustible.

But that didn't mean he didn't see her, didn't keep tabs on where she was and what she was doing. And didn't he pull out this very book almost daily, turn it over in his hand, and trace his fingertips over her author photo? Didn't he turn on the television and watch the morning shows on which she was so often a guest, especially now that *The Price of Ransom* was the talk of Hollywood?

The story was perfect for a book, and for a movie. Five third-graders kidnapped in their school bus. Missing over a month, and then almost killed when a rescue attempt by a group of incompetent mercenaries went horribly wrong.

And no one suspected that the author was a kidnapping victim herself. That the empathy with which she wrote was utterly genuine.

Not one interviewer asked if the project was personal to Jane. If it was catharsis. If it was therapy.

But it was, of course.

Dallas understood that, even if nobody else did.

He understood something else, too. He knew Jane's face too

well not to see it. The slightest tightening in her cheek when a reporter would talk about how, ultimately, the kids were ransomed.

How they got their happy ending.

Just thinking about it made Dallas want to laugh almost as much as it made him want to cry.

The kids had survived, sure.

So had Dallas and Jane.

But that didn't make for a happy ending. Dallas knew that. Jane knew it.

And he was sure those tortured little kids knew it, too.

He started to reach once more for the scotch, and then purposefully pulled his hand away. The night had turned interesting, and he wanted a clear head, no matter how tempting it might be to wash away his thoughts of Jane.

He left his glass on the bookshelf and turned back to face the room. As he did, he saw that the blonde had crept to the edge of the bed while the redhead had actually slipped off and was now walking toward him, her hips swaying provocatively.

He fought the urge to tell them both to get dressed and go home, because right now, he really wasn't in the mood.

But that didn't matter anymore. The Dallas Sykes he'd created was always in the mood. That was the illusion, after all.

He held up a finger to stop the redhead's approach, then cocked his head in disapproval at her irritated expression. "Back on the bed," he said to her. "Your mouth. Her pussy."

When she didn't obey immediately, he moved to stand in front of her. He heard her ragged, excited breathing, and the last of his reticence faded. He wanted this. Hell, he needed it.

Not her, but her willingness. Her obedience.

He slipped his hand between her legs and thrust two fingers inside her. She moaned, a low, passionate sound that rumbled through him, satisfying that deep, primal need.

"Now," he said. "Until I tell you to stop."

She licked her lips, her eyes glassy with desire. Then she moved naked back to the bed and buried her face enthusiastically between the waiting blonde's legs.

A trill of satisfaction cut through him, as he marveled at how eagerly she obeyed. How enthusiastically. They were in his control. As much as Mueller was. As much as the sixth kidnapper soon would be.

"Sorry to interrupt your party," Liam said dryly, when Dallas had retrieved his phone and returned to the balcony.

"Fuck you," he said amiably.

"Appreciate the offer, man, but I think you've already got your hands full."

Dallas almost laughed. Of all his friends, Liam was the one who most understood what Dallas did—and why. But although they'd been on the verge of celebrating just moments before, now the tide had shifted. Despite the attempt at levity, Dallas could hear the hard edge in Liam's voice. The frustration. Even defeat.

He didn't want to ask, but he wasn't one to hide from bad news. "Tell me," he demanded.

"Apparently our Mr. Ortega is on a lot of people's shit lists. Noah just confirmed that local officials are looking for him, along with Interpol and, quite possibly, the FBI."

Dallas bit out a curse.

"It gets worse," Liam continued. "Turns out he's been missing for the last thirty-six hours."

"Someone else got to him first." The words were hard to get out past the tightness in his chest. All this time—all this work—and they missed the prize by just over a day? Fuck that.

"And it's not hard to figure what card he'll play if he's trying to catch a deal."

"Not hard at all," Dallas agreed. "Spill the beans about a

Sykes kidnapping—say that he's certain one happened and that he can point to the man behind it—and Ortega will be some agency's goddamn hero with immunity and a pat on the back."

Inside the bedroom, one of the women screamed in ecstasy.

On the balcony, Dallas closed his eyes in anguish.

He took a deep breath, then raked his fingers through his sex-mussed hair, trying to find some solution. Some magic fix. "If any one of those agencies finds out who the Jailer is before we do . . ."

He didn't bother to finish the sentence. He didn't need to.

For seventeen years, he'd been fantasizing about killing the motherfucker who'd taken him and Jane. He'd sweated. He'd planned. He'd researched and interviewed and wrangled and prayed. And when he'd had every piece in place, he'd started recruiting.

Now Deliverance was in full swing, and at the height of its power. A lean, nimble machine. A goddamn thing of beauty that thrived in the shadows.

Deliverance was about rescuing victims, yes. But it was also about justice. It was also about revenge. And everyone on the team knew that. There was no sugarcoating. No happy trappings of procedure and rules. Deliverance found the bad guys. And it did what was necessary to punish them and bring the victims home.

If the government located the Jailer, it would prosecute.

Deliverance, however, would execute.

And no power on earth could talk Dallas out of that. He'd dreamed of the moment. Played it out in his mind over and over.

The fantasy had sustained him during the long nights in the dark. During the endless hours when he'd been alone. When he'd been tormented. Shamed.

When, ultimately, he'd been broken.

Dallas knew damn well that watching the Jailer and the Woman die wouldn't restore what he and Jane had lost, wouldn't heal what was broken. But it would be just. It would be good.

Maybe it would even be enough.

"I'm coming," Dallas said. "If Ortega's still at large, I'm working the hunt with you. And if you manage to grab him, I want to interrogate the son of a bitch myself."

"Dammit, Dallas—"

"And if the government already has Ortega in custody, then we're going to the mat with Mueller. I want to squeeze every bit of information out of him. What he knows about Ortega. What jobs he's pulled, what cigarettes he's smoked. What women he's fucked."

He paced, his mind whirring. "I want to know everything and everyone. There's no way Ortega bragged only once about a Sykes kidnapping. I want to know what else he said, and who he said it to. I want to know what he knows, and I want to follow where it leads."

"So, what? You're saying you need to be onsite? That you don't trust me to lead this team? That you don't think Quince and Noah and Antonio can do the job? That's bullshit, and you know it."

"Dammit, Liam. Deliverance is—"

"Yours," his friend interrupted. "You think I don't know that? That we all don't know that? Deliverance is your baby, your mission. It's your show, Dallas, and we've all been playing by your rules. Playing to the goddamn letter. And it's been working. But there's a reason you're a ghost in this organization, man, you know that. Hell, you laid down the law yourself. And the first rule is that nobody breaks the damn rules."

Dallas's smile was thin. "I'm not breaking anything. It's just that now the rules have changed." He mentally calculated how long it would take for him to get to the airport in his helicopter and then to Argentina in his jet. "I'll be there in thirteen hours.

And if Ortega's not in a room when I get there, then Mueller damn well better be."

Liam knew better than to argue. "Twelve hours," he countered. "Twelve, or we start without you."

"You won't," Dallas said, because he knew not only his men but his friends. "And I'll be there."

Dallas was pulling on black jeans when the bedroom door opened and Archie entered, holding a leather duffel.

On the bed, the two women—still there, still hopeful—scrambled under the sheet. It wasn't necessary. Archie Shaw had spent forty-five of his almost seventy years serving the Sykes family, and the last ten with Dallas exclusively. He was manservant, valet, confessor, and friend all rolled into one.

Archie's piercing gray eyes had seen it all. But he never shared; he never gossiped. And Dallas trusted him completely.

"I've packed clothes and toiletries for a week," he said, depositing the bag at Dallas's feet. "And another letter arrived this afternoon." He held out the now-familiar pale blue envelope. Even from across the room, Dallas knew that his name and address would be on a white label, the letters printed by an old-fashioned dot-matrix printer. There would be no return address.

"Shall I dispose of it?" Archie asked when Dallas said nothing.

"No." Right now, the letters were an irritation. But he could anticipate the sender becoming dangerous. "Put it in my bag. I'll deal with it later." So far, he'd been unable to glean even the slightest hint of the sender's identity. But one day, the sender would make a mistake. That letter could be the one.

Archie's expression didn't change, though Dallas knew that he, too, was frustrated by these anonymous taunts that had started arriving a little over a year ago. He simply nodded and slipped the envelope into one of the duffel's side pockets. "Anything else?"

"Ms. West called."

Dallas pinched the bridge of his nose. He'd dated Adele West for about six months after her divorce, if dating was what you'd call it. Honestly, Dallas didn't know what to call it other than fucked up.

But that was all over—and he sure as hell didn't want to talk to her now. "Leave the message on my desk. I'll deal with it when I get back."

"Of course, sir." He glanced at his watch. "The helicopter will be here in twenty minutes."

"What would I do without you?"

"Wear the same clothes for days on end, presumably. At least this way I'm providing a service to not only you, but to Mr. Foster and the others as well."

"I haven't gone a day without changing clothes since college." He pressed a hand affectionately on Archie's shoulder. "And thank you."

"Shall I tell your guests that you had to attend to an emergency at work?"

"Hell no. Tell them I got a call from—who's that actress who just got slammed on the internet for making a sex tape?—tell them I'm off to see her. Wouldn't want to start repairing the reputation I've worked so hard to destroy."

"In that case, I wish you godspeed and success. And, Dallas," he added, his voice thick with emotion as he strayed from his usual formality, "come back in one piece."

Dallas's grin was both quick and cocky, but his voice was serious. "I will. I always do."

Archie looked like he was about to argue, and Dallas understood why. Sure, Dallas had participated in missions before—but like Liam had pointed out, Dallas had always been a ghost.

He'd worked behind the scenes in research and analysis. He acted as a front man and liaison, interacting with potential clients by pretending to know someone who knew someone who could help them get their loved ones back quietly. He frequented high end parties across the globe, both to gather intel and to plant listening devices or perform other necessary tasks. And on the rare occasion when he did go on a raid, he was suited up, so there was no chance that anyone would recognize his very well-publicized face.

This time was different. This time he wanted to be in the room. He wanted to look Mueller and Ortega in the eye until he was certain he'd extracted every bit of information that he could from the bastards.

And then he wanted to see them dead. Ortega, who'd been the fulcrum that had pushed Dallas's own life over the edge. And Mueller, who'd blithely snatched so many children—who'd ripped their lives and the lives of their families apart for no more reason than the money and the thrill.

"I'll be careful," Dallas said slowly, his eyes on his old friend. "But I'll get the job done."

Archie tilted his head in acquiescence, like a parent resigned to sending a son off to war. It was an apt metaphor. If anyone knew more than Dallas about Deliverance and its inherent dangers, it was Archie. Stoic, serious, self-possessed Archie, who worked behind the scenes, juggling Dallas's household, his daily life, and all manner of his extracurricular activities, both the real and the spectacle.

As for the latter, Archie nodded toward the far side of the room and at the women who still lounged in Dallas's bed, looking both curious and impatient. "I'll leave you to finish getting dressed and say your goodbyes." He glanced at his watch. "Be on the helipad in fifteen minutes." He didn't wait for Dallas's acknowledgment. Instead he turned, crossed efficiently to the door, then slipped silently out of the room.

"A helicopter?" The redhead pursed her swollen lips into a pout. "You're really leaving?"

"You were eavesdropping?"

Her mouth curved up impishly. "I guess maybe you should punish me."

"I'll add it to the agenda," he said. "But you're right. I have to leave." He checked his watch. He wanted to be on the pad when the helicopter arrived. He didn't want to waste a moment. "You have my cell number?"

"Of course."

"Text me pictures." He shifted his gaze to the blonde. "Text me very interesting pictures."

He took more pleasure in the blush that crept over both women's faces than he probably should, but what the hell. He wanted what he wanted. And if a bad selfie of those two kissing could get him hard—could get his mind off Jane and where he was going and what he was doing—then he wanted it in his inbox. After all, it was a very long flight to Argentina.

He'd just grabbed a black T-shirt from the back of a chair when he heard the light tap at the door. "Come on in," he called, hoping Archie wasn't going to tell him the 'copter was held up.

But when he looked inquisitively toward the opening door, it wasn't Archie's efficient face that appeared at the threshold—it was Jane's. And in that moment, Dallas's heart stopped beating.

He stood frozen, like a fucking idiot, staring at the door as if he were looking at a ghost. Hell, maybe he was. It was more likely that a specter would grace these halls than this woman who'd once lived there.

She wore only jeans and a pink tank top under a transparent, white blouse. Her lush brown hair was pulled back into a messy ponytail, with a few loose strands framing her face. She wore no makeup, and her brown eyes seemed huge against her pale skin.

She looked frazzled and rushed. She looked stunning. And even after all this time—even after fighting against it every goddamn day—he felt desire curl through him, hot and demanding and far too dangerous.

Her eyes found him almost immediately, and he saw her visibly calm, as if he was exactly what she'd been searching for and all she could ever need.

Her eyes were bright, her smile as fresh as sunshine. And for that moment, time stopped and everything was frozen in possibility.

Then the warmth in her eyes cooled, and her gaze flicked down over his bare chest to where his jeans hung on his hips, still unbuttoned, the fly open to reveal the faded black briefs he wore. He felt his cock—already going hard simply from the sight of her—twitch under her inspection. And he wasn't certain, but he thought he saw two spots of pink touch her cheeks.

She didn't meet his eyes, but quickly turned her head, her attention now going to the bed, and the two naked women who were still there, looking defiantly at her, as if they owned his heart. As if they meant more to him than a diversion.

He watched as she licked her lips, then rolled one shoulder, like a fighter about to enter the ring. When she looked back at him, her eyes were flat. "I didn't realize when I walked through the crowd downstairs that you were having a private party up here, too. I guess I should have. That's what you do now, isn't it? That's what you are?"

"It's what I am," he confirmed, though everything inside him wanted to scream that she wasn't really seeing him. That these women—this life—was only a play in smoke and mirrors. A disguise.

And, yes, a defense against her. Because so long as she looked at him with such contempt and revulsion, they were safe. He'd built a wall around himself because it needed to be built. And like those Chinese peasants who'd found themselves bricked in as they built the Great Wall, he, too, was trapped inside a barrier of his own making.

"It's not who you are." He thought he heard a plea in her voice. "It's what you've let yourself become."

A thousand retorts welled in his mind. He didn't voice any of them. How could he, when every word she said was true? When the only thing she got wrong was that he was playing a role? Calculated and planned. And secret from everyone but those who knew him best. And that was a category in which she no longer fit.

She waited a moment, as if she expected him to contradict her, as any self-respecting man would.

When he remained silent, she made a low scoffing noise and shook her head, and the disappointment he saw in her eyes hurt him more than any harsh words ever could.

"Did you come here to criticize me?" He spoke casually as he walked to the bar, hoping she couldn't see how much simply having her in the same room affected him. "Because honestly, a phone call would have been just fine." He held up a clean glass. "Want one?"

He couldn't read the expression that washed over her face. Disgust? Regret? Didn't matter, anyway. It was replaced quickly enough with the fake, polite smile that every child who grows up in the spotlight learns at an early age. The smile that protects them from the nosy press and pushy outsiders.

And now she was aiming it at him.

God, how far they had fallen.

"I should have called first. Obviously." She ran her palms down her jeans, the only sign that she was agitated. And, frankly, he would have preferred if she'd raged at him. It was this polite, level bullshit that was really pissing him off.

"Jane—" He cut himself off, unsure what to say. And so he said nothing, just reached his hand out and prayed she would take the offering.

She didn't.

Instead, she shook her head, and his gut twisted when he saw tears glisten in her beautiful eyes.

"I made a mistake," she said as she turned for the door. "I should never have come to you."

And then she rushed out the door before he could make a move to stop her.

For a moment, he just stood there like an idiot. Then he started to follow. He had to know what she'd come to say. What had driven her to him after all this time. But the blonde's simple question brought him to a halt.

"Who the hell was that?"

Dallas shoved his hands into his pockets, his back to the women and his eyes clenched shut in protest against the truth. The only truth that mattered. She wasn't his lover, not anymore. He wasn't even sure if she was still his friend.

She was lost to him now in every way that mattered. Every way except one. And that was what he had to keep clear. That was what he had to keep in mind. That one connection that still kept them together as firmly as it kept them apart.

"My sister," he said, the word turning like worms in his gut. "She's my sister."

4

Dangerous Jane

Bastard.

I let the word roll through me, pushing me to move faster, to get out of this house that had once held such happy memories, and away from the boy—now a man—who had once been my everything.

I race down the window-lined hall, ignoring the beauty of the moon-dappled ocean that fills the view to my right. Instead, my head is filled with images of his bed, and of the naked women who shared it. *Women,* as in two of them.

Horny asshole bastard.

He's supposed to be hosting a goddamn party, and instead he's hidden away in his bedroom fucking two women. At least I only saw two. For all I know there was another one hidden in the bathroom, just waiting for him to join her so she could suck his cock, just one more in the pile of women he went through. One more bimbo who would write in her journal that she'd joined that exclusive club and the King of Fuck had impaled her with his golden sword.

I grimace at the image, and at the nickname. I'd heard it for the first time tonight as I'd moved through the party trying to find him or Archie. Since I'd crapped out on both counts—earning myself only stares for my so-not-party-ready outfit—I'd decided to let myself into the residential wing and simply wait for him.

Clearly that wasn't my best decision ever.

I push through the heavy wooden doors that separate the private area of the third floor from the rest of the hall and the landing, then slam them shut behind me, the clicking of the latch underscoring my irritation.

The King of Fuck. Christ, now that I've heard it, the phrase is determined to circle in my head, over and over like an earworm, only far more annoying than the most irritating tune.

It's a ridiculous nickname, not to mention demeaning, but the women who'd whispered it had done so with reverence.

And the worst part isn't even how vulgar and stupid it is.

No, the worst part is the way it made me feel.

Not angry. Not disgusted.

Jealous.

God help me, I'm actually jealous. Because those gossiping bitches had been in his bed. They'd felt his fingers stroking their skin, his mouth brushing their lips.

I recall the shiver that had cut through me when I'd first entered his room and found myself face-to-chest with his well-muscled abs that I had once explored with my fingertips. With my lips.

But that had been a boy's chest, and Dallas was a man now. Hard and lean and utterly beautiful.

Objectively, I'd known that. Didn't I see his picture in the tabloids almost every day? But that was print and pixels. Up close and personal was a wholly different experience. In print, he's stunning. In real life, he's a god, or at least a fallen angel, with power and poise and a defiant confidence.

His hair is the color of caramelized sugar, a rich brown with hints of blond. He wears it short on the sides but longer at the top, and that, along with about three days of beard stubble, gives him the appearance of a man who's just come in from his sailboat—or who's just spent long, lazy hours in bed.

He looks like a man who can run an empire. Who spends millions of dollars on his toys.

He looks like a man who can have any woman he wants, and probably has.

A man who enjoys his life.

A man who has long since forgotten about me.

He'd stood in front of me shamelessly, his fly open, his cock straining against his briefs and the denim as his green eyes flashed like the devil.

I'd wanted to reach for him. So help me, I'd had to pretend that my feet were cemented to the floor. And then I'd turned to look at the women, relying on my anger and frustration to keep me anchored.

He'd touched them. Hell, he'd fucked them.

And dammit all, I wanted that to be me.

Except I don't just want a fuck, I want everything. And he and I both know we can't have it. We'd tasted forbidden fruit seventeen years ago, and we'd paid a heavy price.

I don't have the right to want him. Hell, I don't even have the right to be angry with him for shucking off all his talent and education and hard work in favor of the life of a billionaire playboy asswipe.

But I *am* angry. And I *do* have the right. Because even though we don't share a single drop of blood, we're siblings, by law and by adoption.

We're family.

And that pretty much sums up exactly why he's so fucked up.

For that matter, it sums up why I'm so fucked up, too.

I tell myself that I need to get my shit together and get back to Manhattan, and I'm just about to start down the stairs with that goal in mind when I hear the doors open and Dallas call my name.

For a second, I consider running, but I don't. I stop.

A moment later, he's at my side, and I say a silent *thank you* that he's put on a shirt. His hand closes over my elbow, and in that moment of contact a hundred memories flash like fireworks in my mind. His touch. His kiss. His scent.

I jerk my arm away, and I know he thinks I'm angry. But the truth is far more disturbing—it's self-preservation. I can't bear being touched by him. Or, more accurately, I can't bear his casual touch, when I still crave an intimate one.

"I get why you ran," he says gently. "But why did you come here in the first place?"

For a moment I can only stare at him, shocked into silence by his soothing tone, so like a caress and so unlike what I would expect from Dallas Sykes, the Playboy of the Western World.

I watch as his tender expression hardens in the wake of my silence. "Dammit, Jane. You're the one who crashed my party. If you're expecting an apology, you're not going to get it."

For just a moment I allow myself another prick of jealousy. Because this *is* his house now—our parents transferred the title into Dallas's trust when he turned thirty.

It's not the value of the property that upsets me—my Upper West Side townhouse is equally posh, and I love living in the city.

No, what bothers me is the memories, because this house is filled with them. And now they belong to Dallas alone.

"Pardon me, sir . . ."

At first I only hear Archie's voice. But when I step to the side, I can see him striding down the hall toward us.

"The helicopter is approaching the pad," he says. "You really should hurry if you don't want to—oh! Miss Jane." He inclines his head in greeting, and when he looks up, his face is alight with a pleasure as bright as my own.

His hair has gone completely gray and he's gained a few more wrinkles, but his eyes are still as sharp as ever, and I want to run to him just like I did when I was a little girl and he would sneak cookies into my room well past bedtime.

What the hell.

I fling myself at him and give him a hug, knowing it will embarrass him, but not caring in the slightest. I adore Archie, and I've missed him terribly.

I breathe in the scent of his uniform—mothballs and mint—and then back away feeling more centered than I have since the moment I pulled my cherry-red Aston Martin Vanquish up to the valet stand.

"It's a joy to see you here, miss, isn't it, Mr. Sykes?"

I almost expect him to disagree, but I hear the sincerity in Dallas's voice when he answers, very simply, "Yes. It really is."

For just an instant, our eyes meet, and both our guards are down. I want to just stand there, drinking him in. I want to touch him. More, I want him to touch me.

I shouldn't have come, I think. I should never, ever have come.

"I'll tell the pilot you're running late," Archie says, his crisp, efficient voice completely breaking the spell.

I gasp a little, feeling flustered. Dallas, damn him, looks as cool as he always does.

"Miss Jane," Archie says, "it was lovely to see you."

"You, too," I say sincerely, and then watch as he turns and heads down the stairs.

"Why did you come?" Dallas asks again, and his voice is so flat that I have to wonder if I'd been mistaken. If the desire I saw in his eyes was just an illusion. Or, worse, wishful thinking.

I want to tell him that it doesn't matter, but this is the one thing that I won't lie to him about. We suffered through too much together. And while I may not respect the man he's become, I love the man he could have been.

"I got a call from Bill this morning," I admit, then watch his face for his reaction.

It's not hard to miss. He winces. "Your husband."

"Ex-husband," I remind him. "You know damn well we divorced two years ago." William Martin and I were married for almost three years, which was almost three years too long. I'd known from the first week that saying yes had been a mistake. I'd respected Bill, trusted him. And I think I even loved him on some level. But there wasn't passion, not really, and there was never an *us*.

But I'd been lost for so long, trying to hold together all the various strands of a life that was spinning out of control. Trying to figure out what I needed. How I could heal.

I'd thought having a husband would help. A normal life with a normal family.

I hadn't understood then that *normal* isn't something you can play at. It has to be there at the core. But I'm a long way from normal, and I probably always will be.

"You still keep in touch with him?"

"I divorced him, Dallas," I say. "I didn't banish him."

Not like I banished you. I don't say that aloud, though. Doesn't matter. I know he's thinking the exact same thing.

"Bill Martin was never the man for you," he says, and my simmering anger really starts to boil.

"Really? Did you really just say that? Because at least I tried to move on, to grow up. To find something in my life that mattered, and didn't just sit around mourning what I couldn't have."

"Is that what you think?"

"Honestly, I try not to think about you at all. I saw your potential once. I saw your heart. Now, all I see is bullshit. Now all I see is what the world sees—a class-A fuckup with too much money, too much time, and way too little discretion."

He drags his fingers through his hair, and I see the apology on his face, even before he says, "I'm sorry. He's a good man. I shouldn't have—you threw me off kilter," he admits. That, at least, I know is honest.

"Bill's one of my best research sources," I say and hate that the words sound almost like an apology, as if I have to justify continuing to talk with the man who was once my husband and is now my friend.

"For your books."

"Of course," I say. "What else?"

He doesn't answer. Instead, he takes a step toward me. I take a corresponding step back, and feel the bannister press just below my waist. He doesn't relent, though, and there's nowhere for me to go when he closes the distance until only a few inches remain between us. At six foot four, he has a good eight inches on me, and I'm forced to tilt my head back so that I can see his face. I can smell the scotch on his breath. I can see the way his shirt moves with the beating of his heart, a fast rhythm that matches my own.

I hold tight to the polished rail in defense against the unwelcome urge to reach out and touch him.

"And what the hell could Bill have to say that would send you running to me?" he asks.

I lick my lips, knowing how my words will affect him because I know how much they affected me. "Not here," I say, glancing down the stairs to where some of the partygoers have started to drift up to the second floor. "Not where anyone can overhear."

He studies me for a moment, then nods. He takes my arm, and I try not to react as sparks shoot through me from nothing more than that simple connection. I let him lead me down the hall and into the third floor den, a room that I know so well. It's pristine now. The wooden furniture polished, the silk pillows neatly placed. There's a glass coffee table in front of the sofa, and a basket with logs near the fireplace, even though winter is months away.

It looks neat and tidy and relaxing. Not at all like the place where we used to spread our toy cars all over the floor. Where Liam used to set up his train set, and Dallas and I would tie one of my hated Barbies to the tracks before getting bored and racing our Hot Wheels across the polished-to-a-shine floors.

I sigh deeply as the memories flood back, at the same time both welcome and disturbing.

I remember the trips to this house with my mother, Lisa, and my birth father, Colin West. Eli Sykes and Colin had been fast friends since college, and we used to spend weeks inside these walls, the adults doing their thing, while Liam and I— and later Dallas—played and explored.

I recall with perfect clarity the night that I overheard Archie telling Eli that Donovan, Eli's brother, was dead. Lost at sea after falling off his yacht, apparently the victim of too many pills and booze.

And I can still smell the lemony scent of furniture polish that lingered on the sunny afternoon when I'd first seen Dallas. That was the day his strung-out mother had shoved both the boy and a paternity test at Eli. The test proved that the five-year-old boy was Eli's nephew. And Eli kept him because everything about the woman—including the needle marks on her arms—testified that she wasn't fit to raise him.

I'd been five, too, and I'd come to Eli's house with my parents—Lisa and Colin—for one of our regular vacation weeks. I'd held on tight to both my favorite stuffed bunny and to Liam's hand as we watched the drama play out from our hiding place inside this very room's dumbwaiter.

Mrs. Foster, Liam's mother and the live-in housekeeper, was

summoned to help get Dallas settled. She ushered him out of the den, and Liam and I waited until we were sure the coast was clear to sneak out and go look for this mysterious new boy.

We found him in the bedroom next to the one I always used when my family came for overnight visits, and although Eli had frowned when Liam and I had poked our heads in, Mrs. Foster gestured us into the room. "I know it's not my place to tell you what to do, Mr. Sykes," Helen Foster had said. "But I think some playtime with my Liam and Miss Jane may be just what this boy needs."

Eli had considered her words, then looked earnestly at his nephew. "You'll let Liam or Jane know if you need anything? Food, a bathroom, whatever you want." He'd smoothed Dallas's hair and looked into his eyes. "This is your home now, young man. Do you understand that?"

Dallas barely nodded, and when he looked over at me, I smiled, thinking that he was really, really brave.

After Eli left, Liam had gone and sat on the bed, then put his arm around Dallas like a big brother, his dark skin contrasting against the pale little boy. I stood in front of them both holding Mr. Fluffles, my stuffed bunny, tight in my hands.

"So," Liam said, "do you need anything?"

Dallas just shook his head. He had long brown hair that hung in loose curls over his eyes. His oversize T-shirt was gray, but so was Mr. Fluffles, and I knew that both of them were supposed to be white. The boy looked out of place. Lost and terrified. But when he lifted his head and pushed his hair out of his face, I saw his green eyes and thought they were even more beautiful than my mom's emeralds.

I don't know why I did it, but I thrust Mr. Fluffles into his hands. For a moment, he smiled, so wide and happy that sunshine lit the room. Then it faded as he passed the bunny back to me. "He's yours."

"Friends share," I'd said.

"Are we friends?"

I'd glanced at Liam, and we'd both nodded. "Sure we are," Liam had said.

"Forever," I'd added.

Forever.

The hollow echo of my childhood voice seems to fill this familiar, empty room.

Forever?

I'm not even sure what that means anymore. And I sure as hell don't know if Dallas and I are still friends.

Honestly, I don't know what we are anymore.

"Jane?"

His voice banishes the last of my memories, and I realize that I'd stopped right on the threshold, neither in nor out of this room.

"Are you coming?" He's still holding my arm, and I tug it free. The truth is that I don't want to go in—not all the way. I'm too raw here in this house so close to the man I lost. The man I could never really have.

I plant myself by the door, my back against the bookcases that line three walls of this cozy, familiar room. "I'm fine right here," I say.

Dallas doesn't try to urge me in farther. He must understand my hesitation, and I wonder if his thoughts have wandered to the past with mine.

He silently closes the door, then stands in front of me. "All right," he says. "What is it you couldn't tell me out there?"

"You're familiar with WORR, right?" I ask, grateful to get back on topic and away from my memories.

"Of course."

I'm not surprised. Dallas may have morphed into a guy who does nothing but party, but he's still a kidnap survivor, and I'd be shocked if he wasn't at least tangentially aware of the World Organization for Rescue and Rehabilitation.

It's a private group that consults with and provides investigative support to the FBI, Interpol, and the United Nations Office on Drugs and Crime. Unlike UNODC, which addresses all manner of crimes and terrorist activities, WORR's single-minded focus is on rescuing kidnap victims, and then helping to heal their deep emotional and mental scars.

It's staffed by former police and FBI agents, along with attorneys and mental health professionals, among others. It's an incredibly worthwhile organization that I believe in strongly, and I'm glad to know that Dallas is at least aware of it, and that his knowledge of international events isn't limited to what's premiering this year at Cannes.

"Bill left the US Attorneys' office about a year ago to take a top-level position there." I draw a deep breath and cut to the chase. "Anyway, they just brought a guy in for questioning about the Darcy twins' kidnapping."

Dallas's brows draw together. "The Darcy twins?"

"Yeah. Their kidnapping and rescue is one of the focal points of the new book I'm researching, and Bill and some of the other folks at WORR are giving me a remarkable amount of access." He looks so confused that I elaborate. "You know about the kidnapping, right? Henry Darcy's girls? Dad's done a few deals with him."

"Of course I know the man." His voice is tight. "And I also know that the twins have been home safe for over a year. So what does WORR have to do with the Darcys?"

I wave away the question. "The point is that WORR is working the case with Interpol and they've brought in a suspect. A guy named Ortiz—no, Ortega." I glance at Dallas and see how stiff he's become, and I'm certain he realizes that this ties in to our kidnapping. After all, why else would I be here?

"Bill was interrogating Ortega, and the guy says he wants to cut a deal. Says if they give him immunity, he'll tell everything he knows about a secret kidnapping. A Sykes kidnapping. Dallas," I say, when he just stands there, obviously stunned, "he's one of the six guys who grabbed us, and he says he knows who's behind it all."

I wait for the reaction that I know is coming, because it was my reaction, too. I expect to see hope. The possibility of closure. Of answers.

But I don't see that. Remarkably, he looks angry.

"Dallas?"

He puts his head down and runs his fingers through his hair. "Bill knows we were kidnapped?"

I hesitate, my cheeks burning, as he looks up. "Not we," I say. "You." I lick my lips. "You know that the press was never really satisfied with Dad's statement that you ran away from school and ended up in a hospital. Nobody guessed kidnapping back then, but after this, Bill put it together."

"But not about you. He only knows about me. And you didn't tell him that you were there, too."

"He was talking about you and what was said in the papers. And back then, no one paid attention to me. I went to London with the company, and supposedly that's where I stayed when I didn't return to school. And besides," I add, swallowing the bile that has risen in my throat, "they only kept me for three weeks. They held on to you for four more weeks after they let me go. So—"

"So you were there with the family for anyone who was curious to see," he says. "Yeah, I get that," he adds. "Fuck," he says, and there's no denying the anger with which he spits out the word.

I'm absolutely flabbergasted, and I push off from the bookcase and go to him. I start to take his hand, but pull away at the last second. I can't do it. I can't touch him. I can't comfort him. All I can do is stand there and ask him why.

"I don't get it," I say. "This is good news. Why don't you think this is good news?" I hear my voice rising, and hate myself for it. I've spent seventeen years working to control my emotions. To not slide into weepiness or hysteria. And I'm not about to backslide now. "What the hell is going on in your head?"

"You really never told Bill?" he presses. "Never in all the time you were married told him that you'd been kidnapped? Not in all the time that you were researching your book?"

"I—the book was about those kids on the bus. Not about me. I never—" I lick my lips. "I never saw any reason to tell him."

Dallas just looks at me and nods, and I think he sees more than I want him to. I think he realizes that telling Bill would have brought the man who was legally my husband closer to my heart than I could handle. But more than that, I think Dallas knows that telling Bill would have meant acknowledging how much Dallas and I meant to each other in those cold, dark days. And that wasn't somewhere I was willing to go. Not then.

Not even now.

I stand straighter. "This doesn't have anything to do with what I told Bill before." My voice is firm, and I remind myself that I really don't have to defend my marriage. Especially not to Dallas. "It's about now. It's about this Ortega guy."

"You're right. It is. What's hubby going to do?"

His words are so harsh I have to resist the urge to storm out of the room and leave him to his stupid, confusing anger or jealousy or whatever the hell it is. But I tell myself he's in shock. I waltzed in here when he least expected me, when he'd been partying and drinking and fucking, and when he sure as hell hadn't wanted to see me.

I've gotten in his face and laid a huge new reality on his head. Maybe I wanted him to react differently, but what I wanted or expected isn't really the issue. He's got to deal in his own way. I can handle that. I can respect it.

I just don't get it.

But I try. I take a deep breath and I really do try. "He wants to talk to you," I admit. "And he wants to talk to Dad. He wants to pursue it, of course. There's no statute of limitations on kidnapping. He wants to figure out who did this to you. To us," I add softly, because if this does go forward, I'm going to have to tell Bill the truth. "He wants to find the bastard and lock him away forever."

"That's what you want?" he demands. "You want to dredge all that up again?"

"Dredge?" I repeat. "I don't have to dredge up a goddamn thing." My voice is rising with both anger and frustration. How can he not understand this?

"It's right there at the surface," I continue, "no dredging required. I live with it every single day." A tear escapes, but I don't swipe it away. I just look at him. I just stare, not understanding what's going through his head, this man I thought I knew. "Don't you?" I ask plaintively. "Don't you live with it, too?"

I can't read all the emotions that flash like lightning across his face. But I see the pain, and I regret that I've pushed him.

"Every day," he whispers. "Every minute, every hour." He closes his eyes, and when he opens them again he is looking at me honestly, and for the first time in forever I think that I'm seeing him again—the real Dallas. The man who captured my heart without even trying. The man who was my best friend. And, yes, the love of my life.

"I miss you," he says, so softly and simply that my chest tightens and more tears spill out onto my cheeks.

Without thinking, I step toward him. He stiffens, but he doesn't move. I can see the pain on his face, and I want to touch him—and not just to soothe. And, damn us both, it's clear that he wants to touch me, too.

A sharp twang of anger rises through me—not aimed at him, but at myself. Because I should be able to control this desire. To push it down.

But I can't. I've never been able to. That's why I stay away.

Why our time together is limited to family functions and very rare, unavoidable occasions. And even then, we're careful around each other, as if we are porcelain dolls, each afraid of breaking the other.

Our parents believe our distance is because of our shared pain. That being together for holidays and family events makes the ghosts come back.

But that's not really it. I'm not haunted by pain, but by passion.

I feel denied. I feel cheated. Because what was perfect and right and saved us in the dark is forbidden in the light.

I steel myself against this harsh reality. There are so many things in this world I want, but cannot have.

This man is only one of them.

"I—I just thought you should know. But I have to go now." I turn to leave before I can change my mind. I don't make it. He takes my arm and tugs me back, so that I am right there in front of him and he is holding tight to me, his eyes filled with a wild desire, and so help me I just want to fall into him.

Want to, but can't.

"Jane."

I've always thought that my name was as boring as they come, but on Dallas's lips it's a sensual feast. A caress that slides over me, firing my senses and making my skin tingle.

He leans toward me, and for a moment I am lost, floating free on desire and possibility and the fantasy that this could be real and right. But it can't—I know it can't—and I lurch back, then try to pull my arm free, though he holds me in place. I let out a little gasp as he takes my other arm and yanks me even closer, so that there are only inches between us. So that I can feel his heat. So that I can imagine his touch.

And then, so help me, it's there. He still clutches one arm, but with his other hand, he reaches out and brushes my lower lip. I whimper, wanting this. Hating this.

He slides his fingers down, lightly stroking my neck and making me tremble. My breasts are heavy, my nipples tight, and right then all I want is for him to slide his hands lower and lower until he strokes between my legs and relieves the pressure that is building and building, and will undoubtedly make me explode.

This is what I've longed for. What I've dreamed of. Fantasized about. Fought against.

And I'm tired of fighting. I'm so damned tired. I want to surrender. I want to give in completely.

But I can't. I won't. So long as Dallas is pushing, I have to push back. Because giving in would be a mistake. And there are some mistakes that you can't ever come back from.

I jerk my arm, but he holds fast. "Let me go." I'm desperate now, certain that if I don't get free soon, I'll lose my resolve.

"Why?" he demands. "Because it's wrong? Because you can't stand to be near me after what happened between us? Because it's dangerous?"

"Danger? I welcome danger." I meet his eyes and call on all my strength to rip my arm free. I have to run. I have to go. "I just don't want you."

5

Big Fat Lie

It's a brutal lie, and I hate myself for telling it.

But I hate even more the fact that I have to. Because it has to be true. I *can't* want this man. Forget reality. Forget desire.

Forget the fact that I still dream of him after so much time. That I still remember the way his beard stubble scratched the soft skin of my inner thighs. That I wake up imagining him inside me, his face soft with love and wonder.

Forget that he has never failed to make me laugh. Never failed to understand me.

But we're star-crossed, he and I. Like a living, breathing Shakespeare play. And what I want, I can't have.

But I don't seem to have it in me to truly want anything else.

I'm broken, and I have been for years. It's my reality now, and I'm learning to live with it. To turn the angst and the loss around and make it work for me.

It's not easy, though, and it's worse when we're together, which is why we're together so rarely. Which is why I shouldn't have come.

I sigh, already dreading my great-grandfather's upcoming hundredth birthday celebration—a party for which my mother is going all out since this may well be Poppy's last.

We're having it on Barclay Isle, a private island in the Outer Banks that has been in the Sykes family for generations. It's a big island, but Dallas is coming as well, which means even if it were the size of Greenland, it wouldn't be big enough.

Family gatherings are the worst for me. Seeing him. Feeling the tingle in the air from nothing more than his proximity. I attend, of course. Our family isn't that big, and I would be missed. But I go with an escape plan and I stay only as long as I can endure the tension and fight my building need.

One time our fingers brushed at the dinner table from nothing more erotic than the passing of a bread basket, and I'd been rocked by an unexpected frisson of sensual awareness so powerful I actually gasped.

Fortunately, I also knocked over my wine, which not only camouflaged my reaction but allowed me to escape to the restroom, ostensibly to wash out the stain on my dress. But I hadn't cared a whit about my outfit. All I'd wanted was privacy so that I could stroke myself and relieve the hot, thrumming pressure that was pounding between my legs.

Even now, the memory is wild and vibrant, and I feel that growing, needful ache. *Don't go there,* I think. *Just do* not *go there.*

Easier said than done, but I focus on blocking the past and simply getting the hell out of the house.

I've descended the wide wooden steps to the first floor, and I pause to look back over my shoulder to see if Dallas is following me. But the door to the private hallway is still shut, and there's no sign of the man on the landing.

Honestly, I'm not sure if I'm relieved or disappointed.

I continue across the room, pushing past dozens upon doz-

ens of partygoers who have meandered inside, entering through
the three massive French doors that line the east-facing wall.
The throng makes me tense—I don't know these people, and I
don't like crowds. I keep looking over my shoulder to check my
six the way Liam and all my self-defense instructors have taught
me, even though I know it's stupid. No one at Dallas's party is
going to hurt me. But knowing and believing are two different
things, and I've gotten used to constant vigilance.

I look around the room, finding comfort in noticing the details. The usual furniture has been moved out so as to turn this
room into a dance floor with a DJ in the corner and small round
tables set up around the perimeter. Hired waitstaff move
through the crowd with trays of drinks, and I see dessert sta-
tions set up in all four corners of the massive room where my
friends and I used to practice our middle and high school
cheers.

The dessert tables are themed, and I make a beeline for the
chocolate station, cutting across the dance floor and moving
nimbly to avoid arms and legs and dips and shimmies. I also
avoid the stares I'm getting from more than one guest. I'm quite
certain it's not because they recognize me as Jane Sykes, now
Jane Martin, the daughter of Eli and Lisa Sykes. The sister of
Dallas Sykes. And a bit of a celebrity in her own right, what
with the buzz my book has been getting lately.

No, I'm getting stares not because of who I am, but because
of how I look. Everyone here looks like they walked straight off
a Fashion Week runway, and my jeans, canvas sneakers, and
tank top are hardly blending in, even with the designer blouse
I'd pulled on at the last minute. Not because I'd been trying to
dress up, but because I hadn't wanted to face Dallas in such a
skimpy top.

I tell myself I don't care. After all, the women who stare as I
pass and whisper snide comments about my uncoiffed hair

don't really belong here. I do. I grew up here. I lived here. This is my place, part of my identity.

And that's the problem, isn't it? Because here I am in a house that I love, and all I feel is lost. All I feel is alone.

I draw in a breath and focus on the platters piled high with cupcakes and brownies. I grab a cupcake with chocolate frosting and colored sprinkles, and then take a big, glorious bite. As I do, I notice that I'm the only female who seems to be eating anything not from the alcohol or vegetable food groups.

This doesn't surprise me. I got sucked into the low cal–low carb diet obsession about the time I turned thirteen, but all that ended after the kidnapping. When some sick fuck with a god complex decides to feed you only cat food and water for days on end, your perspective tends to shift.

I'm not a glutton, but I don't deny myself food. Not if I want it. Not ever. For that matter, there are very few pleasures that I deny myself these days, with Dallas being the only notable exception.

With a sigh, I tear myself away from the chocolate station and go through the open French doors. I step onto the flagstone pool deck and into a wonderland of decadent extravagance. Everything from the Grammy Award–winning pop star performing on a newly constructed stage just beyond the decking to the prone naked models who are doubling as sushi platters. *Seriously?*

There are just as many people out here, but the crowd is thinner with more space to spread out. All the guests are dressed to the nines, though many of them sport designer swimwear paired with designer wraps and set off by designer shoes. I've never understood why someone would want to wear heels with a bikini, but if the women currently splayed out on the chaise longues or talking in dark corners with well-suited men are any indication, I'm in a small minority.

I pass the bar on one side and the waterfall end of the pool on the other. The lights are on, set to rotate in a pattern of vibrant colors that not only illuminate the floating nudes but also cast a colorful, shimmering glow over the east side of the house. I watch the dancing lights for a moment, my gaze drifting upward to the last window on the third floor—Dallas's room.

I wonder if he's still in there, or if he's gone to the helicopter already, leaving his two guests alone to engage in their own little orgy of fun.

I roll my eyes at myself, irritated at the direction of my thoughts and the extent of my jealousy.

The truth is, I handled this whole evening poorly. As soon as I realized he was having a party, I should have turned away.

Then again, when isn't Dallas Sykes having a party? According to the tabloids, it seems to be a daily event. And, yes, that simple truth makes me a little surly. Because I miss what we used to have, I really do. And I can't help but wonder if he does, too. He practically said as much to me just now, but was it the truth or just a line? Am I now only one of the many women in his life?

I don't really believe that, and yet I wish I could. I think it would make me hate him.

It would be easier if I hated him.

The far side of the pool is lined with cabanas, and I sit on the teak bench outside the first one and watch the show in front of me. Socialites and wannabes mingling and flirting. Women in huddles with secret smiles—and I know that they're all talking about Dallas.

I glimpse a flash of red hair and see the woman who was in Dallas's bed earlier step through the French doors and onto the patio. Her expression is smug, and from the faces that are now turning in her direction, it's no secret where she's been, and what she's been doing.

There are so many stories about Dallas's escapades. So many rumors, so much gossip. I hadn't wanted to believe they were true, but the more I see, the more I believe.

I want to be disgusted—I *am* disgusted—but I can't escape the uncomfortable truth: I want it to be me.

Except I don't—not really. Because the man I crave doesn't exist anymore, and I don't want the man who goes through women at the same pace he goes through scotch.

Somehow, though, I can't quite believe that the boy I loved turned into the man I see.

Finally, I can't take being there anymore, and so I rise to my feet, planning to head back the way I came, back through the house and out the front door to where I left my car with the valet.

I don't make it.

He's right there, standing just past the edge of the cabana. The women nearby have their eyes on him, but he doesn't even seem aware. Instead, he is looking only at me. And as he starts to walk toward me, my chest starts to hurt, and I realize that I am holding my breath.

I exhale, feeling childish and stupid, and force myself to stand up straight, breathe normally, and not look like I'm cornered and trapped.

"I thought you had to catch a ride," I say, because I don't want him to have the first word.

"I do."

I lift a brow. "Then why are you here?"

He glances around, and for the first time seems to realize that we are being watched. "In here," he says, taking my arm even as he pushes aside the curtain that marks the entrance to the cabana.

There's a daybed inside, and a couple sprawled on top of it. They're fully clothed, but their kiss is deep and passionate, and she is straddling his leg and grinding against him in a sensual rhythm.

I feel my own body heat in response, and I make it a point of looking anywhere but directly at them. Or Dallas.

He clears his throat. "Sorry, folks. I need the room. I've got to talk to my sister."

Sister.

And just like that, the heat that had been spreading through me turns to ice, and I stand there frozen as the couple leaves, clothing askew and not looking the tiniest bit embarrassed.

The cabana has a sliding door that provides more privacy than the curtain, and Dallas closes it now, then leans against it as he looks at me.

"All right," I say, trying to sound casual as I sit on the edge of the daybed. "What do you need to talk about?"

"The Darcy twins," he says, which is about as far as you can get from what I was expecting. I must look as confused as I feel because he presses on. "Why is WORR investigating a resolved kidnapping?"

There are so many ways I could answer that, but I go with the most obvious one. "Why the hell do you care?"

I see a flicker of irritation in his eyes. He's not used to being questioned. That's okay. I'm not, either.

"I'm friends with Henry Darcy," he says. "I was there for him when the girls were taken. And I listened as he talked through his decision to keep the authorities out of it and hire a private team to recover the girls. Just like Dad did," he adds, and I can't help but scoff.

"And that worked out so well."

"The team knew the risk," he counters. "And they were trying to rescue kidnapped children."

"Have you lost your mind?" I don't mean to snap, but I can't help it. "Two of the men Daddy hired ended up dead."

And it was my fault. I should never have said anything. Never told my father and his security team what little I knew.

I'd been warned, hadn't I?

But once I was back in my parents' arms, I'd felt safe again. Safe, yes, but so damn scared for Dallas. They'd convinced me that I had to tell. That I had to give the security team every tidbit of information if we were going to recover Dallas.

So I had. And based on a terrified fifteen-year-old's shredded memories, the team had isolated the target and moved in—and I'd suffered for four long weeks believing that Dallas died in that raid, too.

"That's not the point," he says, as if the fact that I got two men killed doesn't matter. As if it was no big deal that he was tortured and traumatized and starved for another month. "I want to know about WORR. Because I'm damn sure Henry didn't give your ex a call and start chatting."

I almost tell him that it's none of his business, but the fight has gone out of me. I feel numb, and the memories of those long, cold days are too close. I want to finish this conversation. I want to get the hell out of here.

"So you know what happened, obviously. The girls went to Mexico with some friends to celebrate their eighteenth birthdays, and they were snatched. Sold into white slavery to some rich asshole in Mexico City. It's pretty impressive that Henry's hired guns found them," I admit.

"It is," he agrees. "After the first seventy-two hours, the odds of getting those trafficked girls back was slim to none."

"You know the stats," I say.

He eyes me levelly. "I pay attention. Like you, I'm interested in the subject."

I say nothing. The truth is, I've made a career researching and writing about kidnappers and their victims. Dallas ostensibly runs several divisions of the family business. In reality, he spends money, drives fast, and fucks hard. I know why I do what I do. Him, I don't understand.

"So tell me the rest," he urges.

"The asshole who bought them got his neck slashed in the raid," I say flatly. "But the team got the girls home safely. Henry told you he wanted to keep the FBI and Interpol out of it. That's what you said, right?" He nods, and I press on. "Well, that decision got the perp killed instead of punished, and Elaine Darcy is pissed."

"Henry's mother," Dallas says flatly.

"She's right up there with Dad as far as old money goes," I confirm. "And with a former US Attorney in her family, not to mention congressmen and judges, she wasn't too happy that her son decided to go the vigilante route." I shrug. "So she got WORR involved. She wanted to know who else was responsible—that's how they tracked down Ortega."

He runs his fingers through his hair. "Christ."

"I know," I say, nodding. "Henry completely screwed up. Those girls could have been killed in the raid, too. But more than that, she wants to find this vigilante group and shut it down. That's one of WORR's mission statements, you know. To try to stop that kind of rogue activity. And it's why I knew about the investigation even before they had Ortega in custody. And then when Bill told me about the connection to us, it just blew me away."

He looks at me as if I've lost my mind. "You knew about the vigilante team and the Darcy twins first? Before Bill told you about Ortega? How?"

"I told you earlier. It's my next book." I shift on the mattress and pull my feet under me, more comfortable now that we're talking about my work. "It's a broader book than *The Price of Ransom*. That focused solely on the one case, but even as I was writing it, I knew I wanted to explore the dangers of vigilante justice. I mean, the Darcy girls could have died. Just like those kids in that school bus almost died because one of the parents hired that asshole Lionel Benson and his team of arrogant mercenaries."

"You're writing about Benson and his team?" Dallas asks, his voice tight.

I nod. Lionel Benson is a dishonorably discharged ex-Army colonel who funneled his particular talents into the lucrative world of vigilante justice. Unfortunately, he was more interested in earning a buck than he was in making sure that the kids he was supposedly rescuing were safe. When he and his team burst into that warehouse to try to rescue the children that had been in the bus, they focused entirely on the one child whose parents had hired them, and in doing so put the other kids at risk.

The supposed rescuers were battled back by the kidnappers, who ultimately received the ransom payment and released the children. Thankfully, the kidnappers were later apprehended by a team of international agents working with WORR.

At the time I wrote *The Price of Ransom*, no one knew the identity of the vigilante team that almost got those children killed. But about a month ago, after two kids in Nevada died in another purported rescue, Benson's team came to light. One of the team was injured during that raid, and when the FBI moved in—thankfully rescuing the surviving children—they also captured the injured vigilante.

Although Benson's arrest was publicly announced, most of the details from the investigation are still confidential. Even so, Bill told me that the captured man is cooperating in exchange for leniency, and that his testimony led to Benson's capture. The witness also told the investigators that Benson's priority during each and every raid was his bank account first, the safety of the child he'd been hired to rescue second. As far as Benson was concerned, any children without a dollar amount attached were collateral damage.

Fucking bastard.

I hug myself as I think about the similarities between Benson and my father, who'd sent in a team rather than contact the authorities because he was more concerned about making sure the press didn't learn about the kidnapping than Dallas's safety. Benson may have been all about the money, but wasn't my dad just as selfish?

Just thinking about it makes my chest tighten, and I have to breathe deep to fight off what I know is a rising panic attack. Finally, I swallow, then look up to meet Dallas's eyes firmly. I'm calmer, but my voice still hitches as I add softly, "You could have died in that botched raid."

"I'm alive, Jane. I'm standing right here." His words are gentle, but they don't soothe.

"No thanks to Dad and his team, though. You weren't rescued. Worse, whoever took us kept you for four more weeks after they let me go. A month, Dallas. And god only knows what they did to you during that time when you were alone."

I expect him to say something, and when he doesn't, I run my hands nervously over my thighs. I know he doesn't remember what happened after I was freed. Over and over he's told us that it is a blank. A gaping black maw in his memory.

The doctors don't know if that's the result of drugs or trauma-induced amnesia. But the bottom line is that he remembers nothing from the time he woke up without me to the day he was finally released in a London tube station. Sometimes, I think that's for the best.

I remember those weeks, though. I remember every minute. Mostly, I remember the fear that Dallas was dead.

6

Falling

The memories come hard and fast now that I've opened the door, and I hug myself as I remember the shock of fear that had slammed through me the night they'd come to set me free. I'd been awakened roughly from sleep, torn away from the warmth and comfort of Dallas's arms.

I'd cried for him as someone yanked me to my feet, then cuffed my hands behind my back. But he had just laid there, his eyes closed, his body eerily still. I'd screamed, terrified that he was dead, the sound of my cry cut short when the sharp sting of a palm landed against my cheek.

"He stays," the Woman had said, her voice a low whisper behind a mask and veil. She moved toward me from where she'd been standing across the room in the shadows. "You're going."

I shook my head, denying the words. I wanted out—dear god, I wanted out so badly—but not like this. Not without Dallas.

"You tell them nothing." The Jailer spoke from behind me,

still clutching my bound wrists. His voice was low and mechanical, processed through a voice changer. I'd seen him only the day we'd been snatched, and the fact that he was here now terrified me all the more. "Nothing you think you know. Nothing you see as we leave. You keep your little mouth shut, and maybe he'll go home one day, too. But you say a word, and we'll know. You say a word, and he's dead."

They'd blindfolded me and taken me out. But the blindfold had slipped, and I'd been able to glimpse a few things. The texture of pavement. The color of a door. I'd heard the chime of a clock tower, the roar of an airplane. The thrum of construction equipment.

There'd been smells, too. The stench of rotten food. The tang of paint. The earthy scent of fresh dirt.

I felt the prick of a needle as they shoved me into a car, and the next thing I knew I was lying under a tree with a cellphone in my hand. I'd called my dad, my fingers shaking with each number I punched, and soon he and my mom and a four man team were at my side.

I'd crawled into my mother's arms, crying hysterically, terrified for Dallas, guilty for being so relieved to be free when he was still trapped. And I'd kept quiet, just like my captors had warned me.

When Daddy asked what I remembered, I told him nothing. I lied and said that I'd gone to sleep in a small, gray room, then awakened under that tree. I said it because I had to. Because I had to keep Dallas safe.

But as the hours ticked by without him, I began to doubt. And the fear that I was wrong to keep the secret ate at me.

"Can you remember anything at all about the last three weeks?" my mother asked as she tucked me into bed that night. "Anything about where they kept you? Sounds? What they looked like?"

"They told me not to." My voice was barely a whisper, but

she heard me. And when I looked up, I saw hope in my mother's eyes.

Within minutes, my father was in the room, too, along with the leader of the vigilante team Daddy had hired. I told them what my captors had said. About how it would be bad for Dallas if I told anything, and so I hadn't.

But they said what I was already starting to believe—that the threat was meant to keep me silent. If I had any information that could help them rescue Dallas, I had to use it. Because for all we knew, they never planned to let Dallas go at all.

They had no leads except me. And I knew that if we wanted to rescue my brother—if I wanted to help the boy I loved—I had to tell the team what little I knew.

And so I did.

It took forty-eight hours and lots of forensic stuff I didn't understand—everything from analyzing the dirt on my shoes to running some sort of diagnostics on the burner phone to pinpointing the location of airports in conjunction with clock towers.

They'd found it, though. My father's money had bought the best, and his team soon determined that Dallas and I had been held in the basement of a semi-demolished building that had been abandoned after funds for a renovation had fallen short.

They'd set out before dawn. I wasn't there, but I heard about it soon enough. How they'd approached silently. How they'd entered the building with the utmost care—and how they'd triggered explosives when they'd moved in.

Two of the four were killed instantly. Another lost an arm and an eye. The fourth had been unconscious for a week, but ultimately recovered.

The building itself had collapsed into rubble.

I felt as though I had, too.

He'd been in there—I knew it. Dallas had been in that basement, and because of me he'd been blown up. Or worse, buried alive.

I'd spent the next four weeks in tears, mourning a boy I was certain was dead. And hating myself for getting him killed.

But he wasn't killed, and now he's standing right before me in a cramped cabana, looking at me with so much compassion that I actually turn away.

"Jane," he says gently. "I didn't die."

"But I thought you had." A tear snakes down my cheek and I wipe it away violently. "For four long weeks, I thought you had, and then they sent that damn ransom letter and it turned out they'd already moved you out of the building." I draw a breath, remembering the wave of relief that had washed over me, coupled with the fear that it was all a cold, cruel joke.

"Jane." He takes a step toward me, but I hold up a hand to stop him. I'm too raw, and I don't think that I can protect myself right now if he offers me comfort.

He stops, his features tightening.

"I'm just making a point," I say. "It was the ransom that got you out. The vigilante bullshit almost got you killed. The way it almost got the kids on the bus and the Darcy girls killed. And those kids in Nevada did die, Dallas. Two children, and that's way too high a price."

Now that I've shifted back to work, I'm starting to get steady again, thank goodness. "Anyway, that was the original core of the book I'm currently writing—Benson's organization and how his idiotic vigilante mission endangered so many kids."

"The original core?" he says. "That's not what the book's about now?"

"It is, yes. But I expanded my focus after Bill told me that there's another organized vigilante group out there offering its services. The thesis is still the damage done by these groups, and why it's so important to shut them down. But I'm examining two sides. The fallout and prosecution of Benson's group on the one hand. And I'm juxtaposing that against WORR's search for this other group that rescued the Darcy girls."

"You're saying it's an active investigation?"

"One of their top priorities," I confirm. "It has been ever since Bill talked with Elaine Darcy and became convinced that there really is a particular organized group out there that's working for diplomats, millionaires, celebrities. People like Dad who don't want the FBI or Interpol involved. And then Henry Darcy confirmed, and—"

Dallas raises a hand to cut me off. "Wait. You're telling me that Henry Darcy admitted to hiring this vigilante group you're talking about?"

"Sounds like something out of a movie, doesn't it? But yeah, he did. According to Bill, Darcy doesn't even know how to contact them. It was all very secret, with burner phones and passwords and complicated contact protocols. But he did hear one thing that he thinks he wasn't supposed to. It's how I got the title for the book, actually." I smile, because the title is freaking awesome. "I'm calling it *Code Name: Deliverance*."

His eyes widen almost imperceptibly, and he looks a little shell-shocked. I'm not surprised. He lived through what I did and more. Every day he's known that he might have died in that raid. Maybe he almost did. Maybe he was unconscious. Maybe fighting for his life.

He knows that I'm the one who provided all the details for a raid that went horribly wrong. And I wonder for the billionth time why he doesn't hate me.

Then again, maybe he does.

Just the thought rips me open, making all the wounds that I pretend are healed raw again. I don't mean to, but I make a little whimpering sound, and Dallas steps forward, his hand out just a little, as if to comfort me. He stops, and I'm not sure if it's because any caress between us is dangerous, or if it's because he knows there's no comfort to be had.

"So now you know why I write." My voice is falsely cheerful. "I get to work out my demons and get paid for it."

"It wasn't your fault."

"Nice words," I counter. "Too bad they're not true."

"Jane." He walks the rest of the way to me, then kneels on the ground in front of where I'm sitting on the bed. This time he does touch me. He puts his hands on my knees, and I draw in a stuttering breath, only now realizing how much I've been wanting his touch. Needing that connection, if only for an instant.

We are face-to-face, and his eyes are full of regret. I can see he wants to say something—and I can also see that he hasn't figured out how.

"It's okay," I say. "I deal. You deal. And pretty soon we'll have some closure, right? I mean surely this Ortega guy will spill about who hired him. And then we'll know why all this happened in the first place."

I already know why, of course. Or at least I think I do. When you're the son or daughter of a high profile billionaire, you're a target. That's just the way it is. And since our kidnappers had made a ransom demand on day one, then kept upping the price, we were probably taken by some militant group looking to finance a coup.

Too bad Kickstarter didn't exist back then.

I actually smile at the thought, and start to tell Dallas, figuring he can use a grin as well. But something in his expression stops me. "What?"

"I really fucked you over." His voice is low and full of pain.

I shake my head, both in denial and in confusion. "What are you talking about?"

"All of it. It's haunting you."

I can't deny it. "It's haunting both of us."

His hands slide up my legs as he pushes himself up to his feet. Just a few inches, but it feels like a caress. And when he pulls his hands away and steps back from the bed, I mourn the loss of contact.

"They came to the school—they came for me. Don't you get it? It's my fault you were taken. My fault we were held captive, hungry and scared and cold."

"No—" I begin, but he won't let me finish.

"It's my fault that this is your life now, that you're stuck in the past, searching for answers in someone else's kidnapping. It's my fault, and I can't make it better. And now Bill is the one who's going to end it for you. Who has Ortega and who's going to find out who's behind this. Who's going to give you closure."

I shake my head. "That's not true."

"It is. God help me, it is."

"Dallas . . ." I stand and face him. I don't know what to say. I don't know how to argue. I don't know what to do, and I feel as helpless as I did those weeks when I was fifteen. As lost as I'd been back then when it was Dallas who had soothed me. And me who had soothed Dallas.

"Do you have any idea how much I want to touch you?" His voice is low, as if he's talking to himself more than me. I can smell the alcohol on his breath, and wonder how much he's had, and how far he might go. "Can you even imagine the things I want to do with you?"

I make a whimpering noise and he moves closer to me, his green eyes like emerald fire. "Being together came close to destroying both of us once already," he says. "But I don't fucking care. You are the memory that gets me through my days, and the fantasy that saves me in the night."

My breath catches in my throat as he reaches for me, then very gently raises his hand to brush a strand of hair off my face. "I know it can never happen—for so many goddamn reasons. I know it's wrong. But I want to taste you again, once more, even if it really is the last time."

My heart is pounding, and I feel prickles of sweat at the back of my neck. My mouth is dry. I feel trapped.

I feel alive.

"Let me, Jane." His voice is rough, and he inches closer. And then—dear god, yes—he brushes the pad of his thumb along my jaw, sending a riot of sparks all through me. "Let me have just one little taste."

I know I should run away. Slap him. Mention our parents. Do something to shut him down.

But I don't.

Instead I just look him in the eyes and say, very slowly and very evenly, "What's to stop you from taking more?"

"You are," he says, as he cups my cheek and I close my eyes, fighting the urge to tilt my head sideways into his palm. "I hope to hell you are. Because I don't have the strength to fight it anymore."

"What if I don't have the strength, either?"

"Then God help us both."

I open my eyes as he leans in. As his lips brush mine.

The kiss is soft. Gentle.

But there's nothing gentle about my reaction. It's as if he has slammed me back against the wall. As if his entire body is pressed against mine. As if his hands are all over me, and I'm opening to him like a flower. Despite everything, I want him. Need him.

He's addictive, this man.

He's dangerous.

And he's right when he says this will destroy us both.

But, damn me, I don't care. It's not a taste of him that I want. Instead, I want to devour him.

I reach up and slide my fingers into his hair as I cup the back of his head and open my mouth, wanting to taste him. To consume him. I don't care if it's wrong. I don't care if it's shameful. Right now, I just want this. I'm like a woman lost in the desert who is suddenly given water, but still can't quell my thirst even though I drink and drink and drink.

But it's only me drinking. Dallas hasn't released me, but he hasn't claimed me, either. He is letting me take, but he has yet to truly taste me.

He is hard against me, and I can feel the timpani of his heart, the beat thrumming through both of us. I shift my hips and brush against his cock, now straining inside the denim of his jeans. The pressure there at the juncture of my thighs sends pleasure spiraling through me, and I grind against him, releasing a little moan right on the heels of his name.

"Dallas."

I don't know if it was his name or my moan of pleasure or the insistence of his cock, but his indecision disappears as he pulls me tighter against him. As he devours my mouth in a kiss so wild I go light-headed. For a moment, I even think that I am flying, but I realize that I am falling backward onto the bed.

He straddles me at the waist, his arms at either side with his hands twined in mine. He bends forward and captures my mouth, then starts to kiss his way down my neck. I'm breathing too hard, my pulse is beating too fast. My skin is on fire and my jeans are far too constricting.

I can manage only one word—*please*. But even then, I'm not sure that I have spoken, especially since he doesn't react, but instead continues his trail of kisses down to the swell of my breast.

He licks the skin that is exposed at the bodice of my tank top, and I gasp and squirm from the wild impact of the sparks that are now ricocheting through me, all zinging between my legs to make me wet and needy and terribly, wonderfully desperate.

Even as the pressure builds, some buried part of me knows

that this is wrong—that it's a mistake. I should sit up. I should push him away. I should stop this.

But all it takes to erase those thoughts is for Dallas to straighten up just a bit. For him to slide one hand along my arm and then over my breast. He finds my nipple through the material and teases it, rolling it between his thumb and forefinger, squeezing so tight that it skirts the line between pain and pleasure, and lands somewhere close to exquisite.

I hear myself make little gasping noises and don't even recognize that it's me. I'm not sure who I am anymore, and all I can think when he violently yanks down the top so that my breasts pop free is that I want to be taken. I want it to be wild.

And, dammit, I want it to be now.

But now that we are doing this—now that I am half naked and throbbing—he is in no hurry. His eyes meet mine as he dips his head to my breast, and I recognize the heat from our youth. It's the light of exploration. Of conquest.

He knows that he has conquered me, all right. And he is enjoying the spoils of his victory.

As if in punctuation of my thought, his mouth closes over one breast while his hand closes over the other, fingers teasing one nipple as his tongue teases the other.

His other hand is still holding mine, but he releases his grip, and slowly trails his fingers along the sensitive skin on the back of my wrist, and then follows the path to my torso. He eases my tank up from the bottom, until the entire thing is like a band beneath my breasts.

I can barely wrap my head around any one sensation as he sucks and bites lightly on my nipple even as his fingers drift lower and lower, along the bare skin of my belly.

I am panting, needing oxygen in defense against the wild onslaught as his hand reaches my jeans and a finger slips under teasingly. I want this—oh, dear god, how I want this.

I arch up, instinctively seeking more. "Fuck me," I whisper, shocked at my boldness. At how quickly all my defenses have fallen away.

For years I have wanted him—this—and yet I've fought. *He's* fought. But tonight, with Ortega in custody, with all the memories rushing back, of the dark, of his hands, of his comfort . . . maybe I just need to get lost. Maybe this is the way to move on.

Maybe I just need the man.

"Please," I beg—and that's when everything shatters.

Instead of tugging down my jeans and taking me hard and fast, he lurches up, releasing my breast, his hands up in the air as if he's pleading innocent to the police. He's back against the wall and he's breathing hard and he's shaking his head.

And it's over.

It's just . . . over.

I hear myself whimper, wanting more. Everything. *Dallas.*

"Please," I repeat, and though I'm still lost in a sensual haze, I am aware enough to see the change in his expression. I don't understand what has happened, but I watch as the heat drains from his eyes.

Suddenly it's not desire I feel, but mortification, and I pull my knees up, then tug my shirt back over my breasts, trying not to see the regret all over his face.

God, I'm an idiot.

"I can't," he says, and I don't think I have ever heard more pain in a man's voice. "I'm sorry. I'm so goddamn sorry. I should never have—I should never have started that. I should never have put it on you to say no. But I've wanted you for so long. Dreamed of touching you for so damn long."

I relax a bit. There's nothing false about his words or the depth of emotion that underscores them. "Then take me," I say before I can remind myself that it's wrong. That we'll both regret it.

He turns his face from me, and I see the way his jaw tightens as his shoulders stiffen. When he turns back, the desire is still there, but it's masked by a fierce determination.

"We can't. I shouldn't have pushed. I should know better than to taste forbidden fruit. And dammit, Jane, so should you. You shouldn't have pushed, either. You shouldn't even fucking want me."

"No," I acknowledge. "I shouldn't. But we both know that I do."

He exhales, as if I'm the one being frustrating. "Look around you, for Christ's sake. You know what I am."

"That isn't you." I taste salt, and realize I'm crying. "That can't be you."

"You knew a boy, Jane. And he grew into a fucked-up man. You more than anyone should know why. This is me, sweetheart," he says simply. "You're looking right at me."

But I don't want to believe what my own eyes show me. Maybe it's my own stubbornness. More likely my refusal to believe stems from guilt. Because Dallas spent four weeks in the dark after I was released. And I know that whatever happened to him after I left him all alone in there must have shaped and molded him, even if he can't consciously remember any of it.

So he's wrong—I don't know why he's the man he is. I can guess, though. In the days before my release the Woman had taken him from me more and more frequently. And when he came back, he'd been tense. Closed off. As if he was pushing fear and anger inside himself.

I don't know what happened when she took him away, but the possibilities that go through my head both scare and sicken me. And I can only believe it got worse after I was gone.

Yet I know this man. I've known him since he was a boy. And I have to believe that there is more to the man. But whether that's because it's true or because I can't live with the guilt if it's not, I really don't know.

He pinches the bridge of his nose. "We can't do this. You

know it. I know it." He looks at me, and his eyes are as hard as stone. "You said in the house that you didn't want me. Dammit, Jane, you need to mean it. You need to believe it. I'm not the man for you. We both know I can't be the man for you."

He's harsh. And he's right. I think about what our parents would say if they found out. I know our father would disinherit us both, but that's not even the worst of it. It's the way they'd look at us, so full of disappointment and regret.

I glance down, every reason that we've stayed apart coming back to me as I struggle to adjust my clothes and look anywhere but at him. A single tear streaks down my cheek, and out of the corner of my eye, I see him take a tentative step toward me.

"Jane."

His voice is so low and gentle that I think I might be imagining it. But I know that I'm not, and mortification spreads over me, heating my skin, stinging my eyes. Sitting like a heavy, horrible weight in my stomach.

"Go," I whisper.

"It's not that I don't want—"

"Please," I snap. I can't let him finish that sentence. It's too damn painful to hear. "Just leave."

For a moment, I hear nothing and know that he is standing perfectly still. I clench my hands into fists, my shoulders stiff, my jaw tight. *Go,* I say in my head. *Go,* I want to scream.

Finally, I hear the rustle of his clothes as he moves away, then the scrape of the door as he slides it open. I count to ten before I turn around, and when I do, I'm alone.

I close my eyes again, and this time it's to hold back my tears.

I stay on the daybed for at least fifteen minutes. Just sitting. Not even really thinking, because right now I don't want to think. I don't want to do anything. If I could, I'd gladly disappear, and I'm incredibly frustrated with myself for losing control. If he hadn't stopped us, I'd be naked on this daybed right now, with his cock deep inside me, and—

I let out a little moan as I think about all the possibilities that go with "and."

The King of Fuck, indeed.

I stand, determined to get myself and my errant thoughts under control. I take a deep breath, run a hand over my clothes to smooth them, and then head out of the cabana.

No one even looks my way. Why would they? I'm his sister, after all, as he so conveniently announced so that everyone in the vicinity could look past my drab clothes and recognize me from the frequent media shots and TV talk show appearances.

If I'd been any other female, all eyes would be on me. Looking for clothing askew. For smudged lipstick.

There would have been winks and nudges, and probably even a secret handshake to mark my entry into the already massive Fucked by Dallas Club.

I should be grateful not to have the attention.

But I'm not grateful at all. Instead I'm frustrated. And I'm pissed. And that reaction just pisses me off more. Because I shouldn't care. I shouldn't want to be part of that club.

I don't want to be a pastime. I don't want to be a casual fuck. Just one more woman in a never-ending stream.

Not that it matters.

Because when you're in love with your brother, how many women he screws is really the least of your problems.

7

Brother & Sister

Jane West couldn't sleep. Her arm ached too much. And all the memories from the day kept jumping out at her when she closed her eyes.

She was going to have nightmares, she knew it. A broken arm and nightmares and a daddy who was getting erased. No, terminated. That was the word. Only not like the cyborg in those movies.

It was her eleventh birthday, and it was probably the worst day of her life.

It wasn't fair.

She heard the light tapping at her door, but ignored it, thinking it was one of the staff making noise in the hallway. When it came again, though, it was louder, and she sat up in bed, smiling for the first time that day. "Come in!"

The door opened right away, and Dallas hurried in, then shut the door quickly behind him.

"I had to wait until everyone was asleep," he said. "And I

couldn't get Liam. The grown-ups are talking in the kitchen, so he's stuck back there in his rooms with his mom."

Jane just nodded. Liam was one of her best friends, too, but right then she really only wanted Dallas.

He climbed onto the bed, a lanky boy of eleven, taller and leaner than most of the other boys in school. His hair was short, and right now it was spiky, probably 'cause he ran his fingers through it when he was worried. Jane knew he'd been worried about her. She could see it on his face, and in the green eyes that had always seemed magical to her.

He had Mr. Fluffles with him, and he passed the bunny to her. "Here," he said. "I figured he'd help."

"He's yours." For some reason, it was really important to her that he keep the bunny.

"Well, duh. But just for tonight I thought you'd need him."

"Oh." She smiled at him, and when he smiled back she forgot a little bit how much she hurt all over.

"So what happened? Nobody's saying anything."

She shrugged. "Daddy called Mom and wanted to take me out today because it's my birthday. Mom and Eli didn't want him to but they let me go anyway because I haven't seen him so much lately."

For the last year, Colin had been serving his second prison sentence, this one for tax fraud, and he'd only gotten out a few weeks ago. Her mom, Lisa, had gotten a divorce after the first time he'd been locked up for something called insider trading, and then she'd married Eli right after Jane's seventh birthday.

"So what happened when you were out with him?" Dallas pressed.

She bit her lower lip, then pulled her knees out from under the covers so that she could hug them to her, along with Mr. Fluffles. "He took me to dinner and that was nice, and then he said he had to see a friend on the way home."

"Were you in the city?"

She nodded. "For dinner. But then we went over into New Jersey. He said he needed to pick up a package and move it somewhere else. So we ended up in this warehouse by the river filled with boxes and crates and stuff."

"Cool."

Maybe on another day she'd think so, but not today. She shook her head. "We got the package, but as we were leaving these guys in suits came in. Daddy started to pull me back, but one of the guys grabbed me by the arm and yanked me toward him, and—and he had a gun."

Dallas's eyes went wide, and he reached for her hand. "Who was he?"

She clutched his hand as she told the rest, not really wanting to talk about it, but wanting him to know. "I don't know. But the guy standing next to him said my daddy owed him money, and if he didn't pay up, he'd be sorry."

"What happened?"

"I don't know. Not really. But Daddy walked with that man to a corner and I could hear them shouting. And then they came back and the guy told the one with the gun to let me go. And he shoved me toward Daddy, but I fell and I heard a crack and it hurt so bad. I think I fainted because then we were in the car and we were almost to the hospital."

"Whoa."

She nodded. Now that it was over, she had to admit it was a pretty good story. She couldn't wait to tell Liam. He'd be impressed, too.

"So what did Mom say to him at the hospital?"

"To him? Nothing. He left while they were putting my arm in the cast. And he didn't even give me my birthday present."

"Oh!" Dallas dug into the pocket of his robe. "I got you one."

She took the little box he passed her and ripped off the paper, then opened it to reveal a shiny golden locket. She looked up at him, delighted. "It's so pretty. And it's a heart."

He lifted a shoulder. "Yeah, well. That's all they had." He didn't quite look at her face. "So open it."

She did, and found two tiny pictures inside. One of her, and one of him. Her heart fluttered in her chest as she gazed at the little images. "It's the best present ever."

"Really?"

She looked at him, and felt weirdly shy when she smiled. "I promise."

"So what happened next? What did Mom do?"

"Well, she couldn't yell at Daddy, but she sure yelled at Eli. Big-time."

"At him? Why?"

"Well, to him, I guess. Said it was the last straw and she wanted Eli to file the papers. She didn't care if it cost them everything, it needed to be done."

"What?"

"That's what I asked. And she said that she was going to have a court terminate Daddy's parental rights. She's gonna sue so that he's not my dad anymore."

"Wow."

She nodded, then swiped away a tear. "And then Eli came to the bed I was in and told me not to worry. Everything would be just fine, because he would adopt me, and I'd have a mother and a father again, all living in the same house."

"Just like that?" he asked.

"I guess so."

"Then that means we'll be brother and sister."

She frowned. "We already are."

"Nope. You're my stepsister. Because Eli and Lisa adopted me after they got married, so I'm their kid."

"I know that," Jane said. She remembered when the drugged-up lady who was Dallas's birth mother had been found dead, and Eli had said that it was sad, but good, because it would make the adoption process go easier.

"And Lisa already had you before she married Eli," Dallas continued. "So we're steps. Eli's your stepfather and I'm your stepbrother."

Jane rolled her eyes. "I know that, dummy. So what?"

"So, if Eli adopts you, then we'll have the same two parents for real. Eli will be your real dad, I'll be your real brother, and you'll be my real sister. Wild, huh?"

Her eyes went wide as she thought about it. "Yeah." She wrinkled her nose. "Is that good?"

He frowned, considering. "I don't know. I guess."

After a second, he shook it off. "You want me to stay with you tonight?"

She nodded. "It's not scary anymore—I mean, I'm home and it's all over. But I think it will be scary in my dreams, and I don't want to have nightmares."

"Okay then." He sat up straight, looking every bit the determined bodyguard. "In that case, I have to stay. And you don't have to worry because I'll protect you. I'll always protect you."

He dropped his robe on the floor and crawled up to the head of the bed in his version of pajamas—flannel sleep pants and a Tower of London T-shirt from his last trip overseas with his parents. Soon to be her parents, too.

He slid under the covers and she scooted over to share her pillow. They both laid on their backs, and he held tight to her uninjured hand.

"Do you think they can really do that? Make my daddy not be my daddy, I mean?"

"I guess so."

"I didn't know you could lose people like that. I mean, just all of a sudden, and then they're no longer who you thought they were."

"Don't worry," Dallas said. "You'll never lose me."

And then he pushed himself up, leaned over, and very sweetly—very awkwardly—kissed her cheek.

8

Mothers & Daughters

My sexy little Vanquish Volante convertible can go from zero to sixty-two miles per hour in just over four seconds. But despite the fact that I want to put distance between me and the Meadow Lane house that I love—not to mention the man—I'm not taking advantage of all that power and speed.

Instead, I'm parked on the shoulder, the engine still running and the radio blasting as I claw my way back from my memories. Sweet, wonderful memories, yes. But I don't need to linger in the past. That boy no longer exists, and the sooner I cement myself in reality, the better.

But it's not even my feelings for Dallas that are the worst of it. No, the worst is that I gave in. That I lost control. Because after the kind of trauma I lived through, control is pretty much the holy grail. That's why I hate crowds. Why I drive too fast. Why I got married. And, yeah, why I got divorced.

I know all of that because I have paid a shit ton of money over the years for a stream of therapists to tell me so. I crave control. I'm scared of the dark. I don't trust easily. I have survivor's guilt.

I am, in other words, a therapist's wet dream. A walking, talking textbook illustrating the emotional damage that follows a kidnapping. So much so, that the storm in my head can provide enough challenge to support a shrink's entire career.

And even if I'm not quite curable, at least the symptoms can be masked, and the chorus line of doctors can feel like they've accomplished something. Because whenever I get twitchy, I have a lovely little rainbow of pills that can take the edge off.

I tap a yellow one into my palm right now—because god knows I lost control in a big way with Dallas.

Big. Major. Huge.

But all I do is stare at the pill, and then I drop it onto the ground beside the car.

Fuck it, I think. I can handle this.

And I really hope that I'm right about that.

I'm just about to pull back out onto the road when my phone rings. I glance at the caller ID, and then eagerly push the button to talk.

"Hey, sweetie." My mom's voice is soft, with just a hint of her Georgia roots, and the moment I hear it, I burst into tears. "Baby?" She sounds freaked, and I can hardly blame her. I love my mom—I talk with her all the time—and even though we sometimes disagree, her calls never drive me to blubbering.

"Sorry—I'm just—" I cut myself off because I don't know what to say. I rub my hands under my eyes and suck in a calming breath. "I'm just having one of those days, and I'm really, really glad you called."

It's true. I am. I'm almost thirty-two years old, and right at that moment, I don't think there's anything in the world that would make me feel better than talking with my mom.

"I'm glad I called, too," she says. "You know you can always call me."

"I know." My entire life, that's been my mother's motto. I can call her anytime. I can talk to her about anything.

For the most part I have. My marriage and divorce. The Hollywood bullshit I've encountered in LA. My panic attacks before media appearances. My never-ending stream of self-defense classes. My frustration with therapists who don't help. And, of course, the nightmares and anxiety that have dogged me for the last seventeen years.

But the one thing I've never talked to her about is the one thing I need to talk about the most—Dallas. What happened between us. How I feel about him. How much the distance we've kept between us now eats at me.

How much I just plain want him, and how hard it is to know that I can't have him.

Doesn't matter how open my mother is or how well we communicate. That is one conversation that is just not happening.

"Why don't I come over?" she suggests, obviously concerned that I'm not elaborating on what's bugging me. "We could make cookies. Watch a bad movie."

I glance at the clock. It's almost midnight. "Don't you think it's a little late?"

"It's not even nine," she says. "And I'm just down the hill on Sunset. I'll ditch Sarah and be right over," she adds, referring to her lifelong bestie.

"You're in LA," I say, as I realize that she believes I am, too. On any other day, the odds are that she'd be right. I've been living for the last four months in an adorable little rental house just off Mulholland Drive. I'd tried working on the screen adaptation of *The Price of Ransom* from New York, but there were so many meetings, it ended up being easier to just make the move.

"We decided to do a girls spa and shopping weekend," Mom explains. "We arrived just in time for dinner, and we're on our way to after-dinner drinks and dessert, but I'm happy to change plans if you want me to come by."

I smile, because that is so my mom, just going with the flow and looking cool and fabulous while she does it. I can imagine her in the back of their hired car, her golden blond hair perfect even after a day traveling, and her linen outfit not the slightest bit wrinkled. Lisa Sykes is always camera ready, always has a smile for reporters, and is pretty much the classiest lady around. I inherited my looks from her, but not her ability to make friends wherever she goes. Personally, I'm happy to fade into the background.

"You can come by," I say, amused. "But since I'm not there, I don't see the point."

"Well, maybe tomorrow then. If you want to join us for massages in the morning you can—wait." I can practically hear her playing back our conversation, including my comment about the late hour. "You're not in LA, are you?"

"I'm in the Hamptons. I just got back to New York today, actually." I am, in fact, only about half an hour away from the house my parents now keep in East Hampton village.

She laughs. "Well, isn't that a comedy of errors? Did you drive all the way out to see me and Daddy? No," she answers herself, "of course you didn't."

She knows perfectly well that I never drive to see them unless I call first. My father is usually traveling—I happen to know that he's in Houston at the moment, working his way through a lineup of meetings relating to the new Sykes Pavilion, a massive, high-end retail, restaurant, and hotel destination that is scheduled to open in just under twenty-two months.

"I came to see Dallas," I admit.

"Dallas?"

I understand the surprise in her voice. She knows Dallas and I have avoided each other ever since the kidnapping. Hell, I even went so far as to beg to go to a boarding school in California, near where my birth father was living at the time, just so that I could get away. Mom absolutely despises Colin now, and she trusts him not at all. Not only that, but she'd gone through a brutal battle to have his parental rights terminated when I was a little girl.

Even so, she let me go. And that simple fact underscores how much she knew I needed distance from my brother after the ordeal was over.

"Why on earth did you fly in to see Dallas?"

"I had to talk to him," I admit. "I should have waited until tomorrow, though. He was occupied." I can't keep the sarcasm out of my voice, and her almost inaudible little *hmmm* shows that she understands. How can she not? She sees the tabloids and gossip shows just like everyone else, and I know she's as disappointed as I am in what he's become.

"Your brother has to deal with his issues in his own way," she says, which is exactly what I would expect a mom to say.

"He's acting like an ass," I reply, which is exactly what a sister would say.

"I guess being an ass *is* his way," she adds, and I remember all over again why I love my mom so much.

"I wish he'd get over it," I grumble.

"You miss him." Her voice is gentle. "You two used to be so close."

She's right of course, but after what happened earlier, I really don't want to go there. So I shift the conversation, because she has as much of a right to my news as Dallas. "I came to see him because—oh, god, Mom—I came because Bill has one of the guys who snatched us in custody. And he wants to trade immunity for the identity of the man who was behind it all."

Silence.

There is nothing but silence on the other end of the line.

"Mom? Mommy?"

I hear the sharp intake of breath, and I realize that she is trying to talk, and that she can't through the tears.

"Oh, god, I'm sorry," I say. "I shouldn't have dropped it like that. I didn't mean to—"

"No." Her voice is raspy. "No, baby, of course I want to know. Of course you can tell me. I was just—after so much time—"

"I know. I can't believe it."

"What did Dallas say?"

I think back to his reaction—his guilt that I'd been caught up in his kidnapping. My guilt that I couldn't save him. That I got out and he didn't. All of it. Every horrible bit of it. I don't know how to tell Mom any of that, though, and so I go with the simplest and truest answer. "I think he was a little shell-shocked. I get that. I am, too."

"And Bill will keep us informed?"

"Of course. He's going to call Daddy, too. He wants—well, he's going to want Dad to press charges."

"Oh."

I frown. I'd been hoping she'd say that Daddy would jump on the chance. But of course he won't. He kept the kidnapping secret back then, so I doubt he'll be keen on it going public now. "You'll talk to him, won't you? If they really do find whoever did that to us, I want to see him strung up by his balls." I wince. I may be an adult, but I'm usually not so vulgar when I talk to my mother.

"I'd like that, too," she says, completely unperturbed. "But so much publicity on you after all this time—it's going to bring back the stress and anxiety."

"Bring it back? It never went away."

"You're doing better, sweetheart, and you know it. You and Dallas both are."

I snort. "That's because he has a harem to help him cope."

I can practically hear my mother pressing her lips together to keep from commenting. After a second, she says, "I'm thinking about your career. About your books. If your kidnapping becomes public you're going to end up in the spotlight in a much less pleasant way. The media will be sympathetic—you and your brother were the victims—but they'll be relentless. Is that what you want?"

"Want? Of course not." I hate the tabloid attention that comes with my family name. Piling on more attention—and for so horrible a reason—sounds like a living nightmare. "But if that's what it takes to punish the person who did that to us, then I'll deal."

"Well, all right," she says softly, but she doesn't sound convinced. "I suppose we'll see what your father has to say."

I don't respond. Because honestly, I don't understand her reaction at all. I mean, objectively I understand why Daddy wanted to keep the kidnapping secret. Our lives were public enough without adding that kind of horrific spotlight. But we're adults now, and if we can catch the man who did this to us, then I want him punished. Even if that means stepping into that circle of light.

My mom clears her throat. "And Colin? Have you told him?"

I know Mom doesn't like the fact that I still see my biological dad, but after the kidnapping he'd been there for me in a way that my parents—who are also Dallas's parents—couldn't be. And although he was a class-A fuckup when I was little, I think he's mostly gotten his shit together.

Mom, I know, isn't so sure.

"I called him from the road and told him the basics," I admit. "He wanted me to come straight over—but he also said he had plans to go to Boston for an overnighter. He told me he'd cancel, but that didn't really make a lot of sense, especially since I wanted to see Dallas. So I told him we could have dinner tomorrow when he gets back."

"Do you really think telling him was a good idea?" I hear the sharp edge in her voice and cringe.

"Mom." My voice is soft. "He deserves to know. I mean, he is my father."

"Not legally."

I exhale. "I know that. And I know he's a screw-up. But he's tried really hard to put his life back together."

My mother snorts. Clearly she doesn't believe me. "Tell that to the IRS agent who called me last week. He's under investigation again."

"Why are they calling you?" I ask, avoiding the real question of whether or not my birth father is backsliding.

"I was married to the man for ten years." I hear the shrug in her voice. "It's hard to escape your past."

I sigh, because isn't that the truth?

"I know it bothers you," I say. "That I see him, I mean. But—well, sometimes it helps."

"Oh, sweetheart." She sounds so lost, and I think again how much it must have hurt her when I'd begged to go to boarding school near him.

"Mom? I'm sorry."

"No." The word is sharp. "You have nothing to be sorry for. You and Dallas went through so much. Lost so much. And—and we all have things we regret. I'm sure Colin has many."

"He does. He's told me so over and over."

For a moment, she's silent. Then I hear Sarah's muffled voice telling Mom to take her time, that she'll wait in the car. A moment later, I hear a car door slam. I expect her to wrap up the conversation, so I'm surprised when she says, "Colin and I—well, we were never meant to be. But—You know that Eli and I had an affair?" She continues, the words sounding like they've burst out of her. "While I was still married to Colin?"

No one had ever specifically told me as much, but years later I figured it out. "Yeah," I say. "I know."

"We broke rules. Hurt people we loved—because even when Colin screwed up, I did still love him. Maybe I still do in some ways even though he makes me so damn angry. But the point is that I don't regret the affair. Not really. Your dad and I were meant to be together. It wasn't an easy path, but sometimes the best destinations require the most difficult journeys."

"Have you been skimming *Reader's Digest* again?" I keep my tone light, a little uncomfortable with such an intensely personal revelation from my mom.

"I swear that's my own original slice of brilliance. And all I'm saying is it was worth it, but it wasn't easy, especially on you kids."

"I guess not. But I don't know anyone with a normal nuclear family these days."

"Well, that's true," she says with a laugh. "But I meant the way we bounced you and Dallas around with marriages and adoptions. Sometimes I think Dallas should have lived with us as Eli's nephew, and you should have simply been Eli's stepdaughter. I think maybe it would have been easier."

I hear her long sigh before she continues. "But he wanted legal heirs. He wanted the picture perfect family package. A wife and two kids to shoulder the Sykes empire once he was gone. We never had the dog, but we all did okay. Didn't we?" she asks, and the question seems so genuine that I wish I was back in LA so that I could give her a long, tight hug.

"Of course we did, Mom," I say, and it's not a lie. My life may be screwed up and I may wish that things were different, but I'm doing okay. I'm surviving, aren't I?

"Well," she says, and I imagine her smoothing her skirt as she gathers herself. "I stepped out of the car to talk, but I should get back to Sarah. And our driver is probably wondering if I've lost my mind. I'll see you on the island this weekend, okay?"

"I can't wait. I love you, Mom."

"Love you more."

We say our goodbyes and I sit for a moment longer. I may not have had the best luck on the father side of the equation—at least not originally—but I won the lottery with my mom.

I turn in my seat and look back at the familiar house that holds so many of my childhood memories. My parents. Colin. Liam. And, of course, Dallas.

He's no longer in there, I know. His helicopter has already whisked him away. And as I look at the well-lit house contrasted against the dark night sky, I can't help but wonder where he's going—and if he is thinking of me.

9

First Kiss

Dallas was cramming his T-shirts into his duffel bag when Jane burst through his bedroom door wearing sleep shorts and a Bugs Bunny T-shirt. She was fourteen now, just like him, and Dallas didn't know if her body had filled out early or late for a girl, but he knew that it was perfect. And he knew that he thought about it way, way too much.

"Liam just told me," she said, slamming the door shut behind her. "Is it true?"

"Guess that depends on what 'it' is."

She scowled at him. "Is Dad really sending you to boarding school in London?"

He wanted to snap back an answer—like, what? Did she think he was packing for fun? But he saw the tears glistening in her eyes and the words died in his throat. It wasn't Jane he was mad at. It was himself. And his father.

But it was Jane he was going to miss the most.

He dropped the duffel and went to sit on the edge of his bed. "Yeah. It's true. I'm surprised Mom didn't call you."

"Me, too." She'd been at a sleepaway girls' camp for the last week. Dallas had been having fun with his friends, too. Mostly jacking cars like the one that had gotten him caught. The one that had his dad sending him away.

"Why did you do that? I told you that Ron and Andy were bad news. Why did you keep hanging with them?"

He couldn't answer. He didn't have a reason. Or maybe he did. Maybe he was just bad like his birth parents. Maybe that's why he did all that shit.

Maybe that's why the only girl he fantasized about was his sister.

"Now they're sending you away from me and it's all your fault. God, Dallas, what were you thinking?" A tear spilled from one eye and she wiped it away brutally. "You're so stupid sometimes."

He exhaled loudly. "It's not just because of the cars."

"What? The drugs, too? I know you smoke pot sometimes, so don't even pretend that you don't."

"It's not the drugs," he said. "And it was only a couple of times."

"Then what?"

He took a deep breath. "You."

Her forehead crunched into a frown. "What are you talking about?"

"Remember a few months ago. The time I fell asleep in your bed?"

"Yeah. So?"

"Eli saw me come out of your room."

"So what? It's not like we ever did anything."

But we wanted to. He almost said it, but he didn't. He didn't need to. She knew it as well as he did.

Instead, he just lifted a shoulder, remembering what their father had said. "He said it was bad." He lifted his hand to bite his thumbnail, then forced himself not to.

"What was bad?" Her voice was almost a whisper.

He swallowed, then focused on his thumb. "The way I look at you."

"Oh."

"He said it was bad, and that if anyone found out it would be worse. He said he'd disinherit us. Disown us." He turned his head to face her. "He said it was a sin."

"How do you look at me?"

He shifted on the bed feeling too exposed. And his skin felt tingly like it did when he jacked off to the thought of her, right before he exploded. He wanted to answer, but how the hell was he supposed to tell her that?

"Dallas?"

"Like I want you," he blurted.

"Oh." She licked her lips. "Do you?"

Oh, god, she was killing him. He sucked in a breath for courage. "Yeah. You know I do."

She turned so that she was looking right at him. "Me, too," she said, and he thought those were the most magical words in the world.

"Do you believe him?" she asked. "That it's a sin, I mean?"

"No. And even if it is, I don't care."

She nodded, as if considering that. "Is he here?"

Dallas shook his head. "In Chicago for the night."

"Can I stay with you, then?"

He wanted to just scream *yes*. But instead he reminded her about the staff. "If anyone sees you . . ."

"We can set an alarm. I'll go back to my room early. But you're leaving tomorrow for good."

He almost laughed at that. "I'm not moving to the moon."

She made a face. "You might as well be. And it's not like we're gonna *do* anything."

He *really* shouldn't feel disappointed. "No. 'Course not."

"But maybe—I mean, do you think—I just—Oh, crap. Dallas, would you kiss me goodbye?"

He didn't answer, at least not in words. But he turned to her and leaned in, his nerves jangling because he didn't know what he was doing. But he knew he wanted this. Her. And when he brushed his lips against hers, it all made sense. It all felt real.

It all felt right.

And as he tasted her—as he explored her wide mouth and soft lips—he thought their dad was crazy. Because this was too good to ever, ever, ever be bad.

10

Mendoza

"We're starting our descent, Mr. Sykes."

Dallas winced as the captain's voice crackled over the intercom, just a little too loud for comfort considering the alcohol and Jane-induced headache he was nursing.

He'd been in the damn jet for almost ten hours now, and she still filled his head. The way she'd melted against him, so soft at first and then so demanding. Christ, the way she'd taken charge of that kiss had made him practically lose his mind. The knowledge that she wanted him—that she was willing to cross all those invisible lines to have him.

He'd known he should resist, but she'd filled him up, made him hard. And he'd been a total and complete goner. And when those soft little sounds she made filled his head, he'd snapped. He'd had to have her again. Had to touch her, claim her.

Oh, dear lord, she had felt so good. Her skin so smooth. Her nipples so damn hard. He rubbed his thumb against his fingertips, remembering the way her skin had moved with each stuttering breath, her desire so open, so evident, it's a wonder he didn't fucking come just from the sight of her.

He'd wanted to strip her bare and spread her wide. He'd imagined her on her knees, her back arched so that her breasts were high and her pussy was wide open for him. He could imagine the taste of her as he teased her with his tongue, and the feel of his palm against her ass when he punished her for coming too early.

He wanted to possess her. To have her. To stroke and cherish her.

And at the same time he wanted to run from each and every one of those desires. Because they came from the dark. From the things the Woman had done to him. The way she'd hurt him, then pleasured him.

She'd fucked with his body and with his head.

She'd broken him, and he'd never—*ever*—wanted to drag Jane down with him. And yet that's what he'd done. He'd practically taken her in a cabana in the middle of his party. And he'd been so lost in the haze of desire for her that he hadn't even realized how far he'd gone until she cried out for him, begging him to fuck her.

He was a complete bastard. He should never have kissed her, never touched her, never opened that door. He'd known it was a mistake, but he'd been unable to resist. And he'd wanted her as much in that moment as he had seventeen years ago when they'd been lost in the dark together.

And that was the real hell of it, wasn't it? Because he could never have her again. Not on any level. Not like he wanted.

He was too broken, and she deserved so much more. And even if he were whole, what would it matter when every touch was forbidden? She was his sister, for Christ's sake. It's not like it could ever be right between them.

He wished he could block her out of his mind, but he knew

that wasn't possible. She'd walked back into his life, and by doing so, she'd marched right into his head. All of his desires. All of his memories. Everything was flooding back, dark and raw and wrapped up in this news about Ortega.

He closed his eyes, hoping that Liam would greet him at the airport with the news that Quince had brought Ortega in, and that the son of a bitch was trussed up in the interrogation room.

Damn, but that would be sweet.

Find the Woman. Find the Jailer. And fucking end this thing.

He wanted the closure. And he wanted the pleasure of telling Jane.

It wouldn't change anything—she still couldn't be his—but at least he could do that one thing for her.

He sighed. He needed to put it all away. He wanted to be sharp when he arrived. Not emotional. Not fucked up.

He took the last sip of sparkling water, then lifted it up for the attendant to take. She came quickly, a pretty girl he'd flirted with on many flights, but never taken to his bed.

"Just an overnight trip this time, Mr. Sykes?"

"That's right."

She knew it was an overnight, of course. She was either making conversation or reminding him that she'd be at the hotel. The lovely Mendoza Elite, an exclusive boutique hotel owned by the Sykes empire. Which meant he could easily find out her room number if he was so inclined.

He wasn't.

He glanced down at his satellite phone, still showing no calls, and resigned himself to waiting until they'd landed for an update from Liam.

The attendant—Susie?—was still standing in front of him holding his empty glass. He wanted to tell her to look elsewhere. To have a little pride. Didn't she read the papers? Didn't she know that he was nothing but a good time? She was sweet and pretty and deserved a hell of a lot better.

But since telling her that would be the same as blowing his cover, he simply gave her a bland smile and started to flip through his notes on a new retail center that was opening in San Diego in the spring.

She cleared her throat. "Well, I hope it's a productive trip. I look forward to serving you on the return flight." She flashed a quick smile, then scurried back to her seat, hopefully to review her contacts and see if there was some nice guy back in the States who'd given her his phone number.

He was seated on the small leather sofa, his duffel tucked beneath the empty space beside him. Now he bent over and slid his phone back into the side pocket. As he did, he caught a glimpse of blue and remembered the letter. He grimaced. Just one more nuisance to add to the steadily growing pile.

He considered continuing to ignore it—for that matter, he considered ripping it up. But prudence prevailed and he pulled it from the bag.

He opened it carefully, even though he knew there wouldn't be prints.

As always, there was a single piece of paper inside.

And, as always, the words on the paper were typed. Needy, clingy, demanding words.

> You're mine, Dallas. You always have been. You always
> will be.
> Why don't you see this? Why don't you listen?
> But I am patient. I've always been so very patient.
> So have your fun.
> Play with your little girls.
> But we both know that it is me you'll come back to.
> Me that you need.

Ice filled him as he read it. He had no idea which of the women who'd been in his bed had sent it—analysis of the paper, font, envelope gave no clue. All he knew was that the letters had started over a year ago, but considering the number of women he'd entertained, that didn't help much.

Each new letter made his gut twist. Because although he knew it wasn't true, each word could have been written by Jane.

Fuck.

He crammed the letter back into the duffel and braced himself as the plane landed, the force pushing him against the back of his seat. He closed his eyes and for just a moment he succumbed to physics instead of manipulating, twisting, and trying to rearrange the world.

Then the plane slowed and the interlude was over. He opened his eyes and waited for Susie to open the door and lower the stairs. The instant he stepped out of the jet and into the sunshine, he knew that something was wrong.

Liam stood on the tarmac, his straight posture revealing his army training, and his expressionless face a reflection of his years in military intelligence—Liam never gave anything away. Not to the world, anyway.

But Dallas could see the shadow on the other man's face, and he knew it meant trouble. Along with Jane, Liam was Dallas's oldest friend. He'd watched the skinny, smart-ass son of a housekeeper grow up into a solid rock of muscle who could make another man cower with only a glance and a scowl.

Liam might look like an absolute badass, but Dallas knew the only time he'd failed to call his mom on a Sunday was when he'd been unconscious after taking a bullet in the shoulder during one of his tours.

Liam knew Dallas better than anyone, and Dallas trusted him more than anyone. And yet Dallas had never told his friend about Jane. About what had happened in the dark. But more than that, about how they'd felt. How he still felt.

None of that mattered now, though. The only thing Dallas cared about at the moment was learning what was wrong.

"Don't sugarcoat it," Dallas said. "Just tell me."

Liam didn't hesitate. "Ortega's dead."

Dallas allowed himself one moment to feel shock. Anger. Fury that the hope he'd been riding on had been so cruelly and quickly ripped out from under him.

One instant to feel lost. Slapped down. Fucked all over again, just like he'd been when he was fifteen. As helpless as he'd been in the dark.

Then he pushed it away. He shifted focus. And he moved on.

He needed to strategize. To plan. And for that, he needed information. "How?" he demanded as they fell in step together, heading for the Range Rover.

"Homemade shiv. His death is considered classified while they investigate, but my source tells me that the bastard sliced his own throat."

Dallas pulled open the door to the backseat and tossed his duffel inside. "They're calling it a suicide?"

"That's the official word," Liam acknowledged as he slid in behind the wheel.

Dallas joined him in the SUV that had been tricked out just like all the vehicles Deliverance used. "You believe it?"

"Do you?" Liam gave him a sideways look as he shifted into gear and cranked the stereo up, so that a riot of hip-hop filled the car.

"Hell, no," Dallas said. Ortega had been sitting on the holy grail—a near surefire bid for immunity. Why the hell would he off himself before at least seeing how his ploy played out?

"Right there with you, bro."

Dallas grabbed a bottle of water from the cooler between them, downed a long swallow. He let the music pound into him as he stared out the window at the verdant foothills of the Andes rising up in the distance, majestic against the bright blue sky.

He needed to think, but right then, he felt numb. Jane. Ortega. The goddamn Darcy leak. It was all just piling on.

He turned to Liam. "This is one hell of a setback—"

"Isn't that a fucking understatement?"

"—but we can work it. Use Deliverance's resources to investigate the supposed suicide."

"I've already got Noah digging around to find out who knew Ortega was in custody," Liam said, referring to the team's computer and tech guru. "That should lead to figuring out how he got the shiv. Not to mention who had reason to want him dead."

"Good." Dallas considered the options. "Any chance Ortega could be the Jailer?"

"I thought you might ask," Liam acknowledged. "It didn't ring for me, but neither one of us is going to rely on my gut when the stakes are this high, so I poked around. Timing doesn't work. He was free as a bird the day you were snatched, but the day Jane was released—and we know the Jailer spoke to her at the site in London—Ortega was in a Louisiana jail, waiting for some asshole lawyer to get him released for lack of evidence. Which said asshole managed a few days later."

"Just as well," Dallas said. "Ortega's already dead, and I want the pleasure of choking the life out of the Jailer with my own bare hands."

"You're thinking the Jailer might be behind the suicide."

Dallas glanced sideways at his friend. "Hell, yes. But we can't bank that. Not yet. Ortega was the kind of slime who made enemies. God only knows how many people would kill to keep him from ratting them out."

"But he'd only threatened one. The only trade he offered was the Sykes kidnapping."

"And that," Dallas said, "is why Ortega's death isn't as much of a clusterfuck as it could be. The fact that someone went to the trouble to kill him is a lead. And a damn good one."

"In the meantime, we focus on Mueller."

"Exactly." Dallas knew that Quince would dredge every bit

of intel about Ortega out of the German fuck. Between that and the intel Noah was gathering, with any luck they'd pick up the trail of breadcrumbs that led to Ortega's involvement in the kidnapping. Not to mention his contact for that job.

It would be slow. It would be plodding. But it was a shot, and until he found the Jailer, Dallas intended to run every lead to ground.

And, of course, there was Jane's bombshell about Darcy to consider. He still couldn't believe the financier had told WORR about Deliverance—and had actually mentioned their goddamn code name. That was a serious breach, but Dallas knew better than to panic. His men were top notch. His organization well-cloaked. The name was unofficial only. And Darcy had nowhere to point. WORR might look, but they wouldn't find.

Jane herself, though, was a different kind of problem. The kind he couldn't dismiss. Couldn't chase down. Couldn't fix.

The kind that got under his skin and drove him to distraction. She was his lifelong obsession, his dirtiest secret, his deepest love.

Bottom line—he wanted her. And Dallas was a man who was used to getting what he wanted.

When they were about five miles from the safe house, Liam reached over and clicked off the stereo. "So what's up your ass?"

"Excuse me?"

Liam gave a slight shrug. "Just noting the attitude, man."

"Fuck you. I don't have an attitude."

"Just calling it like I see it."

Dallas scowled. "Our best lead bled out in custody. If I've got an attitude, I think it's justified."

Liam glanced at him, gave a little shake of his head. "Whatever, man."

Hell. Shit, fuck, damn.

Dallas had no intention of getting into a conversation about Jane. And as for Darcy . . .

He tilted his head back and looked at the ceiling. "I was waiting to tell you until we were all together."

"Tell me what?"

"That Darcy screwed us."

For a moment he saw the fury in Liam's face. Then his friend's lips pressed together and he gave a curt, quick nod.

"Give me the details when we're inside." He nodded at the gate that surrounded the ten acres nestled in the foothills. "Might as well give me a few more minutes before I get really pissed off."

A single push of a button on the Rover's console opened the gate, and Liam blasted through, kicking up dust as he went from the asphalt to the dirt road. From this distance, the house was hidden from sight by a line of trees, but Dallas knew it well enough. His father had purchased the five-bedroom stucco house with the familiar red tiled roof when Dallas was only a boy.

He'd bought it from his dad a dozen years ago, and had made a point of bringing various models and D-list actresses to the property at least twice a year, just to keep up the illusion that the house was now his own private love nest. But in reality, it was so much more than that. Over the years, Dallas had transformed the interior into a state-of-the-art operations center.

It was one of the crown jewels of Deliverance's operational holdings, and just seeing it again—stately, well-camouflaged—made Dallas smile. He'd spared no details in putting together Deliverance, and that care and planning showed in the results.

They'd get results with Mueller, too. He was certain of it.

They parked on the graveled drive that formed a semi-circle in front of the house, then passed through the functionally landscaped front yard. The house was well-secured, though not obviously so, yet easy enough to enter with the proper access codes. They were inside within seconds, stepping into the terra-cotta tiled foyer of what appeared to be a vacant home.

Dallas shifted his duffel so that it hung more comfortably on his shoulder and then headed for the kitchen. Not massive, but well-equipped.

Right then, Dallas had no use for it. He passed the stove and fridge and headed straight to the broom closet. The back wall was covered with a series of hooks on which hung coils of rope, extension cords, copper wiring, and spools of tape.

Dallas took hold of the empty middle hook, turned it ninety degrees, and then pushed. The entire back wall opened on a hidden hinge, and he and Liam slipped through into a second room that, at first glance, appeared to be an electrical closet and storage space.

Here, Dallas opened the electrical panel, flipped three breakers in combination, and turned to see the final door open at the back of the room.

This time he followed Liam, who was already halfway down the stairs by the time Dallas had closed the small metal door that covered the breaker switches and retrieved his duffel from the floor. He eased over the threshold, shut the secret door behind him, and followed his friend down the dimly lit stairs.

The heart of Deliverance's South American operation was two stories down beneath a false basement floor. It was always a shock to the senses to go from the murky yellow basement lighting to the bright, high-tech glow of the main conference area.

Quince stood at one of the map tables poring over what appeared from Dallas's perspective to be an electrical schematic.

"About bloody time," he said, peering at Dallas from over the top of the half-frame reading glasses he wore only when he was focusing intently on a project. He had a lean, hard face and deep-set eyes. Women called him ruggedly handsome, but that was all about the attitude. Most of the time, Quince just looked like a badass.

Now, the badass broke into a smile. "Beginning to think you'd decided to come by carrier pigeon." He came around the table and caught Dallas in a hug, coupled with a hearty slap on the back. "Good to see you, mate."

After Liam, Quince had been the second man Dallas had recruited into Deliverance. His boarding school roommate had risen high in British intelligence, and was currently an active MI6 agent. Dallas had never intended to recruit him—too damn risky. But then Quince had confessed that he'd waited in the dorm for a while, but then decided to follow Dallas that night. That he'd arrived in time to see the kidnappers drag him and Jane into the back of an unmarked van. And that he'd never felt more powerless in his life than he had at that moment.

Dallas had taken a chance. He'd told his friend the truth. And Quince had insisted he join the team. He'd been the riskiest addition, because he'd made clear that he wouldn't come on board without authorization. Dallas had debated for three months then finally given the okay.

Now, one man—and only one man—in the British Secret Intelligence Service knew that Quince worked with Deliverance. The trade-off had seemed fair. Dallas acquired Quince's very unique skill set, and British intelligence acquired certain limited information regarding human trafficking rings and terrorist activity uncovered by Deliverance.

But if it all went to hell, Quince was on his own. He'd be completely disavowed.

It was a risk that Quince had willingly accepted.

Now, Quince shot a quick glance toward Liam. "He brief you?"

"About Ortega? Yeah. I got the memo. Makes the one in the box all the more important," Dallas added, referring to Mueller.

"So are you really planning to have a go at him?" Liam asked Dallas. "Is that why you came?"

"It's why I came," he admitted. And he wanted to—wanted to go in there, grab hold of the hair at the back of Mueller's head, and smash his ugly face down onto the table. He wanted to tie his legs to the chair and jam his heel into the guy's crotch until his balls spewed out his nostrils.

He wanted to make the guy hurt. He wanted to make him pay for what he did to Ming-húa, the scared little boy who was finally back in China with his family. For what he did to every child he'd kidnapped. Every innocent that he'd harmed. That he'd scarred.

Wanted to, but he wasn't going to.

Because Mueller had information about Ortega's jobs, his life, his contacts. Information that might lead to the Jailer. And extracting that information was a job that required certain skills that, thanks to the British government, Quince had acquired.

Dallas would trust his friend, his colleague. He'd take a backseat and let his people do what they were trained to do.

"Dallas?" Liam pressed.

"No," he said. He looked at Quince. "You work. I'll watch."

Quince tilted his head in both acquiescence and respect. Dallas knew damn well that his friend understood what the decision cost him. "All right then."

"I need to fill you both in on something first, though," Dallas added. He paused to gather his thoughts and present what he knew about Darcy as succinctly as possible. "I talked to Jane. She's the one who told me WORR had Ortega in custody."

"How'd she hear?" Quince asked.

"Must've been her ex," Liam said, eyeing Dallas for confirmation. "He heads up a division there now."

Quince aimed a steady gaze at him. "You okay, man?"

Dallas nodded. All of the men in Deliverance knew about

his kidnapping. Knew his sister had been with him. Knew she'd been freed and he'd been left behind to suffer.

And they all knew that Jane and Dallas didn't see much of each other anymore.

None of them, however, knew the real reason why.

Dallas turned to Liam. "Did she call you, too? Did she tell you about WORR and Ortega?" He hadn't thought to ask her if she'd spoken to Liam.

"No. She's been buried in that screenplay, and I've been working in London. We haven't talked in weeks."

As children, the three of them had been inseparable. Now, Liam and Jane were still close, and that was probably the one thing for which Dallas was jealous of his friend.

Jane, of course, didn't know the truth about what Liam did. She thought—as did the world—that Liam worked for SysOps, a private security company that operated under the umbrella of the Sykes conglomerate and dealt with security at the various Sykes retail establishments.

"What did she say?" Liam pressed.

"She told me about Ortega getting caught in WORR's net," Dallas said. "That he wanted to trade immunity for information about our kidnapping. But that's not all of it. She also told me that WORR knows about Deliverance."

"Bloody hell," Quince said.

"That about sums it up," Dallas agreed. "Apparently Elaine Darcy put pressure on her son," he began, then ran down the rest of what Jane had told him.

"And he knew the name? He knows we call ourselves Deliverance?"

"We've never advertised it, but we've never kept it a secret. There's risk involved. We all know that. But code name or not, no client has a clue to any of our identities." They were too careful for that, operating Deliverance through a complicated web of anonymous contact points, untraceable wire transfers, burner phones, and a myriad of other precautions.

"You might want to have a talk with Darcy," Liam suggested. "As a concerned friend. After all, your ex-brother-in-law is at WORR. Makes sense you would have heard the news."

Dallas nodded. "I thought of that. Would be good to know what he's telling Bill. I'll catch him at a party. Or throw one myself."

"Rough gig," Quince said with a cocky grin. "I saw the pictures of you and that actress that were all over the *Post*. Hard life you got there."

Dallas shot him the bird. But he smiled while doing it. Then he nodded to Quince. "On that note, why don't you go show our guest just how hard this life can be?"

"Thought you'd never ask."

As Dallas watched, Quince went to the door and started to slowly raise the lights. First there was only a gray blur. Then it formed into the outline of a man. And then Dallas could see that it was Mueller, sitting in the dark in the soundproof room, his hands cuffed to the table as he tried to look cool and tough, when Dallas knew that he was scared right down to his bones.

His phone vibrated in his pocket and he pulled it out, taking his eyes away from the image behind the one-way glass only long enough to see the caller ID. *Adele*.

For a moment, he was tempted to answer, but she wasn't the woman he wanted or needed.

He sent the call to voicemail, then slipped the phone back into his pocket. Then he moved closer to the glass and watched as Quince entered the room and shut the door behind him, the thud of the steel reverberating even over the electrical hum that filled the tech-heavy room.

He watched as his friend put a small leather case on the table. As Mueller's eyes went wide.

And then Quince opened the case, and Dallas caught sight of the gleam of a steel scalpel and a metal hook.

He saw the coil of rope.

He saw the hypodermic.

And he knew that Mueller saw it all, too.

As if compelled, Dallas took another step forward, then pressed his fingers to the glass. He looked at Mueller's face. At the fear in his eyes.

He was trapped. Alone.

Completely under the power of someone else. His life in their hands, and no one to turn to.

Dallas knew how he felt. He'd been trapped. He'd been terrified. He'd been cold and hungry and lost and afraid.

But unlike Mueller, Dallas had had someone.

He'd had Jane.

11

Taken

Dallas woke in a dark so black he wasn't even sure if his eyes were open.

He was sore—every single muscle. Even his bones. Hell, even his teeth. And his head was pounding like a bastard.

He tried to sit up, then realized there was something around his waist strapping him down. And although he pulled at it and ran his fingers over every bit of it, he couldn't figure out how to get free.

Panic, which had been hiding behind a fog of confusion and denial, moved firmly into the forefront. "Jane!" He could push himself part of the way up, and he did that now, twisting his head around as if suddenly, miraculously, he'd be able to see something despite the inky darkness. "Jane!"

But there was no answer other than the echo of his own voice.

For hours, he struggled and strained. Then he slept. Then he struggled some more. He grew weak and realized he'd had no food or water and his clothes were stinking and filthy. His throat was parched. And for the first time he didn't wonder *when* he was going to get free, but *if* he would get free.

He'd lost all sense of time, but at some point there was someone else in the room. He called for Jane again, but this time, his voice was only a croak, and as he cried for her, someone nearby dropped water into his mouth.

That happened again. And again. Water. Then food. Until his mind seemed to come back and he could focus. His clothes were stiff on him and disgusting, and the strap around his waist continued to hold him in place. His back ached. His shoulders hurt. His feet were cold. But he was alive and they were feeding him and giving him water. He let himself hope. Mostly, he hoped for Jane. That she was alive. That she was safe.

Every time they brought him liquid, he called for her, hoping that his soothed throat made him just that much louder. Maybe she was right there in an adjacent room. And maybe hearing his voice would give her hope. If there was even a chance, he would keep on doing it.

And then, finally, he realized that something was moving in the dark. He called out—"Jane?"—but he knew right away it wasn't her. He knew the way she moved. The way she smelled. If she was in the room with him, he would know.

He strained his eyes to see, but it was still impossible. And this time, when he tried to sit up, he realized that his hands and feet were strapped down, too, and there was a firm palm pressing flat against his chest preventing him from rising even an inch.

The voice was right at his ear. Strange. Distorted. Like it was talking through one of those Halloween voice changers. And the voice alone was at least as scary as all the rest of it so far.

"You think you can cry out? Get away? You're here because this is where you're supposed to be. You're here because this is where I want you, and you will pay."

He felt breath on his cheek, and the voice was that much

closer. He thought it was a man. Not that he could tell much from the voice—not that it even really mattered—but there had been the palm on his chest, too. And it felt masculine.

"The sins of the father, Dallas. And if the man who now calls you son wants you back, he'll have to pay."

This time, it wasn't breath on his skin, but something sharp, like the point of a pencil or the sharp end of a nail, and someone was dragging it back and forth across his neck.

"I bet he doesn't. I bet the man you call Dad doesn't spend even a day looking. I bet he doesn't spend an hour."

His voice shook, but Dallas demanded, "Where's Jane?"

"Jane? Why do you care? You think she wants you now? You think you could comfort her?"

"Yes."

A hard slap cut him across the cheek. "Then you're a fool, aren't you? Don't you know that you deserve this? The fear. The humiliation. Don't you know that it's yours to own? To taste and wallow in?"

He shook his head. "No. No."

"Do you think this is about her? It's your fault she's here. Your fault she was in the way. Wrong place, wrong time, wrong boy, and if she dies in here, if she rots in here, it's all because of you."

His eyes burned. He wanted to cry from the horror of that thought. Even more, he wanted to kill whoever was taunting him. Wanted to reach up and strangle them with his bare hands. But he was strapped. Bound. As immobile as a body in a coffin.

The thought made him shudder.

"Please . . . What do you want? I'll do whatever you want, but don't hurt her."

"What can you do? You can't even scratch your own ass. You're helpless, Dallas. Helpless and alone. And you're the reason she's here, remember? Why the hell would she want you?"

And then the voice was gone, and Dallas heard nothing to mark the departure. No footsteps. No squeak of a door. Just nothing.

Once again, he was alone with his thoughts.

The sins of the father.

The sins of the father?

Could that mean his birth father?

He knew the kind of man his father had been—born to privilege, he'd thrown it all away on drugs and parties. He'd been a fuckup for sure, and when Dallas had acted out, he'd told himself it was bad blood that made him do it. Because that's what Eli thought, wasn't it? Hell, Eli had practically told him he was Donovan's son through and through back when Dallas was thirteen and Eli had found a *Playboy* in Dallas's room with a picture of Jane tucked inside it.

It wasn't a naughty picture. Just one he'd taken of her sunbathing that summer. And although Dallas had never admitted it, his dad had been right about what he'd thought. Because Dallas really had jacked off for the first time in his life to a picture of his sister. And a whole lot more times after that.

What a damn loser he was.

Just like his father. Just like Donovan.

Had Donovan pissed off the wrong people before he died, and now it was Dallas and Jane who were paying for his mistakes?

Or maybe *the sins of the father* referred to Eli? God knows Eli had enough money to pay a ransom a zillion times over.

But if this was about Eli, then why would grabbing Jane be a mistake? Eli was Jane's dad, too.

It didn't make sense.

None of it made sense.

And when he drifted off to sleep, it was on a cloud of confusion and fear.

When he woke, there was more light in the room. Not enough to see colors, but enough to make out shapes. To get a sense of place, not that there was much to see. As far as he could tell, he was in a square room with nothing in it but a filthy mattress on the floor and a thin blanket.

But he wasn't restrained anymore, either. And he was clean. His clothes were gone and he was in a T-shirt and fleece pants and he could walk around, pressing his hand to the gray walls. Smelling the straw on the floor.

Had they drugged him? They must have drugged him.

Then he heard the metal creak of a door followed by a startled "oh!" and then the dull thud of someone hitting the ground.

Jane.

He was at her side in an instant. Holding her. Clinging to her. Rejoicing that she was with him and that she was safe. Mourning the fact that she was here at all. That she wasn't free as he had secretly hoped.

"Dallas. Oh, god, Dallas." She clung tight to him, her arms around his neck, her head pressed to his chest. "I'm so sorry you're here, but thank god you're here."

She tilted her head back to look at him, tears trailing down her face. He wanted to kiss them away. He wanted to get lost in her. To forget everything but her. To make her safe. To keep her warm.

"Why are they doing this?" she asked. "Ransom?"

"I don't know." They must have bathed her, too, because her hair hung in damp strands that he pushed away from her beautiful face. "Now that I know you're okay, I don't even care. You are okay?"

She nodded, but her eyes were still full of fear. "They tied me up. With leather straps. Tied to a tabletop. And they said they were going to leave me. That I was going to starve. And then they left and I was so hungry." She closed her eyes. "I don't know how long they were gone before they came back with water and some crackers. Dallas, why?"

Rage burned through him, and he wanted to kill their captors. The sadistic fucks who had done that to her.

But he forced it back. He needed to comfort. Needed to make it better for her. "It's okay now," he said. "You're with me now. And I told you I'd always protect you, remember?"

He looked into her eyes and saw some of her terror fade, and he felt a surge of power inside him, knowing that he'd given her comfort.

He heard her breath hitch. "Dallas." His name was a whisper. Nothing more. But he knew what she wanted, and he leaned in and brushed his lips over hers in the softest of kisses, the most gentle of touches. And in the hell of where they were, that single touch was good.

"I'm so scared," she confessed.

"Me, too."

They held each other for hours, drifting in and out of sleep. There was a gallon of water in the corner and a single can of cat food beside it. On the far side of the room, the captors had left a bucket and a roll of toilet paper, along with a jug of cloudy water that the Woman had said was for washing only. Drink it, and they'd regret it.

It was hardly civilization, but Dallas had been grateful.

They'd waited until they were desperate to eat the cat food. They measured time by the diminishing water.

"Are they going to let us starve?" she asked when there was no food and only a little water.

I don't know. It was the only true answer, but he couldn't say it. Couldn't even think it.

"I don't want to die."

"Jane, no." The thought of losing her ripped him up, but he was scared when he looked at her. He didn't know for sure, but he thought that it had been about a week since they'd been taken. She'd lost weight in her face and in the dim light, her cheekbones seemed more prominent. Her huge eyes seemed hollow. She was beautiful—she would always be beautiful—but she was turning into a waif before his eyes.

God only knew what he looked like. Sickly and scrawny, most likely. Their captors were making them weak. Making sure they couldn't fight.

Assuming anyone ever came back into their room.

The thought sent a shock of terror cutting through him.

"We're not going to die," he said, the words worthless and stupid and they both knew that. Hadn't they explored every inch of their cell? Didn't they know damn well there was no-where to go?

"Maybe it would be like sleeping," she said as she rested her head on his shoulder. "Maybe it wouldn't be so bad. I think I could stand it, except I don't want to be away from you."

"Don't talk like that." His words were fierce because she was echoing his own thoughts, and he didn't want to think that she'd lost hope, too.

"I just—"

He crushed his mouth over hers to shut her up, and for a moment she was quiet in his arms. Then her arms went around him and she pulled him down, pulled him hard against her onto the disgusting, lumpy mattress.

"I love you," he said when they broke apart, both gasping hard. "I don't want to lose you, either."

"I know," she said. "I love you, too. You know that, right? You've always known it."

"Always," he said, and for the first time since the night he'd snuck out to meet her, he felt alive again.

He felt hope.

He shifted so that he was leaning over her, and she was on

her back. He looked into her deep brown eyes and felt like he was falling. He was hard, but instead of getting off her—instead of trying to hide it—he just said, "Jane."

She didn't answer in words. Instead she tugged him down to her, and then she softly opened her mouth to his.

He lost himself in the kiss, their connection erasing all his fears, masking all the horror. When they pulled apart, he was breathing hard, his cock so hard he thought he would burst.

"Are you sure?"

She nodded, her eyes wide. "Aren't you?"

"I—yeah. Yeah."

She licked her lips and then pulled off her shirt. And god-damn it—god*damn* it—he lost it. He came in his damn pants just from the sight of her pale skin and her round, perfect breasts.

"I'm sorry, I'm sorry."

She shut him up with kisses, and he moaned as she reached for the drawstring of the ugly pants they'd given him, then loosened them so they fell off his hips. They hadn't given him underwear, so he was naked now, and he kicked the sticky pants off and away.

"Just touch me," she said. "Please?"

Oh, yeah. He could do that. He eased her back, then untied the drawstring of her pants, too. He eased them down, whimpering a little when he saw the first hint of pubic hair.

He'd seen naked women before in magazines, but he'd only fantasized about Jane. She was prettier than he'd ever imagined. He wanted to hold her close and never let go. He wanted to be her protector. Her knight. He wanted to do the kinds of things with her he'd only read about.

He wanted to do everything with her. To her.

He wanted to make her forget they were captives. He wanted to escape with her, even if only into themselves.

And, he realized, he was rock hard again.

Sweet.

"Your shirt," she said, and he ripped it over his head and tossed it aside. For a moment, he was afraid *they'd* come in. That he and Jane would get caught. But he pushed the thought aside. He didn't care anymore. He didn't know if they were going to live or die. He was going to do what he wanted. He was going to have the girl he wanted. The girl he loved.

"I love you," he whispered, because he had to tell her again.

"I love you, too." She licked her lips. "Have you ever—"

"No!" He'd never wanted to with anyone else. There was only her. "Have you?"

"I only want you," she said, and he melted all over again.

Slowly, he drew his fingers over her, mesmerized by the way her muscles tightened as he trailed up her belly. He cupped a breast in his hands, loving the way it fit, the way she made that sweet little noise. And when he sucked on her tit, the darker part around the nipple puckered up and she got so tight and so hard that it was like he could feel it, too, in his cock.

She rolled over on her side, and he stroked his fingers down her waist and over her hips as she touched him, first trailing her fingertips over his jaw. "You're getting a beard," she said, then grinned. "It's sexy."

He felt his face heat with a blush. "Yeah, well, it's not like they gave me a razor."

"I like it." She turned her head away as if shy. "I like the way it feels when you kiss me."

"Yeah?"

She nodded, then bit her lower lip as she moved her hand lower and lower until her fingers were twined in his pubic hair and his cock was twitching. And then, when she closed her hand around him, he closed his eyes and groaned.

When he opened them again, she smiled shyly, looking pleased with herself.

"Lay back," he said, giving her a tiny push. "Fair is fair."

She did, and because he wanted to one-up her, he used his mouth to tease her belly. To move lower until her pubic hair tickled his mouth and he slid his hands up to push apart her thighs.

She tensed. "Dallas—"

"It's okay. Let me." He lifted his head, and saw that her cheeks were bright red. "I really want to taste you." He'd seen so many pictures, but he'd never understood why he'd want to taste a girl down there. But he got it now. Right now he thought he would die if he couldn't taste her, couldn't get lost in her.

He didn't wait for her to answer, but when she slowly spread her legs he knew that was her consent. He ran his tongue over her folds, then used his fingers to open her. She was like a flower, and when he found her clitoris and teased it, she made the most incredible little sounds.

She was slick and wet, and he closed his mouth over her, then felt the hard nub of her clit against his lips. He sucked and licked, and he couldn't get enough of her. And then when she started to squirm he *really* couldn't get enough. He kept his mouth on her, kissing and sucking, but added his finger, too, slipping one inside her, amazed at how hot and slick she was.

His cock was rock hard, and he wanted to thrust it in her, but he also wanted to finish this. To keep letting her build. And then, suddenly, she was shaking and crying out his name, and he was so damn hard because he'd made her come. He'd done that for her—given her that escape—and that was just too fucking amazing.

"Please," she said. "Dallas. Please. I want—I want more."

"Me, too." He straddled her and then he pressed the tip of his cock right against her entrance. "It's going to hurt you I think. I'm really sorry."

She nodded. "I know. It's okay. Just—go slow. Okay?"

He tried. But he was so excited. So ready. And in the end he couldn't hold back. "I'm sorry!" he cried when she sucked in air from the pain, but she just shook her head and told him not to stop. That it was okay, that it was wonderful.

Wonderful. The word washed over him right as he exploded inside her, his body quaking violently, wildly. It felt like it would last forever, and when he finally collapsed, sated, beside her, she curled up against him, her legs twined with his.

"Wow," she said.

"You're really okay?" He held her close, wanting to never let her go.

"Really. It hurt, then it got better." She smiled a little shyly. "A lot better."

"I don't ever want to hurt you."

"You couldn't," she said as she curled up against him. "Not really."

"Jane?" he said, after they'd been silent for a while.

"Yeah?"

"Do you want to do it again?"

She eased back, and he could see the desire in her eyes. "Yeah," she said. "I do."

He kissed her, and even though they were in hell, in that moment, he was happy. They might never get out of this room, but no matter what else happened, they'd been able to escape into each other.

For a few wonderful moments, they'd been free.

12

Temptation and Torment

Dallas pressed his forehead against the cool glass and exhaled, feeling lost. Feeling alone. For long days and longer nights he and Jane had been each other's lifeline, the point of light in a dark and horrible world.

They'd escaped into each other, worshipped each other. Found secret triggers to incredible sensations. Nothing was wrong, nothing forbidden. He'd touched her, tasted her, buried himself inside her. And it had felt more right, more real, more mature back in those weeks as a teenager than in any encounter he'd had since.

They'd saved each other then, in every possible way.

So why the hell did it feel like they would destroy each other now?

Behind the glass, Quince was still working Mueller, but Dallas no longer wanted to watch. He needed to be alone. He wanted to take a shower and shake off the melancholy that had come with the memories. He couldn't go there, couldn't go to her.

And regrets were for pussies.

The main room of the operations center housed the tech and the holding cell in which Quince was now doing his job. But there was more to this underground lair. He gave a quick nod to Liam at the computer, then headed out the side door to the hallway that led to the Spartan sleeping quarters, along with the steam room and shower.

He dropped his duffel on the cot in his quarters, then strode to the shower, situated in the only room that had been tricked out for comfort, with high end fixtures and a state-of-the-art steam feature. He stripped as he walked, then shut the door behind him and tossed his clothes on top of the marble counter.

The control panel was mounted in the wall next to the glass shower door, and he turned it on, setting the water pressure to high and cranking up the steam. As the system began to hiss, he leaned against the counter and looked at his face in the mirror—he looked tired. Worn out. And he wondered how much of it had to do with coming so close to finding his kidnapper—and how much of it had to do with coming so close to having Jane.

His phone chirped, signaling a text, and he felt a little jolt of hope in his chest—*Jane?* He turned to pull it out of the pocket of his jeans, now crumpled on the counter, then suffered a stab of disappointment to see that it wasn't from Jane but from Myra. It took him a moment to place the name, only remembering that she was the redhead from last night when he opened the text and saw the short video image.

She was arched back, her eyes closed and her mouth open in an expression that could only be ecstasy. Her breasts were thrust skyward and her legs were spread wide. The blonde's face was buried between them, and from his perspective, Dallas could see the blonde's own sweet, wet pussy between her bare legs as she squirmed and fingered herself, her ass making small circular motions as she excitedly moved her head, blond curls bouncing, while she sucked loudly on Myra's clit.

For a second, he wondered who was holding the camera, but then Myra lifted her head and opened her eyes so that she was looking over the blonde's arched back right at the camera. Right at him. "We made a new friend," she said. "She likes it in the ass, Dallas." She dragged her teeth over her lower lip. "So do I. So hurry back and come play with all three of us."

He sucked in air and realized he was hard. So goddamn hard he thought he'd explode. And not from the video. Not from Myra's sultry invitation. Not from the thought of himself in bed with three willing, eager women.

No, he was hard because he'd been staring at the video and imagining another scene. A different scene.

Him on his back, his hands above his head as he held tight to straps that were secured to the headboard. His body was stiff, his cock as hard as glass. He was on the edge, about to shatter, and as he stepped into the shower he let the image grow clearer.

He pictured Jane's hand curved around the base of his cock. Her mouth taking him in, deep and wet, as her tongue teased the length of him, then pulled back slowly, sucking hard and lingering on the head so that he had to pull tight on the straps in order to battle the urge to thrust up and fuck her gorgeous, wide mouth.

Then she opened for him, taking him in. Deeper and deeper until he could feel the tip of his cock against the back of her throat, and he was so hard, so ready to explode, but he didn't want it to end. This feeling. This knowledge that it was Jane getting him off. Jane giving him pleasure. Jane, and not some substitute female who could do nothing but satisfy an itch, but never satisfy him.

Deeper and deeper she took him, and as she did, her hands cupped his balls, and that was it—that was all he could take.

He let go of the straps before he shot his load—and goddamn if he wasn't as close in the shower as he was in the fantasy—and he pulled roughly out of her mouth even as he grabbed hold of her arms and urged her up to him.

She straddled him, her thighs warm against his ribs. She was wet, and she rubbed herself over his chest, teasing her clit and making soft little moaning noises as she looked him deep in the eyes.

"Is this the way you want it?" she asked.

"God yes."

The corner of her mouth lifted and she rose up on her knees, breaking contact long enough to lean forward and kiss him, then slide her lips over to his ear.

"I'm being awfully naughty. You may have to spank me."

"Naughty?" He didn't think so. She was following his commands to the letter. "How?"

"Because of what I want."

His cock twitched. "Tell me."

"I want your finger in my ass," she whispered. "I want you to fill me when I ride you. And after I come, I want you to tie me down and fuck me hard. My pussy. My ass. I want the ropes to leave marks on my wrists and my ankles." She licked the edge of her ear, and he shuddered. "I want you to use me, Dallas. I want to be everything you need."

Every word rocked him, sending all of his blood rushing to his cock. He wanted this. Wanted her. And with a knowing little smile, she eased back and lowered herself onto his rock hard cock.

He groaned, relishing the feel of being inside her wet heat. She rode him hard, fingering her clit as she moved up and down until he was right on the edge, right about to lose it.

Not yet.

He flipped her over on her back, shoved her knees up near her shoulders, and pounded his cock into her, harder and harder, until all he knew was his growing pleasure and the mingled sounds of their bodies meeting, her moans, then the wild, violent cry of his name as she exploded around him.

And even before her trembling subsided, she begged for more. "Again," she moaned. "Please, Dallas, tie me down and fuck my ass. I need you. I need you every way I can have you."

The words ripped through Dallas, and he came. Harder. Faster. More violently and wildly than he had in forever. As he did he cried out, both from the euphoric pleasure of the release, and from the emotional pain of knowing that it was all a fantasy. Could only ever be a fantasy. He'd never be deep inside her. He'd never fuck her senseless.

He'd never hear her cry his name as she rode out her orgasm.

Because he couldn't ever go there.

And even if he could—

God, even if he could it would never be right. He needed it dirty. Rough. Fucked up.

He'd take her part of the way in fantasy, but even in his mind he couldn't completely sink down with her—and he sure couldn't take her there in reality. Not now. Not ever.

Dammit. Goddamn it all to hell.

He gulped in air and stumbled back to lean against the hot tile wall. The adrenaline flowed from him like the water, and he dropped his head, exhaustion overwhelming him. Only then did he see the threads of red curling toward the drain.

Blood?

Confused, he looked up, and realized that the shower door was shattered. That his hand was bleeding.

Fuck.

He let himself slide to the floor. Let the water continue to run, to dilute the blood. He closed his eyes and sat in the steam, and wished that he could wash away his self-loathing as easily as the water washed away his blood.

* * *

"You didn't return my call."

Dallas paused in front of the cot where he'd been pacing in his room, a bath towel wrapped around his hips, and allowed himself a single moment to regret the decision to answer the phone.

"Hello to you, too, Adele."

"What's the matter, pet?" He could hear the pout in her voice, accentuated by the lingering French accent that she hadn't lost even though she'd moved to the States forty years ago when she was thirteen. "You don't sound happy to hear from me at all."

"It's not you," he lied. They'd broken up four months ago. And although it had been surprisingly hard to break away, cutting himself free from their screwed up relationship—if you could even call it a relationship—had been one of the best decisions of his life.

At least that's what he thought most days. Other days, it was hard. Because Adele had been the only woman he'd ever had in his bed who knew some of his secrets. Who'd go with him into the dark.

Sure, he could blindfold the models and actresses and socialites who sucked his cock. He could tie their wrists together, spread their legs wide and fuck each one hard with a dildo while he sucked her off. He could spank the redhead. He could make the blonde crawl. He could jerk himself off until he came all over the new one's tits—the one he imagined stroking her own pussy as she videotaped her two friends.

But there were limits on what he could do with a woman he would only invite to his bed once or twice, three times at the max. And while a little kink only increased the titillating buzz that he'd worked so hard to foster, what really got him hard wasn't the kind of thing that socialites whispered about to each other over their Cosmos.

He'd told the redhead that he liked his sex fucked up, and that was true. She just didn't have any idea of how fucked up he was talking.

Adele had known. Hell, Adele had liked it.

"My ego is very happy to know it's not me," she said lightly. "But what's on your mind?"

He sighed, knowing she would press. She was trained as a therapist, so being nosy was part of her makeup.

He put the phone down on the cot after turning on the speaker. He'd bandaged his hand, and it ached from holding the damn thing. "It's nothing, really. I've just got a crisis at work I'm dealing with."

She chuckled softly. "Darling, your father would be so proud. I think he believes you run from anything related to your job that doesn't require you to wine and dine an investor's daughter or squeeze some B-actress's ass at a ribbon cutting for a new Sykes department store."

"You've never even met my father."

"Touchy." He could hear her adjust the phone. "I'm sorry. That was uncalled for. But Colin knew Eli well, and still talks about him often."

The mention of Colin, Jane's birth father, was like a sharp poke between the eyes, and he winced, everything that was wrong about his time with Adele coming back to him like a flood.

They'd met in the years following the kidnapping, when Dallas was grappling with the loss of Jane—both her friendship, and the sudden cessation of everything forbidden that had happened between them.

Dallas had gone one day to Colin, whom he'd once thought of as an uncle, and Colin's new wife, Adele, had joined them for lunch. She was in her early forties, twenty years older than Dallas, and gloriously confident and sexy. There'd been an undeniable awareness between them. Not heat so much as attraction, as if they were succumbing to some sort of magnetic power.

They'd danced around it for years, never doing more than flirting. But as her marriage to Colin deteriorated, Adele had become more and more suggestive and aggressive. So that when she and Colin finally divorced, it was almost a foregone conclusion that Dallas would have her in his bed. Or—he still wasn't entirely sure—she would have him in hers.

She was the only woman with whom he ceded some control, and though he didn't understand why, he knew that something about her compelled him. Got him hard, even when he didn't want to be. It was more than her looks. She was beautiful, true, but with her thin, angular face, she really wasn't his type.

Hell, other than Jane he had no type.

He didn't love her. Sometimes he didn't even like spending time with her. Adele soothed the darkest urges in him, but being with her made him feel even more dirty. As if he came away from sex with her covered in a thin layer of grime.

He'd almost walked away so many times, but that strange attraction compelled him to stay. To punish and be punished. Control and be controlled. It was never quite enough—always just shy of satisfaction—but with her he at least came close to the unknowable, unreachable nirvana he craved.

After about three months, she confessed that Colin had told her about the kidnapping. More than that, she'd eased close, brushed her lips against his ear, and told him she could guess his darkest secrets.

She'd been right. About Jane. About what they'd meant to each other. Done with each other.

About everything.

She'd turned her trained eye on him, and she'd seen right through him.

He should have ended it then. Instead, that's when it had gotten even hotter. Dirtier. Kinkier.

He'd needed the release. The escape. The control.

But there were lines he wouldn't let her cross, and when she'd told him it would be therapeutic to pretend that she was Jane—naked and captive and wanting Dallas to fuck her hard— Dallas had balked.

He'd pulled on his jeans, left the room, and hadn't looked back.

That had been four months ago, and though she had called and apologized—though they'd talked casually and exchanged emails and salvaged the friendship, such as it was—they both knew it was over. At the time, Dallas had even considered that it was Adele who'd been sending him the taunting letters, but he'd dismissed the thought. The first letter had arrived a year ago, long before Adele had any reason to be hurt by his departure. Besides, even while they'd been sleeping together, they'd both known it was only sex. Hell, they'd both known it was mostly therapy.

"You shouldn't lie to me, you know," she said cheerfully now. "It's not work that has you tied in knots. I know you too well."

He grimaced and dragged his uninjured hand through his damp hair. "I'm not lying."

"You do realize that Colin and I are still friends. For that matter, we occasionally fuck. Friends do that sometimes, you know."

"Why are you calling, Adele?"

Her laugh was like the tinkling of bells, and he rolled his eyes, not quite able to stay mad at her. Irritation, however, was still lingering.

"I thought you might need a sympathetic ear. Jane talked to Colin, so I heard the news."

"About Ortega?"

"What else? I hope they rip every bit of information they can out of the miserable bastard. I hope they catch and destroy whoever was behind your kidnapping."

Dallas didn't disagree. He also didn't tell her that Ortega was dead. She'd hear soon enough.

"But I didn't call about Ortega," she continued. "I called because Jane told Colin that she was going to go see you. To tell you the news personally."

"She did," he said.

"And that's why I thought you might need someone to talk to." Her voice was soft. Soothing. "Seriously, darling. Are you okay?"

"I'm fine." Even to his own ear, it didn't sound believable.

He heard her draw in a breath. To him, the breath sounded judgmental.

"She's your obsession," she said gently. "You need to let her go."

He looked at his bandaged hand and knew she was right. "You're not my therapist."

"No, but I could be."

"Adele." His tone was reproving.

"What? I'm just saying that I can help you work through it. You need to let the obsession go, but we both know that's hard, especially when this imprint of her is such a huge part of your pathology."

He bit back a curse. Jane wasn't a fucking pathology.

"Don't turn what I'm saying around," she soothed, obviously knowing the direction of his thoughts. "I'm acknowledging that it's difficult. That you need to ease away from her. You can incorporate fantasy for that, and I can help.

"You can tell me all sorts of dirty things," she continued, lowering her voice to a soft, sexy purr. "You can call me her name, you can spread out naked on your bed and I'll tell you what I'm doing—what she's doing. Do you want to know what I'm doing right now?"

"No." But the word was a whisper and Jane was in his head and his hand was around his cock, the towel having dropped away.

"I'm straddling you. And I'm so wet, and you're hard, as hard as rock. And I rise up on my knees right over your cock—*she* rises up on her knees. And then she starts to lower herself until her cunt just brushes against—"

He flinched, then tugged his hand free from his engorged cock. "God*damn* it, Adele." Rage rushed through him. At her, for pushing. At himself, for letting her. "You think I want that? You think I need that?"

"Yes," she said flatly. "I do."

"You're wrong."

"Dallas—"

But he didn't hear what else she had to say. He ended the call, feeling angry and dirty and totally fucking pissed off.

A knock sounded at his door.

"What?" he barked.

Liam stepped in as Dallas was twisting the towel back around his waist. It did little to hide his erection.

Liam raised his brow. "Interrupting?"

"Fuck you."

His friend's eyes dipped down to the towel. "Sorry. My type doesn't have a cock."

Dallas didn't even bother trying to find a snappy comeback. "What is it?"

"I only came to find out if the shower had pissed you off in some specific way, or if you've just taken to casually beating up bathroom hardware." He nodded at Dallas's bound hand. "You okay?"

"Actually, it's not one of my better days."

"You wanna tell me why?"

Dallas just looked at him.

"Don't even give me that," Liam said. "You and I both deal with shit like this Ortega clusterfuck on a daily basis. And, yes, this one's personal. But it's not the kind of thing you'd put your hand through a door about. For that matter, I can only think of one thing that would get you that worked up."

Dallas narrowed his eyes. "What's that?"

"You saw Jane. I'm right, aren't I? She didn't tell you all of this over the phone. She came by the house. She told you in person."

"So what if she did?"

"You could say better than me." Liam took a seat on the cot, as if they were just casually talking, while Dallas walked to his duffel to get dressed. "I don't know the whole story between you two," Liam continued, "but I know a lot. I've seen a lot. And I know you're both hurting. Ironic since you tell everyone that you're staying apart to make things easier. 'Cause that's bullshit, man. All you're doing is making it harder."

"Don't start playing shrink. I've had about all I can stand of that for one day. And honestly, you don't know what the hell you're talking about."

"Maybe not." He shrugged. "I'm just saying that you're my best friend. If I lost you, I'd fight to get you back."

Dallas pulled a shirt over his head, then scowled at his friend. "What is it that you think you know? What is it you think happened? You think we had a fight? A difference of opinion over our kidnapping accommodations?"

"Don't be an ass. And it doesn't matter what I know or what I think or what anybody thinks."

Dallas cocked his head, hearing something unexpected in Liam's tone more than the specific words. "And what *do* you think?"

"Lots of things," Liam said. "I'm a hell of a thinker."

"Dammit, Li—"

"Fuck, man, you know I love you both. And I'll always tell you if I think you're being a prick." He drew in a long breath. "But there are some things you can't—you can't just butt into."

"In that case, don't tell me what you're thinking. Just tell me what you're saying."

Liam sighed, and Dallas thought that for a moment his bad-ass buddy actually looked a little cornered.

"I'm saying that it's not for me to do the thinking on this one," Liam finally said. "But I'll tell you this. Jane Martin is a hell of a woman. And if I was in love with her, there's not a power on earth that could keep me away."

Liam had been gone a full forty-five minutes, but his words still lingered, tormenting Dallas as he tried to read the reports and updates that the team kept shooting to his tablet.

Screw it.

He gave up trying to concentrate. And before he could talk himself out of it, he pulled out his phone.

It wasn't quite midnight in Mendoza, and New York was only two hours behind. Surely he'd find her awake.

He hit the speed dial on his phone. They talked only infrequently these days, but he'd still put her in the first slot. Always had. Probably always would.

The phone rang once. Twice. Five times. And then it clicked to voicemail.

He clenched his fists, hating the feeling of helplessness that one unanswered call could bring. Was she not by her phone? Was she asleep? Was she avoiding him?

He was about to go run on the treadmill—maybe if he exhausted himself his mind would quit thinking about her for five seconds—when his phone chirped with Jane's familiar ringtone.

With one quick motion he snatched it up and answered the call. "Hey."

"You called me?" she asked. "I just saw the missed call on the lock screen."

"I did. Yeah." He rolled his eyes at himself. He sounded like a teenager again.

"Oh. Well, what's—"

"I wanted to say I was sorry again. I pushed. I shouldn't have pushed."

For a moment, there was only silence, and when she did speak, her voice was low, barely a whisper. "No, you shouldn't have. But you weren't the only one pushing. I guess I owe you an apology, too."

"Fair enough," he said. "Apology accepted."

"So was that it?" she asked. "Was that the only reason you called?"

He thought she sounded hopeful, but that might be wishful thinking. And right then, he didn't have a clue what to say. Hell, he wasn't even sure why he called. To hear her voice, maybe. But now that she was on the phone, he was fucking tongue-tied. Him—the man who'd made women melt with nothing more than the tone of his voice and a stern command—couldn't manage to utter a single coherent thought. Because damned if it didn't feel different when it was real.

"Dallas?" she said into his lingering silence. "Shit, are you there? Stupid cellphone, I think the call dropped."

"No." His voice was so low she probably couldn't hear him. "I'm here."

"Are you okay?"

He closed his eyes, done in by the genuine concern in her voice. "No," he said honestly. "I miss you."

He hadn't intended to say that. And, now the words hung there, and he hated how damn vulnerable he felt. He ran a secret covert operation, and yet he was as nervous as a boy calling a pretty girl for the very first time.

"I miss you, too. I really do. But, Dallas, we can't." He heard the tinge of pain in her voice. "You were right to push away the other night. I should never—I mean, we should never have—"

"No." He rushed to correct her. "I'm not saying we should. When I say I miss you, I mean I miss talking to you. Our friendship." He didn't say sister. He couldn't bring himself to voice what they both already knew so well. And the truth was, they'd come at being siblings by such a convoluted path, with the adoption and without a single drop of shared blood, that she'd always been a friend more than a sister.

He thought about the women in the video. Women he didn't care about. Didn't truly want. "I miss that," he continued. "I need it. I'm tired of polite conversation when we're together. I want to laugh with you again."

"We laugh."

"Dammit, Jane, don't pretend like I'm not making sense. You know what I mean."

"I do. I really do."

"And?"

She took a deep breath. "Are you in town?"

A flicker of hope curled inside him. "South America."

"Oh. Well, come over when you get back. We'll have coffee. Maybe play a game."

"A game?" He couldn't keep the amusement out of his voice.

"That's what friends do. Play games. Watch crappy television."

"Is it? I thought friends went to dinner."

"We don't. Too dangerous. Too much like a date."

"All right then. *Resident Evil* it is." Killing mutant zombies never sounded so good.

"I was thinking more along the lines of chess. Possibly Yahtzee."

"It'll be fun. I promise."

He could practically see her making a face. She was terrible at videogames.

"Okay," she finally said.

"Okay."

"Say goodbye, Dallas."

"Goodbye, Dallas."

She laughed. And he realized he hadn't felt quite this light in a long, long time.

He was still smiling when Quince stuck his head through the half-open doorway. "Hey, you got a sec?"

"Any progress with Mueller?"

"Bits and pieces. Right now I'm letting him stew. I've been on the phone with Noah going over the specs for the security system on Ortega's property."

"And?"

"And I think we may have a way in." He passed Dallas his phone, open to an image of a gorgeous woman with lush dark hair and deep brown eyes.

Dallas glanced at the image, then looked up at his friend. "I'm listening."

"Her name's Eva Lopez, and her father owns the land that borders Ortega's. There's a party there tomorrow night. And I think Eva needs to make a new friend."

Dallas grinned. "Let me guess. There's a weak spot on Ortega's perimeter that's accessible from the Lopez property."

"And that's why you run this show," Quince quipped. "You're a bloody genius."

Dallas's gaze flicked back down to the picture. The girl wasn't Jane, but the eyes were similar. The cheekbones as round and perfect. Her mouth wide enough to swallow a man's cock.

He'd meant what he'd told Jane just now—he wanted to be friends. And he also wanted more.

He might get the friendship, but he knew damn well the

more was not only off-limits, but impossible. He wasn't the man for her. He could never be the man she needed. The man she deserved.

He knew all that—hell, that simple, basic truism had settled into his bones. But that didn't mean the wanting went away.

The woman on Quince's phone wasn't Jane, but he could pretend she was. If that's what it took to get him through this assignment, then yes, he could pretend.

It sure as hell wouldn't be the first time. And, goddamn it, that was the job.

That was the role he played.

13

Bastard on Toast

"Dallas Sykes is a goddamned bastard on toast," I say, huffing a little as I try to catch my breath. We've just run three miles in Central Park and now we're back at the Seventy-second Street exit, waiting to cross with the light.

Beside me, Brody jogs in place. "Because he went with some Argentine babe to a party?"

"*Went* to a party?" I repeat. "More like he practically fucked the bimbo on the dance floor." I bend over and wheeze. I hate running—that runner's high myth is a huge load of bullshit—but I force myself to do it, just like I force myself to weight train, practice at the firing range, and go to self-defense classes. I may never be attacked again, but if I am, I intend to do some damage before I race the fuck out of there.

"You saw the picture," I remind him.

"How could I miss it? You shoved it in my face at least five times before we headed to the park."

I scowl, because he's right. I'd been nightmare-free last night, and I'd awakened in a good mood, enjoying a pleasant little Dallas hangover following our conversation. And then I'd turned on the computer, and the first thing in my feed was about eight hundred different pictures of the man I crave, up close and personal with yet another woman who isn't me.

And suddenly my good day was shot all to hell.

I'd saved the picture on my phone and then proceeded to share my pain.

"First of all, I don't think she's a bimbo," Brody says reasonably. "I looked her up on my phone before we started the run, and she's an Oxford grad."

This doesn't make me feel better.

"And second—well, I think we both know what second is."

"That I shouldn't be jealous of who my brother sleeps with? Yeah, we both know."

I sigh, because he's right. Brody usually is. But somehow that doesn't make the pang of jealousy—and of loss—any less painful. And the fact that Dallas and I don't share a single drop of blood only makes it worse, not better. Because if it weren't for those adoption orders, there'd be nothing keeping us apart. But there is. We're siblings. And that makes it not only taboo but technically illegal.

Brody is the only person other than Dallas who knows my secrets. All of them. The kidnapping. What happened between Dallas and me. And all the rest. Because it wasn't just that Dallas and I lost our virginity to each other. If it was just that, I think I could move on. I could—rightly—blame what happened on trauma. On fear. On the need for consolation and human contact.

But it wasn't just that. In some weird way, our captivity was an excuse to physically consummate something that we'd emotionally sealed years before.

And it hurt all the more because once together, fate and circumstance and social mores had ripped us apart again.

Not that I'd told Brody any of that right off the bat. When I'd first met him, I'd just wanted to fuck him. Or, more exactly, I'd just wanted to get fucked. I'd been acting out. Acting stupid. Fast cars, faster sex, and lots of bad decisions.

I'd gone to a bar near Columbia and met him there. He wasn't a student—he'd dropped out the previous semester to tend bar, and he'd made me laugh as I sipped house wine and ate spiced almonds. I'd sat there until closing, taken him home, and let him fuck my brains out.

To say I'd been something of a mess in those days would be an understatement. I'd gone from guy to guy to guy searching for something—someone—to make me whole. To fill the gap left by Dallas.

I didn't find it in Brody, but I did find a friend, and he's been a steadfast one for over ten years now.

"Your problem is that it pisses you off that two seconds after he tells you he wants you but knows he can't have you, he's on another woman's arm, looking like he couldn't care less that it's her and not you."

That is exactly my problem, and I scowl at him for stating it so succinctly. "You're sounding a lot like a shrink this morn-ing," I say. "Trust me, I know. Over the last seventeen years, I think I've had a session with every therapist in the city."

He laughs as we push against the flow of Sunday morning pedestrians flooding out of the Seventy-second Street subway station and heading into the park.

"That why you moved to LA?" he asks as we cross Central Park West, then turn left toward my block. "Fresh blood?"

"And a comedian, too. Who knew?"

"Yeah, well, I may not have a couch, but I'm pretty damn therapeutic for some of my clients."

"That, I believe." Brody's a professional dom, and, yes, I've played the sub on a couple of occasions, thinking it would help.

That it would soothe whatever it is inside me that has shifted off kilter.

The truth is, kink has never satisfied me. It's not that I didn't like it—I actually did, although we never really pushed any boundaries. And we certainly never did bondage. I'd had my fill of being tied up in captivity, and I really, *really* couldn't go there. Just the thought of it brought on a major panic attack.

But even doing the safe stuff, I could never manage to let myself go. Brody said it was because I have control issues, and suggested I top, at least until I felt more comfortable, but that wasn't what I needed, either. It hadn't felt wrong. Just off. As if I was trying out kink for all the wrong reasons, and with the wrong man.

But that was a long time ago in college. Before Bill. Before I started writing.

Now, I'm working out my issues through my words. Or, at least, I'm trying to.

We've reached Seventy-first Street, and as we turn toward my granite and brick townhouse, he eyes me sideways. "You know my door's always open. Best friend discount."

I give him a hug. "I know. Right now I'm good. Or, at least I'm doing okay." The truth is, doing a scene with Brody really wouldn't be torture. The guy is positively gorgeous with his olive complexion, dark eyes, and just a hint of beard at the cleft of his chin. He reminds me of a pirate, and when his shirt is off, I remember why he was Mr. November in a charity calendar some of the city's sexiest bartenders put together back in the day.

Even so, I still wouldn't ever go there again. Brody's married now. And even though his wife is cool with what he does—which, honestly, impresses the hell out of me—that's a line I just can't cross.

I start to head up the stairs to my door, then pause when I

realize he's not following. "No coffee? I was going to make egg white omelets, too."

"Can't. Got a client coming in two hours. I need to get things ready. But you're still coming over tonight, right?"

Brody's wife, Stacey, started a book club about a year ago when she was going crazy after quitting her job as a specialty travel agent. The chemo had made her too sick to work, but despite the nausea and exhaustion, she'd been going stir crazy.

She's in remission now and back at work part-time. Book club, however, still goes on. And although most everyone does the reading, the real purpose is to get together, eat, and gossip. Honestly, it's fun.

"I'll be there. And I'm bringing champagne instead of wine. I landed a spot on *Evening Edge* to talk about *Code Name: Deliverance*."

"No shit? You're not even done writing it."

"I know." I grin. "That's what makes this appearance so amazing." *Evening Edge* is a television news magazine with a huge viewership, and I could kiss my publicist for landing this gig. I'd told her I wanted to do as much media as possible. I may not have the kind of job Bill does, but I think I can make a difference. More than that, I need to. Because I know only too well what kind of damage vigilante involvement can do.

"And they just plucked you up?"

"Not exactly. Apparently *Evening Edge* is doing a segment with Bill. He's coming to talk about WORR and how one of its objectives is to put an end to vigilante involvement in kidnappings. And one of the producers had read *The Price of Ransom* and saw a blurb about *Code Name: Deliverance* on my website." I shrug. "Pretty cool, huh?"

"Cool? It's amazing. When do I set the DVR?"

"The Saturday after Poppy's party. At seven." I do a little jig on my stairs. "I'm so totally psyched."

"You should be. And you do not need to bring any champagne. We will provide all sparkling wine products. Cake may even be involved."

"Sounds perfect. Now go get ready for your client. I'll see you at five." I toss him an air kiss, then head to my door as he starts the Harley he's left parked in front of my building.

I love my house. I didn't grow up here—my mom preferred the quieter life of the Hamptons—and so coming to the townhouse for weekends and holidays in the city felt like going on vacation. The place was built in the late 1800s for my great-great-grandfather. And over the course of the years, the family has seen it through two sets of museum-grade renovations. Truly, the place is as luxurious as any of the fancy hotels I've stayed in throughout my life.

It's a huge house, honestly too much for me. But I couldn't sell it, even if I wanted to, which I absolutely don't. For that matter, Dallas can't sell his Hamptons house, either. Both of the properties are ours to live in for our entire lives, but ultimately, they belong to a family trust.

The kitchen is at the back and I head in that direction, thinking I'll make a carafe of coffee, then take my laptop and go work on the rooftop terrace. I hear the radio, and assume that Ellen, my housekeeper, is working in there despite it being her day off. But when I get there, it's not her trim figure I see at the table by the garden window but a slender man with salt-and-pepper hair.

"Colin?"

He puts down the newspaper and smiles at me, a broad smile that I know has the potential to not only make deals happen, but to get him in trouble.

"I know I say it every time, but I still wish you'd call me Dad."

I pause at the refrigerator on my way to him and top off my water bottle. "I used to." I keep my voice light and teasing, but every word is serious. "You blew it. And I have another dad now."

"I'm still your birth father, little girl."

I sigh and drop into the seat across from him. I've gone from adoring this man to being scared of him to needing him to actually respecting him. He's done a pretty stellar job of pulling himself out of the quagmire of indictments and felonies, bad choices and debt. At least I thought he had until Mom mentioned this new IRS investigation.

Most of all, he was there for me after the kidnapping when I really needed to just get away.

"You are," I say begrudgingly. "But let's not get into it. I'm not in the mood to play the game where we examine how completely screwed up my family tree is. And for the record, I'm not going to ask why IRS agents are calling Mom about you."

He waves a hand. "Routine," he says. "I promise. I'm on their radar now. That's all. Don't you worry about me."

"I'm not. I've got plenty to worry about without adding you to the mix."

"I'm sorry, kiddo. Of course you do." He leans back in his chair and takes a long sip of his coffee. "You went and saw him? After you talked to me?"

Him, of course, is Dallas.

"Well, yeah. He had a right to know that WORR has Ortega in custody. Just like you did."

"And you're okay?"

I take a sip of my water. "'Okay' is a relative term."

"I know it's hard seeing him. You two went through something no one should have to, and those memories will haunt you. Being near him makes it worse, but being away is like abandoning a friend. Am I right?"

I nod. Of course he's right.

His mouth curves into a sad smile. "I still remember the day you gave him your stuffed rabbit. What was he called?"

"Mr. Fluffles." I smile, too. "I wonder what happened to him."

"You can talk to Adele if you need to," he continues, shifting back to our original topic. "We might be divorced, but we're still close. She's an excellent therapist, and it's a short train ride to Westchester. There's no shame if this news about Ortega has sideswiped you."

"It has. But I don't need to talk to Adele. And honestly, it would be too weird."

Maybe legally she's no relation anymore, but from a pragmatic standpoint, the woman was my stepmother. I just can't go there.

"Well, the offer is always open. And, sweetheart, don't get your hopes up."

I frown. "Don't get my hopes up? All I have left is hope." God, I want to wallow in hope, but here Colin is telling me to hold back, and there Dallas was, pissed that it was Bill who caught the bad guy instead of some anonymous federal agent.

"I don't mean it like that." He's been calm through this conversation but now he looks a little flustered, like he's afraid of upsetting me. Frankly, it's probably a legitimate fear.

He starts again. "I'm just saying that while it really is an incredible thing that Ortega is in custody, it's been seventeen years. Even if he does have solid information for the authorities, it might not lead anywhere. You have to come to terms with the fact that you may never know who did that to you and your brother."

For a moment I think he's going to say something else, but all he does is swallow the rest of his coffee and then stand. He heads to the coffeemaker and reaches for the carafe, but he doesn't pour.

"Colin? What is it?"

"You should never have been there in the first place." His

head is tilted down and his voice is soft, so that I can barely make out the words. I watch his shoulders rise and fall as he takes a deep breath. "If Eli hadn't taken you to London . . . if you hadn't snuck away to visit . . ."

"But I did," I whisper. Does he think I haven't thought of that before, a million times already?

"I don't like it. I don't like knowing that you'll probably never know who or why. And somehow it just makes it all worse because it should never have been you."

He lifts his head to look at me. His eyes are red and his voice is thick. "My poor, sweet baby girl. Oh, god, it should never have happened to you."

Later, I am leaning back in the cushioned outdoor rocker and read the social worker's dialogue I just wrote. My intent is for the filmmaker to overlay her voice on top of scenes showing the children trapped and scared in the hot warehouse into which the kidnappers had driven the bus. So while the social worker is giving the parents hollow comfort, the children are terrified.

The trauma of a kidnapping is like the death of a child. It will always be with you. It will haunt you at the oddest times, and there is no defense against the rush of fear, of grief. And, sometimes, of guilt.

I'm not sure if I've got it right on the page of the screenplay, but in my mind, the scene is perfectly clear. The terror. The uncertainty. The cold even in the warmest room, because there is no way to soothe the icy fear that fills your veins and makes you shiver.

I don't know how those kids found comfort, but I survived only because of Dallas. His strength and, yes, his touch.

I sigh, then put my laptop aside and stand. I need to focus on the work. My memories can help me, but I can't let them take over.

I cross to the edge of the terrace and look out over my neighborhood at the stunning townhouses filled with people and their secrets. In a weird way, it's comforting to know that they all have secrets. They all have things they regret, things they want, things they lost. Some have probably suffered more than I have.

I barely know these people, but I know I'm not alone, and it's a nice feeling. I breathe in, wondering if my social worker should say something like that to the parents. Maybe in act two, when—

I catch a glimpse of the outdoor clock and curse. It's already close to four and I'm not showered or dressed. *Damn.*

I hurry back inside and then down the stairs to my bedroom. I know Brody will forgive me if I'm late, but it will drive me crazy. I start stripping off my clothes the moment I'm through my door, and by the time I've crossed to my bathroom, I'm naked.

I get the shower going, and step in. I tilt my head back, and as I let the water wash over my face, I'm still thinking of Dallas. Still thinking of the dark and the terror. There'd been the Jailer, who came to me only once, his face hidden and his voice altered. And the Woman, who brought us food. She always wore a loose, flowing gown like a caftan, so shapeless it was impossible to tell if she was thin or curvy. She kept her hair hidden beneath a hood, and she wore a carnival-style black mask.

After the initial horror of cat food and starvation, she came somewhat regularly, leaving overcooked slabs of meat or cold cans of vegetables on the floor. There were no knives, no forks. And only one bottle of water at a time.

But mostly she stayed away, and in the gray light, Dallas and I lost ourselves in each other.

The first time had been sweet and tender and wonderful despite the hell of our situations and surroundings. It had been an escape. A release.

Hell, sex had been a sanctuary into which we disappeared as often as we could, losing ourselves in each other. Comforting. Soothing. Making silent promises that we would always be there for the other. That somehow, together, we were strong enough to survive.

We weren't always together, though. Sometimes the Woman came to separate us. To take me away to a dark room where I'd be tied to a cement table. Bound and left there for hours, terrified that this was the end. That the bitch would simply leave me there to die.

As bad as that was, it was worse when she took Dallas from me. The not knowing was like torture to me—and, honestly, I think that torture is exactly what they did to Dallas during those long, lonely hours. Because each time they brought him back he would pull away from me. Not forever, but at first. As if he was afraid to touch me. As if each moment they kept us apart was a brick in a wall dividing us, and with each return we had to break through that wall and find each other again.

We did though. We always did. And each time he pulled me close and thrust hard inside me, it had been both a victory and a tragedy. We were alive, yes. But we knew damn well that we might never touch each other again.

Nothing was taboo between us, nothing shameful. We loved each other. And so help us, we were trying to cram a lifetime into those dark days that might be our last. We never thought about the consequences, and in retrospect we were lucky I didn't get pregnant. I don't know why—maybe I'm not fertile. Or maybe I was so thin from near-starvation that there was no way it could happen.

Even if we'd thought about it, though, we wouldn't have stopped. As far as we knew, we'd be dead before the sun came up. But more than that, we needed each other. Hell, we saved each other.

And each time Dallas kissed me—each time he held me close and moved inside me—each time he made me explode so that for at least that moment I was free—I knew that I would always need him. Would always love him.

And somehow, I would always find my way back to him.

Now, in the real world with our past haunting us, I just have to figure out how.

14

Elephant in the Room

I know that I need to get dressed, but when I leave the shower, my mind is too full of Dallas, and my body too tense with the need for release.

I hesitate, but I want this. The touch. The fantasy.

And so I stretch out on the bed, my body damp, and slide my hand between my legs. I stroke myself, slowly at first and then with more purpose, my fingers sure as I draw them over my swollen clit, now wet and slick.

I should get up. I should tear my thoughts from the past— from Dallas. I should be doing about a million things other than masturbating, my legs shamelessly wide and my thoughts on the man I want between them.

But I don't stop. I won't stop.

I want this. I think I even need it. And this time I close my eyes and let myself slide back into the past again.

I think about the night before he left for boarding school and the story he'd told me in the dark about how much he'd craved our first real kiss that night, and how hot he thought I looked even in a stupid Looney Tunes T-shirt.

And I remember the wonder in his eyes when he'd first seen me naked in that dark, dank room, lit only by the dim glow of a flickering yellow bulb.

I think about the way his hands felt, so strong and sure even at fifteen. And I recall the way his fingers had roamed, exploring every inch of me, making my skin quiver. He'd been so sweet the first time, so afraid of hurting me. But I'd welcomed the pain, because it was Dallas giving it to me. Not strangers in the dark. Not shadows and monsters.

I'm so wet, and I buck my hips and quicken the small circles as I stroke my clit, as I think about other times. His touch, his mouth, his cock. I imagine he's inside me now, his body warm against mine, his voice whispering that it will be okay. That we're together. That it will all be fine.

And it's that voice that takes me higher and higher. I cling to the memory of it as I touch myself with more urgency. As I whimper and shift and try to find satisfaction. And then, finally, as I explode, my cry echoing through my quiet bedroom.

I gasp and try to gather myself, but I'm spent, utterly limp. And it's only when I let my head drift to the side that I realize it's now four-thirty and all I've managed is a shower and an orgasm. I have to get all the way to Brody's apartment in the Village by five.

I scramble out of bed and pull on a stretchy cotton maxi skirt and a funky, flowy top I bought on my last trip to London. I'm searching for my sandals and wondering how long it will take to get a cab when the doorbell chime reverberates through the floor.

I ignore it at first, but when it chimes again, I remember that it's Ellen's day off and hurry downstairs. There's a security camera camouflaged inside the porch light, and when I glance at the monitor at the base of the stairs, I gasp.

I'd expected a delivery. Maybe a neighbor.

Instead, it's Dallas.

For a moment I consider pretending like I'm not home. For one thing, I'm in a hurry to get to Brody's and don't really have time to talk. For another, considering what I'd just been thinking—what I'd just been doing—I'm feeling a tad awkward about letting him in. As if he'll be able to smell his scent on me. As if he'll look in my eyes and know that I touch myself while thinking of him.

But I can't quite bring myself to ignore him. After all, I'll be spending time with him on the island this weekend, so I probably could use the practice. And besides, I was the one who invited him over. I was the one who said we should get together. That we should try to be friends.

And now here he is, outside on my stoop.

And here I am, inside eating my words.

I draw a breath, push the button to unlock the door to the foyer, and hurry to meet him.

"Hey," I say as I pull open the door and invite him in. I'm certain my smile is awkward, and I can't help but feel like he's about to take me to prom. It's an awkward, twitchy feeling, but I remind myself that the point of this exercise is to get comfortable around him again. A little twitchiness is to be expected.

"Right. So come on in." My words are really not necessary as he's already stepped into the room, looking like he belongs here. Which, of course he does, as it was once one of his family homes, too.

He's carrying a canvas grocery bag and he holds it up with one hand and reaches inside with his other. When he pulls out a *Resident Evil* game cartridge, I have to laugh.

"You were serious?"

"I'm always serious about zombies." His tone is bland, which only makes me laugh harder.

"You are going to be so disappointed," I say.

"You're that good?"

"I'm that bad," I admit. "Truly. I've got a friend with an old Pac-Man in his living room. Even that's too much game for me."

His lips twitch with amusement—which is unfortunate as I find myself remembering just how they feel against my skin. "This isn't a problem," he assures me. "I like to win."

"Well, then you're going to love playing with me."

"I know I will."

He's looking right at me as he says it, and suddenly the double-meaning of our words is all too clear, and what had been a light banter between us has turned into something much more provocative.

"I—"

I have no idea what I was going to say, so it's good that he interrupts me.

"And there's more," he says hurriedly, reaching into the tote and pulling out a clear plastic bag filled with my favorite snack in the world.

"Chocolate covered popcorn? From Serenity on Seventh? I take back every bad thing I've ever said about you."

He chuckles. "Then it was entirely worth the seven-bucks-fifty." He nods toward the stairs. "Come on. Let's play."

Once again, our eyes meet. Once again, neither one of us acknowledges how we really want to play.

"I'll get drinks and a bowl for the popcorn," I say quickly. "You go get the game set up."

I don't wait for him to agree, I just hurry to the kitchen, press my hands to the counter so I can draw a few slow, calming breaths, and then start to put together a tray.

I hesitate over the wine—because who knows where alcohol will lead, and the point of this evening is to see if we can force a wild lust to downshift to just friends.

Right, I think. *Sparkling water it is.*

I take the tray up to the game room and find that he's already set everything up. I ease in beside him and pick up my controller and try to remember exactly what I'm supposed to do with all these damn buttons.

Fortunately, Dallas takes pity on me and gives me a little tutorial, walking me through the first scene of the game, letting me get used to turning and shooting and punching and all that good stuff.

He also lets me have all the health bonuses we find. Not to mention the ammo.

"Told you I'd always protect you," he says with a grin.

I smile back but, honestly, his words make me a little melancholy. And when he looks sideways at me with a crooked smile, I know he realizes it.

"Should I apologize?"

I shake my head and grab a handful of popcorn. "Just play."

He does, and since we're partners against the zombie horde, I can't actually say he beats me. What I can say is that I died four times in the first fifteen minutes, and by minute seventeen Dallas is laughing his ass off.

"Do I need to tell you how pathetic you are at this game?"

"You really don't," I say as the screen flashes death number five.

"Remind me to come rescue you when the zombie apocalypse happens. Without me, you're zombie food."

I grin happily. This is the Dallas I know. The one I can laugh with and hang with.

And yet at the same time, this Dallas scares me. Because the Dallas who touched me so intimately in the cabana is the one I at least know how to fight, even though sometimes my willpower fails me. I can look at his harem. His ridiculous media antics. And I can honestly say I want no part of it.

But this Dallas is real. This Dallas is mine. He always has been.

And even though I know we need to just be friends, I'm not sure if he and I can ever "just" be anything.

After I die yet another time, Dallas takes the controller from me and switches off the game.

"Told you I was terrible," I say cheerfully, but my smile fades when I see his face. "What?"

"I don't want to tell you because I don't want to screw up a good evening. But you really need to know."

I frown. "Okay. I'm listening."

"Ortega's dead."

The news rocks through me and I'm on my feet in a second. "No, that's not true. Bill would have told me."

"Suicide," Dallas goes on. "And he didn't tell you because it's classified."

"Then how the hell do you know?"

He scowls for a second, as if I've asked him an inappropriate question, but answers anyway. "You know my friend Quince's in British intelligence. He told me, but don't repeat it or you could get his ass in serious trouble."

I nod numbly. "Suicide. That doesn't make any sense." I look at him as if he has answers. And then the real import hits me. "He was WORR's best lead."

"He was," Dallas acknowledges.

"Oh." I feel my knees go weak as all my hope drains away. That they'd find who'd taken us. That Dallas and I would finally have answers.

I'm starting to sag, but Dallas is right there to catch me. I hook my arms around his neck, and as I do, the whole world shifts again. It's no longer me and Dallas and Bill and Ortega. Or even me and Dallas and zombies.

It's just me. It's just Dallas.

Just the two of us and this living, breathing need that beats between us. That we can't erase, can't destroy, can't tame.

He is looking at me, and I can see he feels it, too. And when he bends his head almost imperceptibly I know that he is going to kiss me. And I want it. I shouldn't—I know I shouldn't. But so help me I want this kiss.

But what I want, I can't have, and I close my eyes, put my hands on his shoulders, and gently push him away.

"Jane?"

I shake my head. "Go. Please, Dallas. Could you please just go?"

And, dammit, he does.

"Well, at least you had a good reason for blowing off book club," Brody says after I've told him about my evening game fest with Dallas. I'd actually arrived just as the last member, Leo, was leaving, so I gave him a quick hug, promised I'd read the next book, and then let Brody lead me back to the kitchen so we could talk while Stacey cleaned up.

She's wearing a short purple wig today. After she finished chemo and her hair started growing back, she decided to shave it all anyway.

"Now I can have a different color every day," she'd told me. "And honestly, life's too short not to have fun hair."

She's stuck by that motto, too. According to Brody, they converted the spare bedroom into Stacey's closet, and one entire side is for her rainbow of wigs.

Now, as we sip the celebratory champagne while she moves in and out of the room with dishes and glasses, I realize that Brody isn't the only one who knows my secrets. Stacey does, too. I'd given him permission to tell her when she was doing chemo. He'd wanted to talk with her during the long hours in the chair, and I'd wanted to subtly let her know that I loved her and would share her burdens, too, whenever she wanted to talk.

So even though I've never spoken with her directly about what goes on in my head and my heart, she undoubtedly knows most of it.

"So here's the important question," Brody says. "Did you have fun?"

"I did." I think about it once more, just to be sure. "I really did and I think he did, too."

"So, that's good, right?" Stacey asks. "That's where you two are trying to get? To be comfortable around each other as friends?"

I tilt my head to the side and shrug. "I said it was fun. I didn't say it was comfortable. Just the opposite, actually. I mean, at one point I banged the crap out of my knee because I practically leaped to the other side of the couch when he leaned toward me. Turns out all he was doing was reaching for the TV remote. And then when he told me about Ortega—"

I break off, shivering with the memory of how it felt in his arms. There'd been nothing overtly sexual in the way he'd held me, in the comfort he'd given me. But I'd wanted more. I'd wanted so much more, and I hate the way that wanting him makes me feel. Lost, when I've managed to find my way back in so many ways. Unsure, when I've fought to build up my confidence.

I lean forward and thrust my fingers into my hair. "I'm a complete mess."

"You are," Brody says. "But not as much of a mess as you should be. By rights, you should be seriously fucked up."

"Um, hello?" I point to myself. "Dictionary definition of fucked up sitting right here."

"You're not," Stacey insists. She's a small woman, so petite she makes me think of fairies. But she's fierce, and she's captured me with her pale gray eyes. "You're a survivor. Trust me. I know the type."

"She's right," Brody agrees. "And you deserve better."

"Better would be great," I agree. "How?"

Brody's eyes flick to his wife, then back to me. He exhales loudly, then stands up and starts to pace. "He's become this thing to you." He holds a hand out in front of him, as if in illustration. "Dallas Sykes is your Holy Grail."

I can hardly argue. "So?"

"Get rid of the expectation. Erase the fantasy." He sits beside me and leans forward so that we are eye to eye. Slowly, his mouth curves into a wicked grin. "Fuck him out of your system."

"What?" I say, even though I heard him perfectly well. So well that a little tremor runs through me simply from the suggestion. "All we've been doing for years is fighting this thing, because, hey, that road leads to stress, disinheritance, and a possible felony conviction."

Not that I'm really worried that sleeping with Dallas would land me behind bars. Technically it's criminal incest—I looked it up, and New York law treats adopted siblings the same as full-blooded—but I can't imagine anyone would enforce that since we're not biologically related. But the rest of it is all true.

And god forbid the media found out. That would be even worse than my father knowing.

Brody lifts a shoulder. "Then don't," he says casually, as if this is all just meaningless banter and not a huge barrier that I have to get over or under or around if I'm going to ever manage to move on emotionally.

"Don't?"

"Just keep trying what you did last night. Go to lunch. Go to the movies. Do all those things that friends do together, and maybe it'll get better and you two can just be normal siblings. Best friends. Whatever you want to call it."

I bite the inside of my cheek, anticipating where he's going next.

"But if you don't believe that will work . . ." He trails off. He really doesn't have to say the rest.

I glance up at Stacey. "He's serious. He really wants me—wants us—to do a complete flip?"

"Sounds like it to me," she says, as she hand-dries a wineglass.

"One hundred and eighty degrees, Janie." He nods with the certainty of a man who knows he's right. "You've been living with the memory of something that happened between you that saved you. You needed it then, and you're clinging to it now. And until you let yourselves relive those moments, you're not going to be able to get past the sex and move on to the friendship. Trust me, babe. Fucking Dallas is the elephant in the room, and there's no other way around it."

"I don't think it'll be that simple. I told you what happened in the cabana. The way he made me feel. All that did was make me want him more." And now I'm afraid that if I sleep with Dallas just to get him out of my system, it would be like a condemned prisoner having one last, perfect meal, and then dying.

I'm not sure I'd ever come alive again.

Brody is shaking his head. "No. No, that's because you opened a door and didn't go through it. Go, Janie. Walk through with him, and see if it isn't all better on the other side."

Stacey puts her hand on mine. "I think he's right. Besides, what have you got to lose?"

Nothing, I think. At this point I have absolutely nothing to lose, and potentially everything to gain.

15

Cockblock

Dallas watched as Damien Stark studied the schematic currently being projected onto the conference room whiteboard. He had, in fact, been studying the specs for a full ten minutes.

The plans provided for a device that could be set up externally, but would monitor conversations taking place in a building's interior by sending a series of pulses through the pre-existing electrical system. Theoretically, a single device could allow surveillance of a building as large as the one he was in right now, and he was on the forty-third floor.

It was a remarkable piece of engineering. And as far as the world of surveillance went, it was a game changer.

Considering how long Stark had been studying the specs, it was clear that he knew that.

Finally, he turned to face Dallas, then leaned casually against the wall. "I'm impressed," he said, and coming from Stark, that was high praise indeed. Unlike Dallas, the tech savvy billionaire hadn't inherited his fortune. He'd taken his winnings from the professional tennis circuit and built a multibillion dollar industry with fingers in all sorts of pies, including high tech.

The men had met a few years ago, and now Dallas was an investor in one of Stark's vacation resorts. Today, Dallas hoped to convince Stark to invest in the cutting edge listening device that Noah had designed.

"Impressed is good," Dallas said. "But what I need to know is if you're interested in producing and marketing it on the terms I outlined."

The terms were extremely favorable to Stark, while still providing Dallas the equipment he needed for Deliverance, and a nice royalty to Noah for the design.

"I might be." Stark crossed the room and pulled out a chair, then sat with his legs extended and his fingers steepled under his chin. "I've been intrigued by the concept since you first pitched it. Now, I'm curious as to why you don't use your own resources to build and market it. You have manufacturing capabilities in Asia. And your security division could not only make use of this equipment but could license it to law enforcement."

"I told you before I have my reasons," Dallas said, hoping that he hadn't misread his friend. That Stark wasn't going to push. The truth was that Dallas couldn't run the device through Sykes channels—not without raising the kinds of red flags that would make it impossible for Deliverance to safely and anonymously use the tech. Farm it out to Stark and license it back, though, and there was no trail.

Stark nodded slowly. "I'm sure you do. And I'm sure that you know I have the resources to learn those reasons."

"You do," Dallas said, and the truth was, he'd never gone outside of the circle of Deliverance before. For one thing, it wasn't practical. For another, Dallas didn't trust easily. But for this project they needed the help, and he believed in his gut that he could trust Stark. "But I think you're a man who understands discretion. And who realizes that a man's secrets are his own."

For a moment, Stark simply held his eyes. Then he nodded slowly and stood. "I'll take a look at your terms and get back to you within the week. We'll shoot for a prototype within sixty days."

"Good." Dallas stood, surprised at the extent of his relief. He liked Stark, and although he feared he was being naive, he believed that even if the other man learned about Deliverance, he'd keep the knowledge to himself.

When he returned to his office after walking Stark to the elevator, he found Gin Kramer, his secretary, standing beside his desk holding a clipboard. She held it out for him, then tapped the end of her pen on a signature block he'd missed that morning despite the red flag that clearly ordered him to *sign here*.

He whipped off another signature, then passed the contract back to her.

She tucked it efficiently into the portfolio she'd carried for every one of her twenty-plus years with the company. "Your mother wanted me to let her know when you would be arriving at the island. Tonight or tomorrow?"

"I'll fly to Norfolk tonight, and hire a helicopter to take me to the island in the morning. Can you arrange that for me?"

"Of course."

"Did she say when everyone else was coming?" He wondered if he should ask Jane if she wanted to travel with him. Then again, he wasn't sure he was up to being in such close proximity to her for an overnight jaunt.

"I'm sorry, sir, she didn't. Shall I ask?"

"No. It doesn't matter."

"And I'm supposed to remind you to bring a gift. Shall I pick something up?"

"Already done." He often let Gin pick out corporate gifts, but this was Poppy, and he wasn't about to let someone else select a gift for his great-grandfather. "Anything else?"

"Mr. Foster asked that you call him when you have a moment."

"Will do. Thank you, Gin."

She reached over to straighten the papers on his desk, then turned and slipped out his door, shutting it behind him.

Alone, he stood and stretched, then went to the window and looked out at lower Manhattan and, beyond that, the Statue of Liberty, still majestic despite his perspective from so high above the city.

They were coming up on the end of the fiscal quarter, and before Stark had arrived, he'd spent the morning catching up on Sykes business. Although his father still retained his position as chairman of the board, Dallas had taken over as CEO of the retail side of the Sykes empire five years ago, and he genuinely enjoyed the work. And, because there were Sykes Department Stores all over the globe, the job provided a nice cover for his work with Deliverance.

From the moment he'd stepped into his office this morning, he'd been inundated with contracts, reports, and columns of numbers. But at least the flurry of paperwork had kept his mind off Jane. Because Jane was very much where his mind wandered lately.

He hadn't seen her since the night he'd gone to her house. The night he'd wanted to touch her. To kiss her. To rip off every stitch of her clothing, press her against the wall, and do all sorts of dark and dirty things to her.

He hadn't, and he considered that a victory.

But the desire wasn't fading, and that was a goddamn fail. If anything, he wanted her more. Thought about her more. The scent of her perfume lingered on his clothes. He sipped sparkling water, and she filled his thoughts. Any bus with a video-game ad plastered on the side made his cock ache for her.

And, damn him, in the last week he'd listened to one of her voicemails, then closed his eyes and jacked himself off.

Pathetic.

He pressed his forehead to the glass and counted to five, then stood upright again. *Done. Finished.*

Pity party over.

Time to get back to work.

He returned to his desk, pulled his personal laptop and Wi-Fi hotspot out of his briefcase and set them both in front of him. Then he swiveled his chair so that he could reach the control panel on the credenza behind him, and pressed the button to lock his door.

He fired up the computer, then shot the team a quick summary of his meeting with Stark. After that, he pulled up the most recent reports from his men, pleased to see that the card key he'd cloned to access the Lopez property had worked perfectly and that early that morning the team had breached Ortega's security at the weak point and then accessed the residence.

That was good news, yes, but nothing more than what he'd already anticipated. And since the report was in progress and didn't say what the team had found, he pulled out his phone and dialed Liam.

"What did you find?" he demanded when Liam answered.

"Just writing that up. The place was mostly a shell—we're looking for the real base he used right now—but we found a hidden safe and it had a netbook in it."

"Anything useful?"

"Potentially useful. That's where you come in."

"Tell me."

"The hard drive's encrypted, so we're still working through it, but we found a name—Peter Crowley. You know him?"

"I do." Dallas frowned, thinking of the forty-something real estate developer he'd worked with once or twice before. The man was married with a roving eye and enough money to support at least two mistresses at a time.

He also threw a cocktail party in his Fifth Avenue apartment at least once each month. Ostensibly to meet and greet potential clients. In reality, Dallas was certain he was scouting his next lay.

"Are you telling me he's in bed with Ortega?"

"Undetermined. Ortega leaned toward kidnapping and white slavery, with an occasional side trip to drug trafficking. That sound like the kind of thing Crowley would be into?"

"Not on the surface," Dallas said. "But you and I both know that no one's who they appear to be."

"Yeah, well, Crowley might be squeaky clean. Ortega's vineyard was a viable enterprise, with clients around the globe including restaurants and individuals. Crowley could be in the system as a legitimate client. Until we hack the drive, we can't know, and the encryption is protected. A wrong move, and the data's erased. So we're taking it slow. In the meantime, we'll take a look at Crowley the old-fashioned way."

"What do you need me to do?"

"Get into his house and drop a bug or two. We'll listen. Maybe we'll get lucky."

Dallas chuckled. "And here I thought you were going to hand me a challenge."

Since Liam and his mother were both attending Poppy's birthday celebration, he promised to bring the listening devices to Dallas on the island. They ended the call, and Dallas drew a breath, hating the thought that Crowley, a man he'd done a few real estate deals with could have a hand in that kind of shit. With a frown, he buzzed Gin and unlocked the door.

A moment later she opened his door and popped her head in. "I was away from my desk. Did you need something?"

"Peter Crowley. Have we received any invitations from him lately?"

"There is an endless stream." A smile touched her lips. "I've been regretfully declining. Isn't that what you asked?"

"It was. I've changed my mind. Could you RSVP yes for the next one?"

He thought he saw a flicker of disapproval in her eyes, but she said nothing. Gin Kramer used to be his father's assistant. She'd known Dallas for much of his life, and though she was far too professional to comment, he knew that she disapproved of his extracurricular escapades. With anyone else, Dallas wouldn't care. But he liked Gin, and so he tried to play down the role of womanizing, spendthrift fuckup when he was at the office.

Sometimes, though, it was hard to avoid the reminders.

"Will there be anything else?"

"No. Thanks. Just let me know the date and time."

"Of course." She turned to go. "Oh! Hello, Ms. Martin!"

Jane?

Instinctively, his hand went to shut his laptop, then he tucked it and the Wi-Fi router into his desk. Gin would either not notice or not ask—most likely she assumed he was circumventing the office network so he could surf porn sites.

Jane would ask.

"Gin, it's so good to see you. And I've told you a million times to call me Jane."

From his perspective at the desk, Dallas could see Jane give the older woman a hug. When they pulled apart, Jane stepped into the room.

She wore a tight black skirt that hugged her hips, red stilettos, and a low cut sleeveless blouse that showed off her more than adequate cleavage. The outfit alone put him on notice that something was up with her. She looked hot. Like head-to-a-bar-pick-up-a-guy-and-fuck-him-in-the-hallway hot. She never dressed that way when she knew she was going to see him. Too dangerous, as evidenced by the way parts south of his brain were springing to attention.

"To what do I owe the pleasure?" He kept his voice light, but he was a little concerned by the look in her eye—a combination of terror and fierce determination.

"We need to talk." She shut the door, locked it, then turned back to look at him.

He sat down slowly. "All right," he said evenly. "Talk."

"Right." She sat, then smoothed her skirt, the motion probably camouflaging her nerves. "Right," she said again. Her throat moved as she swallowed, and he found himself remembering that the indentation at the base of her throat had once tasted as sweet as honey. "It's just that—"

The buzz of the intercom interrupted her. "Mr. Sykes, I'm sorry to interrupt, but Mr. Crowley's party is in one week. Next Friday."

"That's fine, Gin. Just put it on the calendar." He frowned. She didn't usually trouble him with the details.

"I would, but you have a conflict. You're supposed to be in Montreal with your father. You're completely booked Friday through Sunday for a number of events related to the opening of the new hotel and retail center."

"Of course," he said and silently cursed. He'd promised his father he'd make this trip, and while his irresponsible heir routine worked well as a cover for Deliverance, the truth was he loved his dad and really didn't want the last ounce of respect the man had for him to be washed away.

But about this, he had no choice. This wasn't just a Deliverance job, this was about Ortega. This was about the kidnapping. This was about Jane.

"Tell my father I won't be able to make the trip," he said, then watched as Jane's eyes widened.

He waited for Gin to answer. "Gin?" he prompted.

"I'm sorry, sir," she said after a moment. "I'm afraid that's something you're going to have to tell him yourself."

The connection broke, and Jane tilted her head, as if trying to get a read on him. "You're blowing off Dad in favor of a party?"

"Crowley throws excellent parties," he said. "You never know who you might meet."

"Right. Of course." She dragged her fingers through her hair, mussing it a bit and making him think of what she'd look like with her head against a pillow and her dark hair spread wide.

But those thoughts vanished when she looked back up at him. All he saw was disappointment, and he wanted so badly to tell her that he wasn't the asshole bad boy she thought he was.

Instead, he said, "So are you going to tell me why you're here?"

For a moment, he thought she wasn't. Then she gave a sad little shake of her head. "Sometimes I wonder why I want so badly to be close again, you know?"

"Jane—" The word came out strangled.

"*No.* Let me finish or I'll never get this out. I don't know why sometimes, but that doesn't matter, because I do want it, Dallas. I miss you so much it hurts. And I'm not even talking about the sex, although god knows I miss that, too."

Her cheeks took on an adorable pink tone and she didn't quite meet his eyes.

"But mostly I just miss *you*. Every day. All the time." She stood up, clearly uncomfortable simply sitting still. "Maybe it's just me—is it just me?" She cast pleading eyes on him. "Because if it is, I'll let it go. But I can't ignore this—I don't know—this *need* between us."

"It isn't just you." He got up and moved around the desk to her side. He reached out and did what he'd been wanting to do for days. Very gently, he took her hand.

And it felt so damn right. So goddamn right.

"It isn't just you," he repeated. "I feel it, too. Hell, I can taste it. I'm aware of everything about you, from the scent of your shampoo to the rhythm of your breathing. All I can think about is kissing you."

"Dallas—" Her voice came out ragged.

"But we can't." He forced the words out, because it was either do that or pull her into his arms. "We both know why we can't."

"I know," she said, and he knew she meant their family and the idiotic law that turned anything sexual between them into a goddamn crime. But there was more to it than that. Because even if there was no taboo, she still deserved a hell of a lot more than a man like him.

"But the thing is—" She bit her plump lower lip. "The thing is that I don't want to just walk away. Not without trying to be friends. But I can't handle this. We have to make it stop. This tension. This wanting."

He cocked his head, a little bit amused and a little bit intrigued. "What exactly do you suggest?"

Her head was tilted so that she was looking more at the floor than at him. "I want you to fuck me," she said softly. Except that couldn't be what she said.

Then she lifted her head and he saw the boldness in her eyes. And the heat. "We need to fuck each other out of our systems."

I want you to fuck me.

Dallas clenched the steering wheel tighter as he flew up the 9A highway on his way to Westchester. It was still early enough that the road wasn't clogged with rush hour traffic, and his Spyder had more than enough zip to let him weave in and out of the scattered cars that blocked his path.

We need to fuck each other out of our systems.

Christ, she'd really said that. She really wanted it.

Hell, so did he.

Need curled through him, and he pressed on the accelerator, jacking the car up by another ten miles per hour, as if he could out-race this persistent craving. He couldn't, of course. It would dog him until he had Jane, which meant that it would dog him forever.

He thought of how she'd looked when he'd said no.

"Dallas, I know it sounds crazy, but—"

"If that's the only way we can get past this and be friends, then I guess we won't be friends."

She'd flinched, as if he'd slapped her. Hell, in a way he supposed he had.

"You don't mean that." Her voice was low. Urgent. "You know I'm right."

At that, he did take a step toward her. "So what if you are? It's still not happening. I'm not a man you want in your bed. You may think you do, but you don't. I promise you that."

She'd lifted her chin and looked at him with fire in her eyes. "Because you like it rough? Because you like it dirty? Don't look so shocked, *brother*. I have ears. And most of the time, you're the best gossip in town."

"Like it? That's the way I need it." He'd grabbed her shoulders. "And I am not—do you hear me?—not dragging you down with me."

"Dallas—"

He'd heard the break in her voice and wondered if maybe he'd gotten through to her.

"Just go," he'd said. "Just turn around, walk out the door, and go."

He ran the scene over and over in his head, wishing each time that the ending was different. But like every other woman in his life, she'd obeyed.

Unlike every other woman, she'd walked away.

Fuck.

He'd left Manhattan in a crappy mood, and the mood still lingered as he pulled into the drive of the perfectly restored nineteenth-century Westchester County mansion. He stalked to the door, realizing he probably should have called first, and rang the bell.

He expected Adele. But it was Colin who answered the door. "Well, Dallas. So good to see you, son." He stepped back so Dallas could enter, then clapped him on the back. "I've been thinking we should make plans to meet and catch up."

"I'd like that." Before the kidnapping, Colin had fallen off the family radar. Not surprising since the court had terminated his parental rights, and Eli had adopted Jane.

But when Jane begged to be closer to her birth father after the ordeal, Colin had slid back into the Sykes's orbit. He was still mostly estranged from Eli and Lisa, but both Jane and Dallas made it a point to see the man.

Originally, Dallas had simply wanted a conduit into Jane's life during those early years when she'd been too raw to see or talk to him. Over time, though, he and Colin had developed a genuine friendship, and Dallas was grateful that Colin had never become aware of the strange, yet undeniable, sexual tension between him and Adele.

Now, he followed Colin into his ex-wife's sitting room, professionally decorated in hues of ivory and beige.

"Adele didn't mention you were coming."

"She didn't know," Dallas admitted. "You heard about Ortega?"

"The suicide?" Colin shook his head sadly. "Jane told me."

"It's been weighing on me," Dallas said, which was true. "I thought I'd talk to Adele," he added, which was not. Talk, in fact, was the last thing on his mind.

"Well, your timing is perfect. I was just on my way out."

He knew that out of politeness he should urge Colin to stay

a bit longer. He didn't. Right then, he wasn't in the mood to be polite.

"Colin?" Adele's voice drifted in from the back of the house followed a moment later by the woman herself. She wore a silk robe tied around her waist and, from the way the material clung to her breasts and hips, not a thing on underneath it. "I thought you'd gone. Did you—*Oh*. Dallas! What a lovely surprise."

She came closer, then pressed a palm to his arm as she airkissed him.

"I'm on my way out now," Colin said. "I'll see you next week." A flicker of a smile touched his lips as he skimmed his eyes over her.

When the door was shut and locked behind him, Dallas raised his brow.

"What?" she asked innocently. "I told you we still sleep together sometimes. Just because we couldn't survive marriage doesn't mean the sex was bad."

"I didn't come to talk about you and your ex," he said. "I came because—"

"Of Ortega. Yes, I overheard." She crossed the room to the sofa and sat, then indicated that he should join her. He did, sitting slightly sideways so he could look at her directly.

She did the same, and as she turned, her robe shifted, revealing one creamy thigh. And almost revealing more. Though in her fifties now, Adele had stayed in incredible shape. He sometimes wondered how much of it was real and how much was surgical. She once told him that she'd been in a car accident in her twenties and had done several rounds of plastic surgery. For all he knew, she'd kept it up over the years.

"But it's not really Ortega that's bothering you." She looked straight at him, as if daring him to argue. "It's Jane."

He didn't deny it. He didn't say anything.

Adele tilted her head to the side as she studied his face. "I'm right." She scooted closer to him, making the robe ride up just a bit more, so that when he glanced down he could see the shadow at the apex of her thighs. "She's why you're here. Why you're with me."

He lifted his chin so he could meet her eyes and saw the hint of a smile.

"Did you sleep with her?" she asked.

"Christ, Adele."

She pressed her hand lightly on his knee. He felt the weight of it through his slacks. The heat of it.

And right then, he absolutely hated himself.

The fucked-up reality was that he had come for this. Not to talk about Ortega. Not to rely on her professional expertise to help him with Jane. But for *this*. Because he'd wanted the release. Because she was the one woman he'd had in his bed who knew what he really wanted. *Who* he really wanted.

The one woman who was kinky enough to indulge his fucked-up fantasies.

But now that he was here, the real truth was undeniable: He didn't really want this. He didn't really want her. Not now. Never again.

And the weight of her hand on his skin seemed overbearing.

"It's a simple question," she said.

He pushed her hand aside and stood. "No. I didn't sleep with her."

"Mmm." She turned on the sofa and stretched her arms out on either side of the couch. She was still covered, but the sash of the robe had loosened, and it seemed to Dallas that even her wardrobe was participating in her effort to taunt him. To remind him that he'd driven all the way out here because he was so screwed up he'd thought another woman could take his mind off Jane.

"You may not have slept with her," Adele said. "But you wanted to."

It was a statement, not a question.

He answered anyway. "We're just friends. Or, at least, we're trying to be."

"You're not *just* friends, *mon chéri*. Any man who's slept with his sister isn't ever going to be *just* her friend again. You may not have sat on my couch, but you've seen enough therapists over the years to know that."

"Fine." He crossed the room and leaned against the wall. "We're trying to overcome our past. We miss each other. We're trying to find our way to some version of normal."

"Who do you think you're talking to? That's bullshit and we both know it."

"Adele—"

"No." She stood up and started walking toward him, the robe loosening with every step. "You want her. That's why you came." She was only steps away, the sash undone, the robe open and flowing around her. Her breasts were small but high, and her body was toned, sleek and slim like a dancer. "Let me give her to you."

He told himself he didn't want to go there. His cock, now uncomfortably tight in his pants, argued the point.

"Stop being contrary," she said softly. "You know I'm right. It's her who's got you hard, not me."

He couldn't deny the truth. And as she leaned back and let the silk slide off her shoulders to pool on the ground, he knew he should get the fuck out of there, but right then he couldn't seem to work up the impetus to move.

She tilted her head up and smiled at him, her eyes filled with mischief. Then she gently cupped her hand over his cock, so goddamn hard it was painful.

"Fuck me," she whispered. "Imagine I'm her, and fuck me."

He wanted to—he hated himself for how much he wanted to. He wanted Jane in his head. He wanted to imagine that he was buried inside her.

But no way was he going there. She deserved better. And, dammit, so did he.

Roughly, he pushed Adele away, right as she was tugging down his zipper. "Dammit, Adele, I told you no. I'm not doing this. *We're* not doing this."

For a moment, her eyes flashed with anger. Then her face calmed, and she smiled. "Good," she said, as if he was one of her goddamn patients. "You're making progress. But you still haven't fully dealt with the fact that she's never going to be more to you than your sister."

She ran her hand lightly over the curve of his jaw. "Until you let her go, Dallas, you're never going to heal."

16

Island Girl

"He told me to go."

I'm sitting at Brody and Stacey's kitchen table sipping coffee and reliving my moment of extreme mortification.

"Well, what did you expect?" Brody asks. "That he'd strip you naked and bend you over his desk?"

I try very hard not to whimper simply from the mental picture of that very thing.

"For goodness sakes, Gregory." Brody's given name is Gregory Allan Brody, but god forbid anyone but Stacey should ever try to use it. "You're the one who put this crazy plan in her head. Now you're saying you expected it to backfire?"

Since Stacey is currently my ally, I don't point out that she had seconded the crazy plan.

"That's not what I meant," he says. "But come on, Jane. I've never even met the guy and I know he won't do anything to hurt you. Not on purpose. And you aren't just two people deciding to have a good time. He's your brother, which makes it a big fucking deal, no pun intended."

"We don't share a drop of blood. I don't care what the law or our parents or all of society says. It's stupid."

"Doesn't change the fact. Doesn't erase the taboo."

I glance up at Stacey and then over to Brody. "Then let me just second what your wife said. You're the one who suggested this in the first place."

"And I stand by my suggestion. I'm just saying that my take on this guy is that he's a gentleman—"

"Do you *read* the tabloids?"

He narrows his eyes at my outburst. "As far as you're concerned, he's going to tread carefully."

I resist the urge to throw my arms up in defeat. "So where does that leave me?"

He spreads his hands and shrugs, looking more like a Jewish mother than a half-Irish bartender-turned-dom. "You want a fuck, you're going to have to make the first move."

I scowl. Because frankly, I thought I had.

"There's my pretty girl!" Grams, my dad's eighty-year-old mother, holds out her hands to me and urges me over.

She moved to Florida three years ago after Gramps died, and I don't see her nearly often enough. Now I hurry into her arms and give her a big hug. She seems more fragile now, and the knowledge that I will probably lose her soon keeps my smile from blooming all the way.

She peers at me with eyes that seem tiny now, lost in a wrinkled face that has never seen plastic surgery. "These are my battle scars," she told me once after a friend pointed out that Grams could easily afford the best. "Do you know how much work it was to live a good life? Why should I hide it?"

"What's that frown for?" she asks me now, her hands cupping my cheeks.

I shake my head and glance over at my mom. "I just miss you, I guess." I lean over and give her another big hug.

"Well, that's because you don't visit often enough. Millions of dollars in a trust fund and you can't hop a plane to Florida once in a while?"

She's grinning when she says it, and I know she's only teasing. But she's right. And I make a promise right then and there to visit more often.

"Where's the guest of honor?" I ask. Poppy is Grams's father-in-law, and although he'll be one hundred years old tomorrow, he still does the *New York Times* crossword puzzle every Sunday, even though his hand shakes too much for him to write the answers in himself.

"Your dad told Becca to take a little break and took him down the boardwalk to the beach," my mom tells me. Becca is Poppy's live-in nurse and crossword helper, and has been for the past twenty years. Which pretty much makes her one of the family.

"Oh. I guess I'll go catch up to them." I look around the room. There are five bungalows on Barclay Isle along with the main house, which is where we are now. It's the most understated of all the Sykes family homes, which isn't saying much. It's six thousand square feet with walls that actually open so that the entire downstairs can be converted into an outdoor living area that flows out onto the flagstone patio.

I've always loved it here. The water is beautiful and warm. The sky is blue, and there's privacy. So much privacy.

Even on a weekend like this where there are over a dozen people in the house, there's still always room to get away. As far as I can tell, that's what people are doing, because while I see my great-uncle talking with his oldest son by the window, I don't see my uncle's wife or any of their three grandchildren, all of which are about my age.

I wave to them, but don't pause to talk as I head toward the patio, intending to follow the boardwalk until I find Dad and Poppy.

My mother's voice stops me. "You should grab a bite before the staff takes the buffet away."

I nod, then apologize again. "I didn't mean to be so late," I say. It's already after noon. I dropped my bag at my bungalow—the one I've used ever since my parents said I was old enough to have my own space—and then headed to the main house. "I left New York before dawn, but I had to wait for the helicopter in Norfolk. Mechanical issue."

"You're here now," Grams says. "That's what matters."

I smile, thinking how comfortable it is to just be hanging with family. How different than the way it felt with Dallas at our game night. He's family, too, but it wasn't easy like this.

No, Dallas Sykes is in a category all by himself. Brothers with Benefits, I think, then curse my own stupid, sick sense of humor.

I draw in a breath, because now that he's on my mind, I have to ask. "What about Dallas?"

"He's been here all morning," Mom says. "I think he was disappointed you weren't here yet. He went back to his bungalow about an hour ago. Said he had to make some calls."

I nod. "Did Mrs. Foster come with you?"

Mom smiles. "Of course. And Liam's coming this afternoon, too."

I don't even try to hide my pleasure. I haven't talked to Liam in weeks, and it's been even longer since I've seen him, and I really do miss him terribly.

"What about Archie?" He and Mrs. Foster are the two family employees with the longest tenure.

"He's here, too, of course. How would your brother survive without him?"

Frankly, I think Dallas would survive just fine. But I don't say it. Dallas may be a fuckup, but there's more to him than he likes to show, I'm certain of it. What I don't understand is why he's so willing to let people see the screw-up and not the competent man.

That, however, isn't a question I'm going to contemplate right now.

"I'm going to go meet up with Dad and Poppy and then go catch some sun and read." The idea sounds like heaven, actually. I don't get the chance to veg as much as I'd like, and I'm looking forward to a few hours of downtime.

"Have fun. Dinner's at six. Poppy eats early," she adds in response to my raised eyebrow.

"And the party's tomorrow at noon, right?"

She tells me it is and I give her another hug, and then one more for Grams before I grab a couple of wine coolers for my tote bag. Next, I head onto the patio and then over to the wooden boardwalk. I'd taken the opportunity to change when I'd dropped my luggage at my bungalow, so I'm already set for my beach outing.

I have a paperback in my tote bag, along with a towel, a water bottle, and some sunscreen. And now I have the wine coolers, too, which is always a plus. I'm wearing a pink V-neck T-shirt over my bikini top and a scarf wrapped around my hips like a sarong over the bathing suit bottom. I take off my flip-flops and tuck them in the tote, because it's much easier to walk on the beach in bare feet. I'm not worried about splinters. The boardwalk is well-trafficked, and after so many years, it's as smooth as stone.

I see my dad at the end of the boardwalk standing beside Poppy's wheelchair and hurry down to them and give them both a hug. Poppy's smile is wide and toothless, and he reaches out a shaking hand for me. I take it, then wish him a happy birthday.

I stand there for a while, just talking with my dad and great-grandfather, and the conversation is light and easy. For a while after the kidnapping, I was uncomfortable around my dad. I'd been so angry that he'd kept the authorities out that it had caused a rift between us. He'd seen the change in me, of course, but I'd never explained myself, and I know he thinks that I was just dealing with the horror of being kidnapped.

Over time, I've learned to deal with it. My dad is who he is. Rich and arrogant. A man who likes his privacy. And I get that he thought he was protecting us by keeping the whole thing out of the papers. I don't agree—I think he holds as much blame for Dallas's extra four weeks of torment as I do—but I came to terms years ago, and I'm glad. Because even though we disagree at a fundamental level about his hiring vigilantes, I do love my parents and I don't want a wedge between us.

The thought makes me sigh. Because there's still one potential wedge, and it's a huge one: Dallas and me and the secrets we are keeping.

I chat a bit longer and then say my goodbyes. I walk in the surf for a few minutes, then cut back up toward the house to get the little golf cart I'd left in the driveway. The bungalows are scattered over the island so that every space has privacy. Mine is at the very end of the island, with an amazing view of the southern coastline and the wide vista of the Atlantic.

It's also just a few hundred yards from my very favorite spot, a small cove that Dallas, Liam, and I discovered when we were kids. It's difficult to access, as that beach is surrounded by small, rocky hills instead of the dunes that are so prevalent on this island. We'd climbed over looking for tide pools, and when our parents had realized where we were they'd banned us from returning.

Too dangerous, they'd said. We could twist an ankle and end up stuck. We could scrape a knee on the sharp rocks and get blood poisoning. We could get trapped when high tide came in.

Of course we swore we'd stay away.

Of course we returned almost daily.

It's the best beach on the island, in my opinion. And as I carefully navigate the rocks to get to the cove, I feel a pang of melancholy. I miss my best friends, and I don't know how to get either of them back.

I haven't really lost Liam, of course. But distance and his crazy work schedule mean that when we see each other it usually feels like a drive-by encounter.

But I'm terribly afraid that Dallas may be a lost cause, and soon I may have to accept the horrible truth that we can never be more than family. Not friends. And certainly not lovers.

I don't want to think of that now, though. I just want to relax and soak up the sun, and as soon as I'm over the rocks, I find a place for my towel and spread it out. I take off my T-shirt and untie my sarong, then put them both in the tote bag so they won't get horribly sandy.

As the sun arcs over the island, I devour half the book along with my wine coolers. I want to keep reading, but the heat and the alcohol are making me sleepy, and I close my eyes and let myself drift, my mind filling with those particularly vivid dreams that come between sleep and wakefulness.

These dreams, of course, are all about Dallas. His touch, his kisses. Fantasies mix with memories, and by the time I drag myself back to the present, my skin is tingling, and not just from the warmth of the sun.

I stay on my stomach for a minute just to re-orient myself after my nap, and that is when I realize he is there. I don't see him—my head is down—and I hear nothing but the crash of the waves against the shore.

Even so, I am absolutely certain, and I very slowly lift my head and look around.

He's standing perfectly still on the sand, just this side of the rocky barrier, and he is looking at me with such fierce longing that my body trembles from the force of it.

He's wearing a faded blue T-shirt and khaki shorts. Like me, he's barefoot. He looks both casual and confident, a man at home in his own skin. A man who knows what he wants and is used to taking it.

But even so, he doesn't make a move. Doesn't say my name, doesn't walk to me. He just watches me, as if there is no place he'd rather be and nothing he'd rather be doing.

You're going to have to make the first move.

Brody's words fill my head, as if brought to me on the ocean breeze. He's right, of course. I know he is. Isn't that what I did in the cabana when I turned his chaste kiss into something wild and hot? And didn't we come damn close then to what is now my ultimate goal?

My stomach flutters, but those butterflies are inconsequential compared to my wine cooler–induced boldness.

I know what I want. More than that, I know what we need.

But oh, dear god, if he pushes me away again . . .

He won't, though—I know he won't. I recognize the heat in his eyes. The same heat I feel. That same grinding, consuming desire.

He's just waiting for me to make a move. It would, of course, be rude not to comply.

Slowly, I stand, the bikini top barely covering my nipples as the triangles of material hang loose from the string tied around my neck. I reach up and I pull the bow, then let my top fall free.

Even from this distance, I can see the way his throat moves. Emboldened, I take a step toward him, then another. I look nowhere but at him. At his eyes that are watching me so intently.

"Don't pretend this is a chance encounter," I say. "We both want the same thing."

He doesn't answer, but when I raise my hands to my breasts and tug on my own nipples, I can see the way his cock strains against his khaki shorts, and just knowing that I am making him hard sends a surge of power through me.

I take my hands from my breasts then reach for the ties on either hip that hold the front and back triangles of my very tiny bikini bottom together. Just two simple bows, and I release each in unison, then shift my stance, spreading my legs so that the material falls to the sand, and I am left standing in front of him completely naked—and completely vulnerable.

"You know what I want," I say as I slide my hand down my belly to my pubis. I'm waxed, and so there is nothing at all hidden to him. I go lower still, and my fingers touch wet, swollen flesh. Standing here, exposed like this, has not only set my nerves on fire, it has made me more aroused than I have ever been in my life.

"You want it, too," I say boldly, then bite my lower lip as I slide a finger deep inside.

Dallas's eyes never leave me, but his hand is at his crotch, and I gasp a little as he unzips his fly and pulls out his huge, fully erect cock.

I feel a tightening in my core—a visceral reaction to the sight of Dallas stroking himself. Of Dallas watching me. My pussy throbs and my fingers slide over my too-wet clit.

He's stroking his cock hard and fast, and I can hear the sound of skin against skin, of his low groans, and it just makes me tighter. Closer. I press harder, moving my fingers in small circles, concentrating on my clit. I'm desperate now, and I don't think I could stop if I wanted to.

So help me, I don't want to.

I let my gaze flick from the heat in his eyes to his hand on his cock, stroking and tugging. I see the muscles in his lower abs tighten, and I feel my pussy clench around my fingers.

He's watching me.

The thought is so damned erotic, and I'm close—so close. I know he is, too, and I want to shatter. Hell, I *need* to, and when the first tremors ricochet through me, marking a coming orgasm, I whisper his name.

That is all it takes. He explodes in front of me, shooting thick streams of come into the sand, as he arches back, his body tense, and his eyes never leaving my face.

I cry out, too, my knees going weak as my own orgasm rips through me, shattering me, and I fall down to the ground, not quite believing we'd just done that, but unable to escape the simple truth that it was one of the hottest, most erotic things I've ever done in my life.

"Dallas, oh, Christ, Dallas. That was fu—"

"Fucked up," he finishes. "Yeah. That was most definitely all fucked up."

There's an edge to his voice, almost anger.

"I'm sorry, Jane. I'm so damn sorry."

I don't reply—I haven't got a clue what to say. I just sit there and watch—in shock, in surprise, in absolute total disbelief—as he tucks his now-soft cock back into his shorts, turns around, and climbs out over the rocks, leaving me alone and naked in the cove.

17

All Fucked Up

All fucked up.

Wasn't that what he'd told the redhead? That he liked his sex fucked up? Dirty? Base?

And it was true. It was so damn true.

But not with Jane. He'd never wanted to drag her down like that with him. So what did he do the first chance he got? He jacked off to the sight of her masturbating, just like he would have done with any of his other women. Just like he'd so often ordered them to do so he could get release. So that he could keep that tight hold on the way that sex played out in his bedroom and at the club.

He should never have given in, but he'd been so hard, and she'd looked so damned amazing. He knew what she'd been doing—her idiotic idea that they needed to fuck each other out of their systems. It wouldn't work. He'd never be rid of the want of her, the need of her. But today, she'd been trying to force his hand. To make him take the lead.

In a way, he supposed he'd done just that.

He ran his fingers through his hair, frustrated because he didn't know where to go with this. They were on some damn sexual merry-go-round, and they were going to have to figure a way off if they wanted to have any sort of relationship at all. He couldn't fuck her and he didn't want to lose her, and he was all out of options.

A dull ache was building in his head, and he went to the bar and poured himself a scotch, just to take the edge off. He'd intended to sip it, but instead he slammed it back, then poured another. His cock was stiff again just from the memory of the way he'd gotten off while watching her finger-fuck herself. He figured he'd toss this second drink back, too, and then go take an ice-cold shower and see if that helped.

He stripped off his shirt, then did the same with his shorts and briefs. He wasn't even out of the small living room when he heard the door open. He cursed himself for not thinking to lock it—when did he ever on the island?—then turned instinctively, expecting Liam.

Instead, he saw Jane. A wildness in her eyes and raw fury on her face. "Just who the hell do you think you—"

She stopped cold, obviously just now seeing him, and her strangled little gasp made his already heated skin burn even hotter.

He watched as she gathered herself. Blinking a little and then biting on her lower lip as her eyes roamed slowly over him.

He didn't think she did it on purpose, but when she reached his eyes, she actually licked her lips, like he was her own private candy stash. The thought curled through him, along with a delicious fantasy of how he'd like to order her to suck him off.

Fuck.

"Don't you knock?"

He saw the debate play across her face, along with an innocent pink blush that made him want to turn her over his knee and spank her, just to see if he could get the exact same color on her ass.

The indecision on her face lasted only for a moment. Then she burst forward as if she'd been shot and wrapped herself around him, her lower abs warm and soft against his cock, her mouth hard and hot on his.

He should have pushed her away right then, but he no longer had the strength. She'd won, maybe, but he'd damn well make the victory his own.

Wildly, he took her, kissing her deep. Hard. He slid one hand under her hair and untied the simple bow that held her bikini up. Then he slid his hand down and repeated the process with the bow at her back.

The two triangles of material stayed put—held tight by the pressure of her breasts against his chest—but he knew they would fall away if he stepped back, exposing her to him.

He didn't step back. Not yet. Not when he could still savor the moment.

Now, instead, he focused on her mouth. He slid one hand up and held her throat so that she couldn't step back, couldn't move. She could only open her mouth to him and give him what he wanted. And she did, her low, whimpering sounds of pleasure shooting straight to his cock.

With his free hand, he cupped her ass, then found the scarf's loose knot at her hip and untied it. He let the silk fall away, anticipating repeating the process with her bikini bottoms. But she was bare beneath the scarf, and that naughty boldness made him smile and kiss her deeper.

As his tongue explored her mouth, his palm cupped her bare ass and pushed her tighter against him so that the movement of their joined bodies stroked and teased his cock. The friction sent waves of pleasure rolling through him, taking him closer to the edge until he was on the verge of coming right there. Right on her stomach, her tits.

And that's when—*finally*—some tiny spark of reason cut through the sensual haze and he pushed her away from him.

With a sigh, he started to reach down to pick up his shorts. She got there faster, grabbed them, then tossed them across the room.

"What the—"

She indicated her own naked body with a sweep of her hand. "Fair is fair," she chirped.

Oh yeah. He'd love to turn her over his knee.

He closed his eyes and willed himself not to think about her ass. Or any part of her at all. She was wearing him down; he knew it. And he needed to get back control. "You should go." He spoke firmly in the kind of voice the women he invited into his bed obeyed. The kind of voice that gave inarguable orders to his team.

"Not happening," she said, apparently immune. "I'm tired of waiting, Dallas. I'm going to take what I want."

"You don't want this." Why the hell couldn't she get that through her skull? "You don't want me. I can't give you—"

"What? Everything? You think I don't know that? What we are to each other? Why it can't ever work, *ever*?" She stepped around him and headed for the bedroom.

He stood for a moment, a little irritated but mostly amused.

"Of course I get it," she continued. "And if I have to be just your friend, just your sister, then okay. Fine. I can deal with that. But we can't even get there because of the damn elephant in the room."

She sat on the bed, her legs spread just enough so that he could see how wet and swollen she was. She patted the mattress beside her. "You want me—don't you even think of denying it. And I want you. And so I'm here to take what I want, and then maybe, just maybe we can get our heads clear and move on."

"Don't you get it? There is no fucking you out of my system. I can't—"

He stopped, his mouth tight and hard, then took a deep breath and tried a different tack. "You will never be out of my system, and you have no idea what you're asking."

"I know I can't live like this. Everything wild and scattered. My emotions all over the place. I hate it, and one day I'm going to hate you, too, for making me feel this way."

"Maybe you should. Maybe I deserve it."

"You're not the one who deserves it," she whispered, as a shadow crossed her face.

"No," he said, remembering what she'd confessed in the cabana. That she blamed herself for those extra four weeks he'd been held. "Don't even think that."

She looked up at him, and now her expression was hard as steel. "Then take my mind off it. Tell me what you want, Dallas. Do you want me to lay back? Do you want to watch while I touch myself? Do you want me to suck your cock?" She glanced toward him, where the cock in question was enthusiastically answering both those questions in the affirmative. "Well," she said with a smile. "I guess so."

He stepped closer to the bed.

"This is what you want?" he asked. "For me to treat you like one of those women who fall into my bed? Who gossip that they've had me and whisper about the size of my cock?"

"Well, it's definitely worthy of its reputation."

He wasn't amused. "Jane."

"Yes." She lifted her chin. "That's what I want."

"You don't even have a clue what you're asking. If you knew what I did with—"

"Then show me. Pretend I'm your little Oxford grad Argentinean girl. Or that bitchy redhead from your party. Do you kiss them, or is that too personal? Maybe you just fuck them."

He scoffed. "That's the last thing I do."

"Then show me what you do first."

He almost laughed, but the sound caught in his throat as

she stood and came to him. "Do you order them on their knees?" she asked as she went onto hers. "Do you fuck their mouths?" She brushed the tip of her tongue along his glans, then took in just enough to tease.

And then, without warning, she opened her mouth and drew him in so deep his balls brushed up against her chin.

Lust and self-loathing combined inside him, an explosive combination, and he reached down, grabbed her under the shoulders and practically tossed her back to the bed.

She stumbled, then sat. "Dammit, Dallas, I—"

He was in front of her in a second, pushing her back so that she was lying flat on her back with her knees bent and her legs hanging over the bed. He stood between her legs as he leaned over, then pressed his hand against her mouth to keep her quiet as her eyes fired with anger.

"Spread your legs," he ordered, and saw the anger recede and her eyes go wide as she processed his words and then complied.

He kept one hand on her mouth, and with the other he teased her inner thighs, stroking slowly as he moved higher and higher to her bare pussy. She writhed under his touch, frustrated that he wasn't stroking where she wanted. That he was taunting and teasing.

He intended to do a lot of that.

With a small smile, he pulled both his hands away.

"Don't stop," she begged, and the need in her voice made him even harder. "Don't you dare stop."

"Slide up," he ordered, and she hurried to comply as he got on the bed beside her, then straddled her, his cock rubbing provocatively over the mound of her sex.

"Dallas." His name was almost lost in the desperate whimper.

He leaned forward to stroke her breasts. "I should toss you out of here, and lock the door."

"Maybe." Her breath was ragged, filled with anticipation. "But you won't."

"Why not?"

"Because we've tried staying apart and it doesn't work. Because you want me. Because I'm naked and wet for you, and that makes you hard."

He closed his eyes in defense against the truth. "Do you have any idea how much I've wanted this? How often I've imagined you laid out naked for me?"

Her throat moved as she nodded. "Of course I do."

Of course she did.

He was in her fantasies, too, and that simple, straightforward realization pushed him forward, past the voice in his head that said it couldn't work. That there couldn't be a happy ending and this woman in his arms couldn't make him whole.

Probably true. But right then it just felt so damn right.

And maybe it would be right. Maybe this time, because it was her in his bed, it really would all be right again.

She was laid out like a feast for him, and he leaned forward to take a nibble, grazing his teeth over her tight nipple, and then sucking on her breast. She squirmed in pleasure, and the soft noises she made only fueled his desire.

He wanted to taste the rest of her, and he started to slowly drift down her body, biting and kissing as he moved lower toward heaven. As her gasps and sighs became more desperate.

She arched up as he teased her navel, and he could make out her soft, whimpered words. "Don't stop. Please, please don't stop."

He had no intention of stopping. He'd wanted this, needed it, for years.

Hell, forever.

He kept his head down, his attention on the soft skin of her abdomen as he kissed his way lower. But he felt her fingers when she twined them in his hair. When she pushed him downward, urging him to move faster, to taste her and take her higher.

Which was exactly what he intended to do.

He slid lower on the bed, then teased her inner thighs with the tip of his tongue. He held her tight as she writhed, obviously coming undone from the pleasure he was giving her.

Slowly, he kissed his way up, then laved her pussy with his tongue. She tasted sweet and smelled of sex, and in the moment when he closed his mouth to suck her clit, he remembered the first time he'd done that very thing. Her trusting innocence, his fumbling exploration. And the wild, incredible union they'd felt when she'd exploded in his arms—and they'd both managed to escape the dark. Even if only for a moment.

Now he knew his way around a woman's body better, but no woman had tasted like Jane. Had responded like Jane. And as he teased her with his tongue, he thrust two fingers inside her, filling her, urging her, making her struggle against his hold on her as she tried to ride up to passion.

And then he felt it. That distinctive tremor as she cried out and bucked and exploded beneath him, and oh, holy crap, the look on her face. Passion. Pleasure. Bone deep satisfaction.

He was the one who had given her that. And he couldn't understand how anything as exceptionally right as this moment could be wrong.

"Dallas," she murmured meeting his eyes. "Hi. And wow."

He chuckled, amused, as he moved up her body, and then let her taste her own desire as he kissed her hard and deep.

"More," she whispered when he broke the kiss. "Please. I want you inside me."

He could see the heat spike in her eyes, and he could feel the way his cock tightened with just the thought of it. The wonderful, incredible thought of it. Hell, he could already imagine what it would feel like to bury himself inside her and he was so damn hard right now—and she was so incredibly wet—that he could probably fill her up with just one, hard thrust.

And here she was, spreading her legs wider, opening herself to him. She was ready, so ready, and he had longed for this moment for more than half his life.

He had to do it. He had to take her.

Urgently, he moved over her, hard and ready. The feel of her against the tip of his cock was beyond incredible, and as she bit her lip and urged him to *please, please hurry,* he used his fingers to open her. He was trying to keep control. Trying to overcome that urge to just thrust hard toward heaven. He knew better. He knew he wanted to take it slow.

He pushed against her, just a little bit—and oh, Christ, she felt so good, and he held her hips so that he could go deeper, and then—

And then he lost it.

Lost everything.

Control of himself. Of the moment.

Lost his goddamn erection.

A wild burst of fury and self-loathing shot through him and he lurched back off the bed.

"Dallas? No, please." She propped herself up on her elbows. "We need this. Please don't stop. Please."

"*This?*" He cupped his soft, useless dick and watched her eyes widen from the harsh tone of his voice.

At first she only looked confused, but then she twisted so she could see him better. She was looking at his face at first. Then her eyes flicked down and he saw awareness—and shock—bloom on her beautiful face.

"Is this really what you want?" He couldn't keep the self-loathing out of his voice.

"Dallas—" He heard the pain in his name, and the confusion.

"I thought—I'd hoped. Oh, fuck, Jane, they destroyed me. But I kept you in my head when they—" He couldn't say it. Hell, he couldn't even think about what the Woman had done to him.

He shuddered from the memory, then pushed it away. "All these years, you've been my light." He thought of Adele telling him that if he wanted to actually manage to fuck her, then he should think of Jane, because surely he'd keep his erection.

But he wouldn't try. He would never sully Jane like that.

And now it turned out that even Jane herself wasn't enough for him to keep it up.

He shook his head, disgusted with himself. Embarrassed. Lost.

"Dallas, it's okay. It's not—"

"What? Important? The hell it's not." He drew in a breath, then laughed at the dark irony of it all. "You think we should fuck each other out of our systems? Well, guess what. It's never going to happen. *Can't* happen."

He clenched his hands at his sides, trying to forestall the urge to put his fist through the wall out of sheer frustration. "I'm broken and I'm your brother. And I can't be the man for you."

He didn't wait to hear what she had to say. He didn't wait to see her expression.

He just turned and went into the bathroom, then shut the door behind him. He turned the lock, then slid down to sit on the floor.

Right then, that was about the best he could manage.

18

Gone, Baby, Gone

And the award for worst handling of a moment ever goes to me.

I frown as I hesitate outside the bathroom door, my hand poised to knock. I don't though. Because I don't know what to say.

I sigh, hating myself for being sideswiped and confused. For not realizing he'd lost his erection and assuming he was just taunting me again.

And my face—oh, god, I know I must have looked shocked, and that sure as hell isn't the way to look around a fragile male ego. But even when my mind had clicked to reality, I still couldn't quite believe it. King of Fuck, after all.

I play back his words in his head. *They destroyed him?*

He kept me in his head when they what?

I was his light?

What does that mean?

Except that's not a question I really need to ask. I know only too well what it means. They tortured him. They broke him.

The Jailer. The Woman.

They destroyed him.

I think of all those long weeks after the botched raid—when we didn't know if Dallas was alive or dead. Was that what they were doing? Ruining an innocent boy for fun? For punishment? For the sin of sleeping with his sister?

I don't know, but I think that must be true.

Every therapist I've seen over the last seventeen years has listed survivor's guilt among my many diagnoses. I've always known it was an accurate assessment, but only now do I fully understand the depth of what he suffered without me. I still don't know exactly what they did to him—until just now I'd believed that he didn't remember what they did to him.

Now I know differently. He remembers, although he'd sworn otherwise.

I suspect that he remembers everything. Every horrible moment.

They destroyed me, he'd confessed. *But I kept you in my head.*

I tremble with the memory of those words. He still wants me, even though he should hate me. Because I'd been safe at home while he'd been left behind to suffer.

And I really don't know how we move on from here.

Reluctantly, I get dressed again. I gather my spilled tote and then pause by the bathroom door. I don't know if he'd rather talk to me or be alone, but I can't stand being quiet any longer.

I knock softly. "Dallas? Dallas, will you please come out and talk to me?"

He doesn't answer, and I close my eyes and exhale, sad for him and for us. And, yes, scared, too. Because I'd thought that we were moving forward, and now I think we're farther back than when we started.

I head to the front door, step out into the late afternoon sunshine, and immediately wish I'd stayed locked up inside.

My parents are right there, strolling along the little path that runs through the island's interior.

My mom smiles and waves, but my dad's expression is thunderous. I'm terribly afraid I look guilty, but turning the other way would look even worse.

So I take a deep breath and put my acting skills to the test. "Hey!" I say, waving. "I was bummed I missed Dallas at breakfast, so I thought I'd come say hi."

"I hope he doesn't miss dinner," my mom says.

"I don't know what he's planning," I say. "He was on some sort of work call." My voice sounds cheery and overly perky. "I told him I'd catch him later."

I give my mom a hug and my dad a kiss on the cheek. "I'm going to go change for dinner. I love you," I say, again in my chipper voice that I can't seem to turn off. I give them a little wave and then it's all I can do not to sprint to my bungalow.

19

Sins of the Father

Dallas heard the door slam and called himself nine kinds of a fool. He should never have tested his limits with her.

For that matter, he should never have kissed her, should never have touched her.

They'd had their moment when they were young, and they needed to both just get over it. They were chasing fantasies, and it was going to destroy them both.

He stood up and leaned against the bathroom counter, then looked at his face in the mirror. What the hell was wrong with him, anyway? He was a strong man. He ran a billion dollar empire. He headed up a covert organization. He wasn't weak. He didn't shirk from the hard shit. When he had a project or a mission, he did what had to be done to make it happen. Emotion didn't enter into the equation.

So why had he let it with Jane?

Because he'd wanted her.

Because she'd wanted him. Or at least she had until she'd

learned this new truth about him. God only knew what she thought of him now.

But just because they wanted didn't mean they could have, and they'd been torturing themselves for years.

He didn't know how to stop. He didn't know how to rip open his heart and pull her out.

But he had to figure it out.

Because if they kept on like this, he'd just end up dragging her down. And he loved her too damn much to watch that happen.

He rubbed the back of his neck in defense against a rising headache. He'd never truly gotten used to his cock failing on him, but he certainly wasn't surprised anymore. Every time— every goddamn time—he lost his erection at penetration. In fact, he rarely even tried anymore.

But that wasn't all of it. Hell, he couldn't even fuck a woman's mouth and get off. She could suck him until the end of the world, and it wouldn't make a goddamn difference. For that matter, he couldn't let her jack him off with her hand or her tits.

He came by his own hand or not at all, and there was no therapist, no drug, no goddamn magic cure. He ought to know—he'd tried every fucking thing.

This was who he was—who his captors had made him. And he'd gotten damn good at making sure the women in his bed were satisfied. Hell, it had become a point of both pride and camouflage. If they walked away feeling thoroughly fucked, the likelihood of them realizing they hadn't actually been thoroughly fucked was significantly less.

But over the years, some part of him had believed that Adele was right—that it would be different if he was with Jane. Now even that had proved to be bullshit.

He sighed. He'd said all along she deserved more. She deserved better. And although he hated the thought of her in another man's arms, he knew that's where she belonged. She was his sister. Maybe not by blood, but that didn't change the reality. And the reality was that he shouldn't even be thinking about whether or not his cock could make her happy.

A sharp rap at the front door startled him from his thoughts, and he pulled on the pair of gray sweatpants he kept on a hook behind the bathroom door and went to answer it. Once again, he assumed the guest would be Liam, and once again he was wrong.

His father stood on the threshold, his hands in the pockets of his plaid golfing slacks, the ones he wore when he wasn't at the office even if there was no golf course in sight.

"Dad. Hey." He knew he sounded confused, but that's only because he was. He stepped aside and gestured for his father to enter. "What's up?"

"Am I interrupting your phone call?"

"What?" The moment the question was out of his mouth he realized his mistake. Obviously his father had bumped into Jane doing a version of the Walk of Shame and she'd covered for them both. "No, I've been off for a few minutes. About to make a couple more, though." He looked at his wristwatch for good measure.

"Hmm. Good to catch you between, then," his dad said, not taking the hint. "I've been hoping to grab a few moments to chat with you."

"Great. Do you want something to drink? I've got OJ and sparkling water in the fridge. And the bar is stocked if you want something stronger."

"I'm fine." Eli crossed the room to the one leather armchair, then waited for Dallas to sit. He chose to stand.

"Well, I just wanted to say that I'm proud of you, son."

"Oh." Dallas took a seat on the ottoman. Whatever he'd anticipated his father had come to say, that wasn't it. Especially since Dallas had only yesterday told his father he was backing out on the Canadian launch events next week. "Well, thank you, sir. I'm very glad to hear it."

"I don't approve of your string of women, but you've been through the kind of hell I can't imagine. I know you have to work through that, probably for your whole life. So while I don't like it, maybe I understand it. At least a little."

Dallas wasn't at all sure where this was going, so he said nothing. Just sat on the ottoman and waited for his dad to keep talking.

"And while there've been a few times when you've missed a business meeting in order to—well, in order to engage in one of your liaisons, on the whole you're doing a good job running your divisions. You're an asset to the empire, Dallas."

"Thank you." His gratitude was sincere. But he was still waiting for the other shoe to drop.

"I'm your father, and I'm very proud to be. Sykes blood flows in your veins, Dallas, but you and I both know that it's not my blood." Dallas nodded slowly as his father's meandering path became more clear. "My brother made some terrible mistakes during his life. Bad choices. Choices that ruined him."

"I don't remember anything about that, sir. I was very young." That was true enough. Dallas had only been five when his birth mother—who he remembered only as smelling of cigarettes—had left him in the Hamptons.

Eli nodded. "You were. And I consider that a blessing." He stood and went to the bar to pour himself a scotch. "You didn't have enough time with Donovan for him to taint you."

Dallas noticed that Eli didn't mention the trouble that Dallas got into in high school. Experimenting with drugs. Theft. He'd been a fuckup and it had gotten him shipped overseas, and at the time, Eli had been more than willing to blame Dallas's behavior on bad blood.

Honestly, Eli had been right.

Dallas really didn't have any genuine memories of his birth parents, but as soon as he was old enough to read, he'd made it a priority to learn what he could. He'd found nothing about his birth mother. But about Donovan—his birth father and Eli's brother—he'd found plenty.

If it was illegal or immoral, Donovan Sykes was there. A bad boy straight out of central casting, Donovan had fucked anything that moved, been arrested for possession of both heroin and cocaine, had partied with Hollywood stars, raced high-end cars down the Pacific Coast Highway, and basically offered himself up as the poster child for irresponsibility.

At first, Dallas had been disgusted with Donovan. But then, as he got older and started to have sexual thoughts about his sister, Dallas had been disgusted with himself. More than that, he'd feared Eli's rejection, because hadn't Eli written his brother off even before Dallas had been dumped on his doorstep? What was to stop him from writing off his adopted son, too?

Dallas had tested the limits of Eli's love. He'd done drugs—mostly pot, but he'd experimented with harder stuff once or twice, too. He'd stolen cars. And, yes, he'd gotten himself off to thoughts of Jane.

And through all of it, his father had been there for him. Yes, he'd tossed around the "bad blood" insult, but he hadn't tossed Dallas out on his ass—instead, he'd sent him away. And while being shipped off to boarding school had pissed Dallas off at first, he'd come to understand that his parents were trying to pull him back to them, not push him away.

Not that he'd realized all of that at the time. But during the last seventeen years of therapy he'd talked about more than the kidnapping. He was well aware of his litany of issues, and he knew that he'd conquered many of them.

The ones that still lingered were the deepest and the darkest, with Jane right down there in the center. A place he really didn't want her to be, but where she would remain until he could somehow exorcise her from his heart.

And that, he knew, was never going to happen.

His father returned to the chair, pausing in front of Dallas long enough to hand him a drink, which Dallas took gratefully.

"I'm sorry, sir. I'm not really sure where you're going with this."

"I just want you to remember that, like it or not, he's your father, too. So think hard when you move through your life, son, about whose footsteps you want to follow."

Was this about his public lifestyle? Or was it about Jane? Was his father simply giving Dallas some fatherly advice on how to behave in the world of business? Or was he issuing a subtle reminder that his threat to disinherit still lingered?

He met his father's eyes. "I don't ever want to disappoint you or Mom."

"I know you don't, son. And that's one of the reasons I'm so proud of you. I just thought I should tell you. I don't think I tell you often enough."

Message delivered, Eli stood. "Well, then. I should probably go see what your mother's up to. Will we see you in the main house for dinner?"

Dallas thought of Jane. More, he thought about how he really didn't want to run into her, not after what just happened. He was too raw. Too goddamn mortified. "I'm not sure," he said. "I've still got to run through my call list. I may just grab a sandwich and visit with Poppy later."

"Sounds good." As they walked to the door, his father started rattling off some thoughts about an upcoming company retreat. Dallas barely even listened. Instead, his thoughts were on Jane. On Deliverance. On Adele and the dark places into which he so often sunk.

And he knew that whether or not he wanted to, inevitably he would disappoint the people he loved.

* * *

Liam was coming toward the bungalow as Eli was leaving, and Dallas left the door open so his friend could enter.

"Good trip?" he asked, as Liam shut the door and crossed to the bar. He dropped his leather messenger bag on the floor and pulled down a glass.

"This place is a pain in the ass to get to," Liam complained. "Especially if you have to crisscross all over the globe to manage it." He poured a shot of tequila and drank it straight, an affinity that Dallas neither understood nor shared.

"I saw Poppy, though," Liam said. "He's pretty spry for a hundred."

"That he is." Dallas joined him at the bar and poured his own drink. Frankly, he could use it.

"So where's Jane?" Liam said. "I figured she'd be here."

Dallas looked at him sharply. "Whatever you think you know, you don't." He didn't want to talk about it, tiptoe around it, or even fucking think about it. Not now. Not yet.

Liam held up his hands, signaling surrender. "No need to bite my head off, man. I was just wondering about her."

"Yeah, well here's a suggestion. Don't."

"What bug crawled up your ass?"

"This conversation is finished, Foster."

Liam cocked his head. "Yes, sir, Mr. Sykes."

He waited a moment, just studying Dallas, then he bent to the bag, pulled out a small box wrapped in plain brown paper, and passed it to him. "For Crowley's party on Friday. Three bugs. Office. Foyer. Living room or the bedroom. Bedroom's better, obviously, but harder to pull off. That's it. Nothing you haven't done a dozen times before."

Dallas nodded, then set the package aside. For a second, he hesitated, not wanting to be crossways with his friend. But all he said was, "Thanks. I'll call you when they're set."

"Then I guess we're good to go." Liam hoisted the bag back onto his shoulder. "I'll see you at the party tomorrow, D."

And then he walked to the door and headed outside. And Liam Foster, one of Dallas's closest friends in the world, didn't once look back.

20

Silence

The last strains of "Happy Birthday to You" are buried under the cacophony of the entire family laughing and whistling and generally cheering Poppy on into the next century of his life.

Almost the entire family, anyway. Even Liam and Archie and Mrs. Foster have joined in the festivities.

Dallas, however, is conspicuously absent.

As the clapping fades, Poppy grins at all of us—toothless because he spit his dentures into the sand this morning and Becca says they're still disinfecting—and then holds out his arms so that we can each come in close for a big birthday hug.

I go after my mom, and as he hugs me tight he thanks me for the giant book of old *Times* crossword puzzles. "I figured after all this time it would be like doing them for the first time," I tell him.

He taps my nose. "And that's why you're such a smart girl."

I step away so that my great-uncle can move in, and take a

look around, partly so I can decide who to visit with next, but mostly because I'm looking for Dallas. He, however, is nowhere to be seen.

We're on the patio by the pretty, grotto-style pool, with Poppy in the place of honor at the big outdoor dinner table. My mom has wandered off toward the fire pit and Liam is chatting with his mother. I want to talk to him, but I know they spend precious little time together these days, so I head over to join my mom, since I don't see her nearly enough, either.

"Hey, sweetheart." She smiles at me and holds out her hand. "Did you have a relaxing time on the beach yesterday?" She pokes my shoulder, testing for sunburn. "You wore sunscreen, at least."

"Always." My fair-skinned mom is what they sometimes call a Georgia peach, and she's drilled the need for sunscreen into my head since birth.

"Were you able to chat with Dallas at all?"

I frown. "What?"

"Yesterday, when Daddy and I bumped into you. You said he was busy on a call."

"Oh. Right." I shrug and hope that my guilty expression isn't visible to Mom-radar. "To be honest, I still really want to talk to him about some stuff. Do you know where he is?"

"He joined Poppy for breakfast—gave him an amazing book of old *Times* crosswords," she adds with a small smile. "You two always did think alike."

"Breakfast? Why? Where is he now?"

"Back in New York handling some sort of problem at work," she says. What I hear is, *He wanted to get away from you.*

"Oh. Well, I guess I'll just have to catch him in the city." I try to keep my voice light. As if this is no big deal. As if Dallas and I don't have huge things to talk about.

"So does the fact that you went to his bungalow and are

planning to see him in the city mean that things are getting easier for you two?"

And isn't that a loaded question?

"Easier," I say, letting the word sit on my tongue while I try to figure out how to answer. "A little. Maybe. I mean we're trying. Or, at least, we're trying to try." I lift a shoulder. "We miss each other a lot, we really do. But I'm starting to think that we're never going to get past what happened."

"You two used to be so close," she says with a sigh. "Two peas in a pod. And then—well, it's just so unfair that something neither of you had any control over could change the direction of your lives like that."

"Yeah, but not much about a kidnapping is fair."

"Mmm," she says, and for some reason I get the impression that we're talking at cross-purposes.

But before I can press, Mom hooks her arm through mine and starts heading to the boardwalk. "I hope you know how proud I am of you."

I grin up at her. "Is this our annual mother-daughter talk?"

She bumps me with her hip as we walk down the boards toward the beach. "Don't be impertinent when I'm being serious." She pauses and draws me to a stop with her. "You've had to overcome a lot, baby. And I know that Eli and I weren't—"

She cuts herself off and frowns as she closes her eyes, takes a breath, and then begins again. "The kidnapping destroyed your father and me, too, and while that is no excuse, I know we weren't there for you as much as we should have been afterward. I still look back on those days, and all I recall is feeling numb."

"Do you think I don't understand that?"

"I just—I just wanted to say that at the time I was hurt when you wanted to leave and go away to school. And that was unfair of me. I was still raw from the battle with Colin, and I knew he hated me for asking the court to terminate his parental rights.

And then just three years later when I wanted you home where I could pamper you, there you were asking to go live near him. I was angry and I was confused and I was hurt."

"Mom." I swallow. I've sort of known all that, but she's never outright told me before. "I just couldn't be around Dallas. Seeing him every day. Remembering every day."

I drag my toes across the sand-covered boards remembering how I'd snuck into Dallas's room the first night he'd been home. I'd spooned against his back and just held tight. I'd wanted more—so much more—and I know he did, too. But when I'd whispered his name, he'd shaken his head. "I can't," he said. "*We* can't."

He'd rolled over to face me, and I saw the pain in his eyes. "What we had inside, we can't have it anymore. You know we can't."

"I know," I'd whispered. "But—"

He'd shut me up with a kiss. Our last kiss for a long, long time. "It has to stay locked up, Jane. If our parents found out . . . hell, if anyone found out."

I closed my eyes, but I nodded. Because he was right. We were free, and that was good. But what we'd shared had been left behind, locked up inside those dank, gray walls. And that simple truth had come close to destroying me.

The next week, I'd begged my mom to enroll me in boarding school near Colin. And, thankfully, she'd reluctantly agreed.

"It was never about getting away from you and Dad," I tell her now. "You know that, right? It was just that Dallas—"

"Was a reminder. I understand. I do. I did back then, too. And I wanted the best for you. I was glad you could get away, go to a place where you could heal. But sometimes even when we know we're doing the best for our kids it still hurts. I wanted to be the one to kiss you and make it better."

"Mom." I blink away tears. "You always do."

She starts walking again. "I really didn't bring any of this up because I thought we needed an emotional cleansing. I just wanted to say that now things are different. For me, I mean. I understand that Colin was there for you in a way I couldn't be. And the truth is that I will always be grateful to him for that. He could have walked away. From you. From all of it. But he didn't. He stepped up to the plate. And even though he and I don't talk anymore, I thought you should know that I am grateful to him for that. And that I really am glad that you and he have a relationship."

My chest feels tight, and I nod, afraid to speak in case I start to cry.

"You okay?"

"I love you, Mom," I say and start leaking tears.

"Well, good." She hugs me, and I cling tight. "Because I love you, too."

When we break apart, we walk off the boardwalk and onto the sand. She points north, up the beach. "Walk with me?" she asks. "We can look for seashells."

"I'd love to," I say. And even though I know that my mom may never know all the secrets of my heart, I don't doubt that she loves me. And in this moment at least, I'm content to do nothing more than hang with her for a while.

I'm tossing the last of the toiletries in my weekender bag when Liam calls from the front of the bungalow where I've left the front door open for him, as he'd promised to swing by with a couple of beers.

"Back here!" I reply. "Open me one, would you, and I'll be right there." I zip up my bag, glance around the room to make sure I haven't forgotten anything, and head into the living area to meet him.

He greets me with an ice cold beer, and even though I'm much more of a wine girl, when I take a swallow I can't deny that it feels good on my throat. I sit down on the couch and he sits next to me, and I realize that I'm grinning.

"Something funny?"

"Not a thing," I admit. "I just haven't seen you in ages." I hugged him earlier, but I do it again now. "I wish Dallas was here," I say without thinking. "The three of us together would—"

I cut myself off, then shrug. It's been a long time since the three of us have hung out like we used to.

"Did you talk to him at all while he was here? And do me a favor and answer that without chewing my head off."

I raise my brows. "Why would I chew your head off?"

"Because there's a lot of that going around." He stands up to get another beer from the fridge where he stashed the six-pack.

"You're going to have to give me a little more to go on."

"Why don't you tell me what's going on with you and our boy, Dallas?"

I cross my arms over my chest, because that is a hell of a broad topic—and not one I'm keen on getting into with a helicopter on its way.

"It's just that I went over to his bungalow last night, mentioned you, and the fucker practically bit my head off. You two have an argument?"

"I wouldn't exactly call it that. But I'm pretty sure he left this morning because of me. Not because of a business thing."

Liam looks straight at me. "What's going on, Janie?"

"Not a story that's mine to tell," I assure him. "Let's just say that I'd hoped we could maybe stop avoiding each other. But I think we're back to square one. Or maybe square negative one hundred and one." I shrug. "I texted him earlier today to check on him. No reply."

"Gotcha." He leans forward so that his elbows are on his

knees and his beer is held tight in his outstretched hands. His head is down, and he looks like a guy who is thinking deep thoughts, or wrestling with a sticky problem.

When he looks up at me, I can see that it's the latter. "What?" I ask.

"So what are you going to do?"

"Do?"

"You guys are trying to work it out. Trying to repair a friendship or a family quarrel or whatever the hell you want to call it. And he just up and runs away. What are you going to do?"

"I—I don't know."

"Then you're a lame-ass friend, baby girl."

I leap to my feet. "Dammit, Liam. It's not just—"

"I don't fucking care about your excuses, do I?" He stands, too, completely dwarfing me. "Because it's not about excuses. You have one question to ask yourself, and that's 'Do I want that boy in my life?'"

He grimaces in that cocky way he has. "Right now, he's acting like such a prick that I wouldn't be surprised if the answer is no. But if it's yes—" He takes a breath, and I watch as he visibly calms. "If it's a yes, you fight for him." He pulls off his ball cap so he can rub his hand over his buzz-cut head.

"I lost a lot of friends in Afghanistan, you know. Really lost 'em and can't get 'em back no matter how much I might want to. Don't lose one of the people who matters most in your life, Janie. Not if you can help it."

Tears sting my eyes as he looks straight at me. "And if that means you fight, then fuck it, that's what you do. If you think he's worth it, then you have to go to the mat."

21

Sexting

You have to go to the mat.

For about the millionth time since I left the island last night, Liam's words fill my head. I'd taken them to heart and sent Dallas a text message before I'd climbed into the 'copter.

Now, I read over what I sent for the umpteenth time, trying to decide if I could have worded it differently. Somehow written it in a way that actually got through his thick skull. But honestly, it says what I wanted it to. He's just ignoring it.

I get why you're upset, why you backed off and walked away. But don't stay away. You don't want to and I don't want you to. We can try again. We can try a hundred times.

Or we can not try that at all. That's okay, too. I just want you. YOU.

Please don't think so little of me that you actually believe what happened makes a difference in how I feel—in how much I need you.

You know me better than anyone. Surely you know that, too.

So far he hasn't answered, but I open my texting app for the hundredth time that morning and check again. Just in case my phone forgot to beep in signal of an incoming message.

There is, of course, nothing.

Since I'm already looking at my phone, I decide that I probably should check my email, since I haven't even opened it since Saturday when I left for the island.

It's mostly subscription crap or unsolicited newsletters and I barely glance at each message as I slide it off the screen and into the archive.

And then there it is.

D.Sykes@SykesEntUS.com

J—

We can't play this game. More important, *I* can't, for a lot of reasons, and you know every single one of them.

I don't want to write you out of my life—hell, I already miss you. But we have to find a way to move on, and if cold turkey is what it takes, then that's what we do.

Hate me if you want. Maybe that will make it easier.

Your brother,

Dallas

For one minute I let myself consider the possibility that he's right. After all, we've lived at arm's length for years and survived. But that's all it was—surviving.

And now that I've touched him, talked to him, just plain been with him again, I know that I don't want to just survive anymore. I want to live. Fully and completely and with Dallas—my best friend. And, yes, my lover. Forbidden fruit be damned.

Honestly, the thought that he thinks differently—that he

could just turn back to that emptiness, pisses me off. Either he's lying about how he feels about me, or, more likely, he's willing to sacrifice both himself and me on the altar of lost erections, bullshit incest laws, and ridiculous social taboos.

Idiot.

Damned, stupid idiot.

For just a moment, I let myself rage at him. Then I very calmly and deliberately squeeze my fury down into a neat little box and I tie a pretty red bow around it.

Done. Finished. Nothing to see here. Just move along.

Because anger doesn't do me any good. I want to go to the mat, yes, but I'm not interested in stomping on his face when I get there.

But now that he's officially thrown down the gauntlet, I'm faced with the biggest question of all: how exactly do I fight a man who just won't engage?

"Easy," Brody says when I present him with that very question at Starbucks three hours later. "The same way you got him in bed with you on the island."

I've told him the whole story up to the real reason for the lack of follow-through. I figure that's the kind of thing Dallas wouldn't appreciate me sharing, and so I blamed it on an attack of conscience.

"I jumped him in his bungalow after we watched each other masturbate on a beach," I say flatly. "I'm thinking reproducing those circumstances won't be easy."

"Mental masturbation," he says with a grin. "Sexting. Send him naughty pictures and even naughtier suggestions. Eventually, he'll either block your texts or fuck you blind."

I frown, because at the moment I think the blocking possibility is very, very real.

But I also don't have a better idea.

Unfortunately, I also can't think of what I want to say that doesn't sound like I write porn scripts. I enlist Brody's help again, but he makes my porn-a-licious sext attempts sound like a Disney movie.

"Well, I can't help you if you don't press send," he says after I reject his fifth attempt. "If you won't text him then go back to door number one and accost the boy."

"Unfortunately, he's not in the habit of forwarding me his daily agenda. And while I could monitor Twitter and chase him all over town, I really don't think that's my best option."

It's only Wednesday morning, but already the King of Fuck is back in business, and Twitter is lighting up with Dallas sightings all over the city, with a different bimbette—or two—on his arm at each and every location.

"If I knew ahead of time that he was going to be somewhe—"

"What?" Brody asks.

"A party," I say as I congratulate myself on my own brilliance. "Turns out I do know at least one place he's going to be."

I take my phone from him and start typing out a new text.

You say you don't want to play the game. You say you want to move on. But I know better. Because I know you. I see you with all those women, and I see what no one else out in Twitterland does.

I see you watching me. Imagining me.

I'm right, aren't I? You slide your palm over a brunette's ass and you pretend it's mine.

You cup a blonde's tit and you remember your mouth on my nipple.

Do you slip your fingers in their panties on the dance floor? I bet you do. And I bet they're wet for you. But not as wet as me. And while you finger-fuck them to Lady Gaga, you remember the way it felt when your tongue made me come.

Don't try to deny it. I know it. And I'll see you soon and prove it.

I glance at Brody, whose mouth is hanging open just a little. "Shit, woman. Who are you and what have you done with my innocent little Jane?"

I roll my eyes, because I have never been innocent. "Just expanding my palette," I say as I think about how incredible it felt to masturbate on the beach with Dallas watching. "Trying new things."

I read my draft text again, and I'm just about to send it, when Brody's steady voice stops me.

"Wait."

I tilt my head, confused. "Not the right tone? I thought you liked it."

"No, that's not it. Shit, Jane," he adds, then runs his fingers through his hair. "I'm about to break some rules that matter to me, I want you to know that. But the truth is, you matter more."

He looks flustered, and I don't remember Brody ever looking flustered.

"What the hell, Brody?" I don't even know what the trouble is, and yet I'm worried. "What is it?"

"You know I take clients to The Cellar."

"Sure." I've never been, but I'm familiar with the downtown kink club. "So what?"

"What goes on there—*who* goes there is confidential. Telling someone who's not a member is grounds for expulsion. So I shouldn't be saying anything at all. But I love you, and I want to make sure you know what you're walking into. It was one thing to fuck him out of your system, but if I'm reading you right, now you're hoping to fuck him right into your life."

"I am," I say, a little bit numb as I process everything that Brody is saying—or, more accurately, *not* saying. "You're trying to tell me that Dallas is a member."

"He's a dom."

I raise my brows. "Professionally?"

Brody laughs. "No. But when he plays, he tops. He's not there all the time, but often enough that I've seen him. Never spoken to him, don't know him personally, and I don't think he's into the lifestyle so much as he's into control."

"That doesn't surprise me."

"And that control translates to kink."

"What kind of kink?"

"I don't know. That's my point. I've heard rumors that he's got a playroom set up in that fancy Hamptons house of his."

"Really?" I think about the huge basement that used to house a Ping-Pong table and a variety of freestanding video-game machines. I haven't been down there in ages, and now I'm wondering just how Dallas has redecorated it.

"Just what I hear, although he must not use it all the time—you told me he was with those two girls in his bedroom, right? But I doubt it's gathering dust. So you need to think about that. If you start this thing, are you willing to follow where it leads?"

I know Brody is thinking about our sessions and my less than enthusiastic reactions. But the truth is that the thought of getting kinky with Dallas is already making me wet. I can imagine him blindfolding me. Spanking me. Flogging me.

And, yes, I know that he may like it a lot darker than that, but the question isn't what Dallas likes, but where I'm willing to go.

With Dallas, I'll go to the ends of the earth.

With Dallas, I think I might—*might*—even be able to do bondage.

I meet Brody's eyes, then rise up out of my chair so that I can kiss his cheek. "Thank you for telling me. It means the world that you did."

Then I sit back down and very firmly—very deliberately—I send my reply to Dallas.

I catch Brody's eye, and he's grinning. "Guess that answers my question," he says.

"Guess it does." I get up to make a cup of coffee. The truth is, I don't expect to hear back from Dallas soon. Maybe not ever.

The phone pings before I've even poured the cream.

Don't play these games, Jane. You won't win, I promise. And it's a losing battle. We can heal apart. Together, we'll just keep fucking each other up.

I'm so euphoric that I prompted such a quick reply that I don't even care that he's trying to shoot me down. My reply is swift and firm:

We never fucked each other up. We healed each other. And I think you know it.

I'm about to send it when Brody snatches the phone from my hand. "Hey!"

"Just wait."

He taps out an additional sentence, and as he does my hand goes to my mouth. "Okay?" he asks.

I nod. Honestly, I love it. And at this point, I have nothing to lose.

(P.S. I'm going to still play this game. You can't stop me, but a spanking might punish me.)

He sends the text and then grins at me. "So where is this party, and do Stacey and I want to go, just to watch the show?"

"Don't even think about it," I say firmly. "I'd be a nervous wreck. As for where, I'm just about to find out."

This time when I pick up the phone it's to dial Gin Kramer.

"Ms. Martin," she says. "What can I do for you?"

"I was hoping you could help me. I'm so scattered. But I

know that somewhere on my desk is an invitation to a party that Peter Crowley is throwing, and I can't find it anywhere. Didn't you RSVP for Dallas when I was in his office the other day?"

"I did, yes. What do you need?"

"Just the time and the address. And if you wouldn't mind sending in my RSVP?"

I imagine there will be a guest list with the doorman. And anyone who RSVPs through Dallas's email account will be added without question.

"Of course," she says. "And it's this Friday at eight in his apartment on Fifth. I'll email you the address so you have it handy."

"You're wonderful," I say, then hang up and look at Brody. "Friday," I announce. "It's countdown time."

22

Game On

Dallas was on edge, and it didn't have a damn thing to do with the fact that he'd just bugged Peter Crowley's office while the man himself stood only five feet away, sipping scotch and ogling the woman on Dallas's arm.

It didn't even have anything to do with the fact that the woman, a sweet girl named Nina who just landed herself a role in *Chicago*, had noticed his stiff cock, assumed he was thinking naughty things about her, and promised to give him a blow job as soon as they found a quiet corner.

No, Dallas was on edge for one reason and one reason only—his sister had just sent another text message. And he was going out of his mind until he could get to his phone to read it.

He said it again, hard and harsh in his head. *Sister.* Because if this little game of hers led to its obvious conclusion, then they both needed to understand what they were getting into. All of it. No pretending like it wasn't fucked up. Like law and society and all its stupid taboos didn't exist.

Like their parents would look the other way.

He thought he was on edge now? He was the picture of calm and cool compared to what he would be if the tabloids got wind of the dark and dirty Sykes family secrets.

And the real hell of it was that right then, right there, he didn't fucking care. There wasn't any room in his head to care. It was too full of her. Too full of Jane and her delicious mind fuck.

He was seated in one of the guest chairs in front of Crowley's desk. His date, Nina, was in his lap, her hand lightly stroking his cock. And, just like Jane had predicted, he was imagining that it was her.

He knew he shouldn't look right now. Jane's name would be right there at the top of the text.

But goddammit, he had to see what she said, and so he reached into his jacket pocket, and then glanced at the phone as discreetly as he could while Peter Crowley continued to talk about the real estate market on the Upper East Side and Nina continued to stroke his cock.

I'm not wearing any underwear.

Oh, holy Christ.

He closed his eyes, counted to ten, and tried damn hard to gather himself. Then he tapped out a reply.

Prove it.

He'd told her he wasn't going to play, but who was he kidding? He'd never block Jane's texts. And he was anticipating them so much now that he got hard just from the chime that signaled her incoming messages.

She'd sent three yesterday. One had been a selfie of her in

the shower, obviously done on a timer. The glass was steamed, so that he could make out nothing more than the outline of a woman's form behind the fog.

He'd known it was her—and he'd jacked off to the image twice, then taken his own shower.

That evening, another text had arrived, this one a picture of the lingerie she was going to sleep in. A tiny babydoll gown and matching panties of the barely there variety. He'd imagined her in his bed wearing both—and then he'd imagined ripping them off her body and teasing her mercilessly, taking her just to the edge, but not letting her come. Not, at least, until he was ready.

The last text had done him in, and he'd gone to bed early simply so that he could fall asleep with his cock in his hand and his mind on Jane.

Changed my mind. Sleeping naked. Fingering myself. Thinking of you.

There'd been no image, but it didn't matter. He could see the picture clear enough in his mind, and he'd thought about calling her and describing everything he wanted to do to her. Every reaction he wanted to elicit. Every pleasure he wanted to see played out on her face.

But that wasn't the game, and he hadn't called.

Now here he was at this party with a lovely and willing young woman who had made it perfectly clear that she would do whatever he wanted. Be whatever he wanted.

Except she couldn't be Jane.

He exhaled and gave Nina's hip a little squeeze, signaling her to stand. Maybe he couldn't get his mind clear of Jane, but he could at least get his damn job done.

He'd placed the bug in the foyer as he'd arrived. Not hard.

He'd just dropped a few coins, bent to pick them up, and attached the adhesive back of the small, round bug to the leg of the marble table right by the entrance.

The second one here in this office hadn't been a challenge, either. He'd pressed it to the underside of one of the many shelves in the room, tucked into the back corner where it wouldn't be noticed.

With luck, both would remain indefinitely. After all, with Noah's tech, the bugs wouldn't be found by any currently existing electronic surveillance sweep equipment.

The third was the trickiest, simply by virtue of the location. Liam had said either living room or bedroom, but Dallas knew damn well that the quality of the intel would be a thousand times better if he could get it in the bedroom. So that's what he intended to do.

He stood, then curved his hand possessively around Nina's rib cage so that his fingertips cupped her breasts.

"So if you're looking for a place near the park . . ." Crowley was saying, still going on about the real estate market.

"You'll be the first one I'll call," Dallas promised. So far the man had said nothing to suggest that he had any ties to Ortega's criminal activities, and maybe he didn't. But that was the point of the bugs. So that the team could listen and learn. And maybe, just maybe, kick-start an investigation that had stalled with Ortega's death.

"In the meantime," Dallas said as he pinched Nina's nipple just enough to make her moan and Crowley's jaw drop, "I was hoping for a little favor."

"Of course." Crowley's eyes were glued to the girl's tit. "Anything."

"I've got a . . . cramp. My lovely friend Nina's going to help me work it out. Perhaps we could continue this conversation in a few minutes?"

"I—what? Oh. Well, of course." The man was stuttering, which didn't surprise Dallas. It wasn't the way polite business chats normally concluded.

"Pleasure talking with you," he said as he released Nina, then moved across the room to shake Crowley's hand. Then he turned and headed for the door. Just for show, he actually snapped his fingers as he said, "Nina, with me."

A flicker of envy bloomed on Crowley's face as Dallas strode out of the study, the petite brunette hurrying after him.

He'd gone only a few steps into the living area where the party was in full swing when he saw her.

Jane.

He actually stopped and stared, acknowledging to himself that she'd truly scored points with this move. He'd had no idea she was at the party, and yet there she was, talking with a woman who'd almost certainly given Dallas a blow job in the back of a limo a few years prior.

Jane had noticed him, too, and now she lifted her head, looked right at him, and smiled very slowly. A second later, she lifted her phone, tapped the screen, and winked at him.

An instant later, his phone chimed. He tugged it out of his suit pocket, opened the app, and just about lost his shit.

It was a photograph—and not the kind of photograph he would ever have expected of her, although after their moment on the beach, he wasn't as surprised as he might have been.

It was a photograph of her pussy, slick and wet. And of her finger teasing her swollen clit.

It was dirty and hot, and the camera flash made it clear that this was the kind of shot that skewed toward porn, not art. And Jane had sent it. *Jane.*

He almost came right then.

And it was clear from her smile that she knew it.

He'd always assumed she'd be shocked by the way he liked

to play. That the Jane who was willing to get fucked up with him lived only in his imagination.

But she'd turned his perception around, and he couldn't deny that he liked this new reality.

He didn't know how far they could go—how far *he* could go—but he was willing to find out. Because there was one thing Dallas knew better than anyone. And that was how to satisfy a woman in the most creative of ways.

And that's when it clicked. When he knew what he wanted.

He'd continue to play her game all right. Hell, he looked forward to it. But from now on, he was going to be the one in charge.

You're being a very bad girl.

I read Dallas's text and smile to myself, feeling both powerful and turned on.

I am, I text back. *But not as bad as I can be.*

It takes a few seconds for him to respond, and in that time, I realize that he's no longer standing by the door to Crowley's office. I frown and look around for him, then see him heading down the far hall with his hand on his date's ass.

I tell myself that's part of the game, but that doesn't stop the jealousy from curling inside me.

I excuse myself from the woman I'm chatting with and go to the bar, because right now I really could use a glass of wine. But my phone buzzes on the way, and I step into a quiet corner and eagerly retrieve it.

Did you see the woman I was with? Do you believe me when I tell you that I'm imagining she's you?

I answer immediately: *Yes.*

I wish you were here.

Yes, I text. *So do I.*

Go into the bathroom. Pull up your skirt. Sit your bare ass on the
toilet seat and touch yourself. Don't stop until I tell you to. But
don't you dare come.

I read it twice. I'm pretty sure I moan both times.

I look around and see the powder room. I hurry that way,
step inside, and lock the door behind me. I lean back against
the door and breathe hard. I'm aroused—so damn aroused. My
nipples are hard, my pussy is aching for release.

I want Dallas. Hell, I need him. His hands, his mouth.

But at the same time, I want this, too. This game that we're
playing—and the way that he's shifting it around, telling me
what to do now. I don't want it to stop because I like the way it
makes me feel. Like I'm falling into him. Like I'm surrendering
to him, but it's not scary and it doesn't make me crazy. Instead,
it makes me feel safe.

I do as he says. I put the toilet lid down, then pull up my
skirt. I'm not wearing panties—he already knows that much—
and the porcelain feels cool against my skin. I close my eyes
and slide my finger over my clit, then bite my lip as a flurry of
sparks shoot through me. Just a tease for now. Just a promise of
better things to come.

I'm so wet that my inner thighs are slick, and I'm throbbing
because I want him so much. I'm getting close, too, and so I
slow down.

He told me not to come, and I'm determined to obey.

Finally my phone pings, and I use my free hand to answer it.

Are you there? Does it feel good?

I tap the microphone button so I can dictate my answers because he told me not to stop. "Yes," I say, and my words print in the text box for him.

My phone rings, startling me. It's him, of course, and I answer immediately.

"Dallas?"

"She's sucking my cock right now."

I suck in air, his low, sensual voice doing a number on me. But it's his words that have me thrusting two fingers inside myself, my reaction shocking me—but there's no denying my full-blown arousal.

"Sucking me off while she listens to me talk to another woman. While she knows I want to fuck another woman."

I add another finger and writhe, closing my eyes as I do. Imagining it's his cock.

"Does that turn you on? Knowing another woman's mouth is on me? Knowing that I'm pretending she's you?"

"Yes," I whisper.

"Yes, what?"

"It turns me on."

"Are you wet?"

"God, yes."

"How can you tell?"

I lick my lips. "I'm finger-fucking myself," I admit. "I'm imagining it's you."

"Good girl," he says, and his voice is strangled. "I'm going to send you a video. This woman on my cock who should be you. I want you to ride your fingers while you watch. I want you to come."

"Okay."

"Don't say, 'okay,' baby. You say, 'Yes, sir.'"

I moan, even more aroused by this new order. "Yes, sir," I say obediently. And then, "Dallas?" I cringe a little, because I'm so blatantly breaking this new rule, but the question is important.

"Yes?"

"The video won't—I mean, you're not going down on her, are you?"

"Do you want me to? Do you want me to eat her out and pretend it's you?"

"No." The word comes fast. Immediate.

"Good answer, baby."

"Dallas, this really is fucked up."

"Sweetheart, we've barely scratched the surface."

I swallow, wondering just where this could lead.

"Watch the video," he orders. "Get yourself off. Then go home. Wait for me in your living room. In the leather recliner. No reading. No watching television. And no touching yourself." The command in his voice is like a caress. "I'll come to you."

"When?" I am breathless.

"Will you wait for me?"

"Yes," I promise. I think right then I'd wait forever.

"Then does it matter?"

I say nothing.

"And, baby? Wear a silk robe. And don't wear anything under it."

23

Together in the Dark

I came so hard in the powder room watching that video. Watching another woman suck his cock. Pretending I was her. Knowing that Dallas was pretending the same thing.

Listening as he groaned. As he murmured, "Christ, I want you," and I knew he was talking to me, not her.

I touched myself as he tugged his stiff cock from her mouth and then pushed her back onto the bed. He kept his phone in one hand and wrapped his other around his cock as he told her to lie back. To pull up her dress.

She was bare beneath, and I imagined that was me. That I was lying back on the bed, my dress up around my tits, my legs spread wide and willing. My chest felt tight, and I realized I was afraid he was going to fuck her or go down on her despite what he'd promised me.

And although I was surprised to realize that some tiny, perverse part of me actually wanted to watch him do just that, I was relieved when he didn't touch her at all. Instead he stood over her, the camera on his erection. On his hand. On his cock.

His words made me dizzy. "Only you, baby. Only you." And when he came on the anonymous woman's belly, I actually screamed from the hard, wild violence of my orgasm.

It was kinky. It was fucked up. And it was an absolute, total, unexpected turn on.

As soon as I'd pulled myself together enough to stand, I'd fixed my clothes, grabbed my purse, and headed straight for the door.

I thought he would be right behind me—I assumed he would rush in the moment I was through my door, throw me down, kiss me hard.

I thought he was as crazy for me as I was for him. As hot. As wild.

I thought there was no way he could wait, because waiting was torture and he wanted relief.

I thought wrong.

He didn't come right away. He didn't come in ten minutes or thirty or sixty.

At ninety minutes, I was starting to get irritated.

At two hours, I was starting to get pissed.

And now, when my clock chimes that it is one in the morning, I fear that everything about the night was wrong. That he doesn't want me. That he wasn't turned on. That he is off somewhere fucking that bimbo, and that he was simply playing a game to get rid of me or to prove a point. Though god only knows what that point is supposed to be.

That I'm a fool, maybe?

That when he said we weren't going to do this I should have listened?

I remember what he said in his email: *Hate me if you want.*

Is he trying to make me hate him?

Finally, I can't take it anymore. I stand up and stretch—my legs are sore from not moving for so long—and then I tighten the sash on the damn robe that he'd ordered me to wear, the bastard.

I stalk up the stairs thinking I'll take a quick shower to cool my red hot mood, and then I'll crawl under the covers and sleep for a year. Or at least until tomorrow afternoon when I have to go to Midtown to tape my television appearance.

I consider firing off a nasty email to my darling asshole of a brother, but I decide not to. He'll be expecting that. Let him think I didn't wait at all. Let him think I didn't even notice that he didn't show. That I really don't care.

Dammit, dammit, dammit.

And while I'm at it, damn Liam Foster for convincing me to go to the mat. Because all that did was get my hopes up. All that did was cement just how much it matters to me.

Because I do care, dammit. I care and I want.

And now I'm hurt.

And Dallas is the one person that I don't want to hate. That I can't hate.

But after tonight, I think that I should hate him.

My bedroom is dark when I yank open the double doors, just the barest glint of city light peeking in around the edge of the shades that Ellen must have pulled down when she was cleaning. Odd, because she knows I like to wake to the sun.

I'm about to cross to the light switch when I realize my mistake. It wasn't Ellen who did this. It was Dallas.

"How did you get in?" I ask the dark room.

"You disobeyed," he says from the far corner. "I think you've forfeited any right to ask questions."

I turn toward the voice as a wash of light sprays over him from the reading lamp he's just switched on. He's seated in my burgundy leather reading chair, still wearing the suit he wore to the party, a half-empty crystal tumbler beside him.

"I told you to wait downstairs."

"I did." My heart is fluttering. I'm actually nervous about what he's going to do about my disobedience. More than that, I'm incredibly turned on, and I wonder if he can see how hard my nipples have become under the robe from all the way across the room.

His brows rise. "And yet here you are. Why?"

"I was angry," I admit.

"Is that all?"

I lick my lips. "I was jealous."

He nods, but he doesn't tell me about the girl. He doesn't tell me where he's been for the last three hours.

I start to ask him, but I swallow the question. Not because he told me I hadn't earned the right, but because I don't want to know the answer.

"Take off the robe," he says. "And then walk to me."

I lick my lips. "Dallas."

"Do you want me to make you come?"

The question is so unexpected it shocks me, though under the circumstances, it really shouldn't.

"Yes," I say, because he would know any other answer is a lie.

"Then I want no hesitation. No argument. Walk to me, Jane. I want to see you move. I want to watch you and anticipate touching you. I want to study your body and ponder the best way to get you off."

Oh. Well, okay then.

I untie the sash on the robe, then push the silk off my shoulders so it falls to the ground. Naked, I walk to him. I move slowly, and with each step I'm becoming more and more aroused. And I can see by the bulge in his slacks that he is, too.

When I'm a few feet away, he unzips his slacks, takes his cock out, and starts to stroke it. He's huge and hard, and I imagine him filling me—and I hate that I want that because I don't know if he will ever be inside me. But that's just one part of everything I want with this man.

Right now, I just want this moment. The way I feel, so sexual and alive. And the way he's looking at me, his jaw tight as if he's working to hold everything in. His cock rock hard. His eyes so focused on me I can feel the heat.

"You are so beautiful," he says. "So beautiful. So sexy. So goddamn hot."

I lick my lips and keep walking.

"Tell me you want me."

"I want you."

"Tell me I can do anything to you."

My pulse kicks up. "You can do anything to me."

"Should I punish you? You were supposed to wait for me, Jane. How should I punish you for being such a bad girl?"

"Any way you want to," I whisper, and I hear his low chuckle.

"Good answer," he says. "But you don't mean it."

I'm right in front of him now, and I stop. "Yes, I do."

His mouth curves up. "Baby, you don't have the slightest clue what 'anything' means with me."

The way he says it gives me chills, and I can't help but think that he's right. Brody's given me an idea, but I don't truly know. And I wonder if Dallas is going to show me.

I really want him to show me.

He stands, his cock tucked away again. He is right in front of me, still in his perfectly tailored, extraordinarily sexy five-thousand-dollar suit. He looks like a man who owns the world. A man with the confidence to have any woman he wants. A man who asks for and expects obedience. A man who will punish those who get in his way.

He's a man with demons, and this is how he fights them. He knows that. He owns it.

I'm a woman with demons, and I've been searching for years for a way to fight back. Hiding behind a laundry list of crutches, everything from meaningless encounters, to a bad marriage, to pharmaceuticals.

Now here I am, naked and submissive in front of the man I've wanted my whole life, and I can't help but think that the weapon against my demons was him all along. And all those years I spent running the other way were wasted.

He puts his hands on my hips and starts to ease them up, the slow movement of his skin against mine making me crazy. When he gets to my breasts, he cups them, and they feel heavy in his hands, my nipples so hard and tight they are almost painful.

"Maybe I should take my hands away," he says. "Maybe I should punish you by not touching you. By making you crave, but never have. Is that what you want?"

I shake my head.

"Then tell me how to punish you," he says. "Tell me what you think you deserve."

I swallow, completely unsure. I have no idea what he expects. "Spank me?" I suggest, though it's hardly a punishment when the thought of his palm on my ass makes me wet.

For a moment, I think he's disappointed in my lack of imagination, but then his smile blooms. "Very appropriate. I've been thinking about turning your ass the same shade of pink as your cheeks when you blush for me."

"You've really thought about that?" Just the idea sends shivers through me.

"Baby, I've thought of a lot more than that. Come here."

He leads me back to the chair, and once he's sitting, he bends me over his knees. I've never actually been spanked before. Even when I tried kink with Brody, we didn't go there. But I've read about it. And I've wanted it.

Honestly, I've wanted it from Dallas.

But though I expect a smack on the ass, it doesn't come. Instead, he rubs my rear, then thrusts his fingers deep inside me. I moan at the unexpected intrusion and it feels so damn good I actually start to hump his fingers.

"That's it, baby," he says. "You're so close. So close to exploding for me. Can you feel me inside you? Can you feel how tight you are around my fingers? How much your clit throbs as it rubs against my slacks?"

His words only make this hotter, and I can feel him inside me, and my clit is so hard, so ready, and I can feel the tightening in my groin that signals a rising orgasm, and I'm right there, right there, right—

He pulls out his fingers and smacks my ass so hard that I cry out.

But I also come harder than I ever have. He thrusts his fingers back inside me and my core clenches around him, milking him, and yes, I do wish it was his cock, but this feels so damn good that right then I don't care. I just want more and more and more.

When the tremors fade, I am limp and exhausted. It's past two now, and I am spent. He lifts me up and very gently carries me to the bed. He pulls back the covers, puts me in, and then gets in beside me.

"I thought you were going to punish me," I murmur.

"Who said I was through with you?" He brushes my cheek and his touch is so gentle that I want to purr with pleasure.

"Thank you," I whisper.

"For what?"

"For giving in. For playing my game. For this." I prop myself up on my elbow. "I missed you so much. My friend and my lover."

"Not your brother?" He says it simply, but I can hear the harshness.

I reach out and cup his cheek. "My brother, too. The whole package, Dallas. I just missed you. It's so unfair."

"It is," he agrees. "On so many levels."

"Dallas—" I know where his mind has gone. "Don't you get that it doesn't matter? I've never felt like this before. Sexual. Playful. Who else could I do this with? Be like this with?"

"No." He presses a finger to my lips. "If we're doing this— whatever this is—you need to really understand that I may never be able to fuck you the way I want. The way you need and deserve. And there's no pill, no medication, no special oil that's going to change that."

"I just told you it's okay. And it really is. But don't say never. We have a crazy history, I get that. But if you can do it with all those women, then—"

"No."

I frown because I don't know what he means.

"No? But tonight with that girl. After the video, weren't you with her? And all the other women?" I'm completely confused.

"I sent Nina home in a limo," he says.

"Then where were you?"

"Not here." His grin is just a bit wicked. "Making you crazy."

Since I can't argue that, I skip over it. "But you have a repu-tation. And in your bed—I saw those two women, and—"

"None of them," he says firmly. "Not one."

I don't say anything. I just stare at him, because I don't un-derstand at all.

He leans in and captures my mouth with his. The kiss is long and deep and I feel it all the way down to my toes, so in-tense that I feel like I'm floating. So passionate that I feel like I'm melting.

When he breaks the kiss, his expression is gentle, and he is looking at me as if I'm the most precious thing in the world to him. "Never," he says. "I've never fucked any of them, though at first it wasn't for lack of trying."

I push myself up to a sitting position. "But—but you're—" I cut myself off because this isn't easy to talk about. Except that's stupid, so I try again. "But you're hard. Like rock hard."

He half-smiles. "Nice of you to notice."

I roll my eyes. "I get why it happened with me," I say. After all, we have a history—a dark history and so much of a guy's performance is in his head. Any girl who reads *Cosmo* knows that. "But with other women . . ."

"I swear to you, Jane, you're the only woman I've ever been inside. And yeah, I hate it. Maybe I'm not as strong a man as I'd like to believe, because even though it shouldn't, losing my goddamn wood—not being able to fuck—it makes me—"

He cuts himself off, but I know what he was going to say. Makes him feel less. Makes him feel broken.

Isn't that what he'd told me? That he was broken.

"But everyone knows you fuck around," I say. "You're practically famous for it."

"Smoke and mirrors. An illusion. Just like a magic show."

"I don't understand."

"I've been building that reputation for years. It's important to me."

"Why?"

"What could be more important to a man who can't fuck than the reputation of being the best there is?"

It's a reasonable answer, and I certainly can't argue. But at the same time it doesn't quite ring true for me. But why he wants the reputation is his business. What I'm really curious about is how.

"What woman is going to admit to being the only one not fucked by the great Dallas Sykes?" he asks, when I beg him to explain. "And honestly, no woman has left my bed unsatisfied. So on the whole I think they're getting a pretty good bargain."

"I am sorry," I say. "I know it can't be easy. And this is going to sound terrible, but I'm glad it's not just me. On the island, after what you said, I thought I was the only girl you couldn't fuck."

I shift so that I am sitting up with my knees to my chest.

"You said stuff that night about how they destroyed you, but you kept me in your head. So I guess I thought that it was just me. I guess I thought you blamed me."

"Oh, baby, no."

"You do remember, don't you? All these years you've said that you don't remember anything between them releasing me and you being ransomed. But it's not true, is it? You do remember, and you were alone." I feel a tear spill down my cheek. "You were all alone without me."

He pulls me close and kisses me. My lips. My cheek. My brow. He strokes my face and looks into my eyes. "Jane. Oh, god, Jane."

For a moment, he just holds me. Then he gets up and walks to the window. He stands there for a little bit, just looking out. When he speaks, his back is still to me. "I do remember," he says. "The truth is, I haven't forgotten a single moment of those days in the dark. Honestly, I wish I could."

24

Sweet Dreams, Dark Nights

My heart hurts simply from the pain in his voice. "It's okay," I say. "You don't have to tell me."

"Honestly, I don't think I can. Not all of it. Not at once."

I want to stand up and go to him. I want to touch him. But his back is still to me, and I don't know if going to him would help, or would simply draw him back inside himself.

"It was the Woman," he says. "It was only her. He may have watched, I don't know. But she was the one who was there. Always there."

"After I was gone?"

He turns from the window, and his eyes are full of pain. "Before, too, but it was more after."

"When they took you away from me," I say flatly. "You'd come back and be so distant for a while. I thought—I thought they were doing something horrible to you."

"They were." He draws a deep breath. "I was terrified they were doing—stuff—to you, too."

"She tied me down. Arms and legs spread-eagled and then

bound with those leather straps. And she'd strip me first so that I was naked."

"Oh, baby. Like what they did to you that first week. You should have told me back then. You must have been so scared."

I nod, hating the memory. Hating how afraid I'd been, but I hadn't wanted to make it worse for Dallas. "She'd call me a slut. A whore. But it was all better when they shoved me back into the cell with you, so I never wanted to talk about it. I just wanted you. And she never touched me except to tie me down. Did she touch you?"

His laugh is harsh. "Yeah. You could say that."

I swallow, because I don't want to hear this. And at the same time, I do. I want to know because I want to help him heal.

For a second, I think it's a moot point. He's silent, and I think he may be done talking about it. Then he begins to speak, so softly I have to strain to hear. "The room was always dark, and she always wore a mask. But not the carnival style she would wear when we were together. This one kept her mouth free. She liked to use her mouth," he adds harshly.

"The first time she made me get undressed, then strapped me to the wall. Bare cement. Metal hooks that held the straps. She bound my legs and ankles. She jerked me off until I came— and then she whipped my cock and my balls until I begged her to stop."

His voice is flat. Toneless.

I realize that I am biting my fist.

"She'd start over again, and every time I came, she punished me." He closes his eyes, takes a deep breath, then opens them. When he looks at me, his expression is fierce. "That's how it started." I watch his throat move as he swallows. "Those were the easy days. The ones that came after . . ."

He breaks off with a shudder and I can no longer stay away. I move into his arms and hold him tight, tears streaming down my face. "Don't think about it," I order. "Just hold me."

He does, and I cling to him, and suddenly I'm shaking with sobs. I can't stop, and I'm choking as I try to catch my breath.

"Oh, sweetheart. Baby, it's okay."

I cling to him, letting him stroke my back until I can pull myself together, ashamed that I have lost control. "I should be the one comforting you," I manage to say through my sniffles and sobs. I pull back so I can see him through the blur of my tears. "I'm so sorry."

I reach out and cup his cheek, needing that connection. I know that he hasn't told me everything—I could see the shadows in his eyes as he edited his words. But he has told me enough to know the truth. And the truth is horrific.

"You should have told me," I said. "Back then. You should have told me what she was doing."

"And bring that nightmare between us? Never? Even in that hell hole, being with you was perfect. No way was I going to spoil the bubble we'd built around us."

I nod, because I understand. I do. In a small way, hadn't I done the same?

"But afterward, when you were free? Why did you lie?" I ask. "Why have you always said you don't remember?"

"It was too much," he says. "Too hard. Too everything. And I couldn't process it. And I didn't want Mom and Dad to know. Or you," he adds before I can ask. He takes my hand and we walk back to the bed. "I was ashamed, even though I knew none of it was my fault. And I think even back then I understood that it had changed me."

"Changed you?"

He sits on the edge of the bed, his hand tight in mine. "I'm not the boy from the dark, Jane. The dark's inside me now. The things she did. The things I do now."

"You started to like it," I say. I'm not horrified. I'm not shocked. I'm just numb.

"Like? I don't know. But I started to need it."

He rakes the fingers of his free hand through his hair. "When I told you I was broken, I meant it. I'm fucked up, baby. I do fucked-up things. And I never wanted to taint you with that."

I shake my head. "Don't do that. Don't make it sound like I'm something you're going to get dirty. Don't put me on a pedestal, Dallas."

"I'm not. But I also don't want to take you down with me."

"You mean kink, right?" I don't tell him I know that he goes to The Cellar. That's not a confidence I can break.

"That's a nice, polite term for it," he says, and a little frisson of excitement cuts through me.

"But maybe you need it," I suggest. "Maybe you need the dark—the kink. Maybe it excites you. Maybe it gets you hard." I squeeze his hand. "Maybe you need it to stay hard."

He lifts our joined hands and brushes my knuckles over his lips. "That's what I'm afraid of. Christ, I don't want to have this conversation."

I lick my lips. "What if I want it? Not the conversation," I clarify, "but, well, what you do. Maybe I want to do it, too."

He looks at me silently for a moment, and there's an edge to his voice when he finally asks, "What are you saying?"

"Just that I'll go there with you. You won't taint me, Dallas. I want to. Whatever you need, I want to give it to you."

His smile is sweet but a little sad. "I don't think you understand what you're offering."

"Tonight was a little kinky," I point out. "And it qualifies as one of the hottest nights of my life."

"We played tonight, baby. That's not the dark I'm talking about." He brushes a strand of hair off my face as he looks into my eyes. "I don't want sex with you to conjure ghosts. I don't want what she did in my head when I'm with you."

I shudder, just the mention of the Woman giving me chills. She knew what Dallas and I were to each other almost from the beginning. I didn't realize it at first, and I never told Dallas. I was afraid if he knew we were being watched, then he would stop coming to me. Stop making love to me. And I needed it.

Even when the Woman would bring a whispered comment along with my food—"You little slut, you're a whore, you're cursed, you incestuous little bitch"—I said nothing to Dallas. But the Woman only spoke to me. Just words. Hurtful, yes, but not physically.

But god only knows what else she did when she had Dallas alone.

"You can talk about it with me, you know. Whenever you need to."

The corner of his mouth rises in an ironic smile. "I thought I just did."

"I mean about the rest."

I see the haunted look in his eyes and know that he may never say a word to me.

"You don't have to," I assure him. "But I want you, Dallas—and I will take you however I can get you. Even so—and I'll only say this once—I admit I want to feel you inside of me again. And I know you want it, too. So if going into the dark together is what you need, then I will. I'll go in with you."

I take a breath, because I've been talking too fast and the words are spilling out on top of each other. "You need to be in control, and I need to let go. And if this is what we need to do for us to be together, then I will stay in the dark with you."

"Together," he repeats. He doesn't have to explain what he means. The truth is that we both know that for us *together* is a hell of a lot more complicated than working through sex. *Together* means secrets. Complications. Lies and misdirection.

And I will do all that and more if it means I can have Dallas. I will do anything. Everything.

I squeeze his hand and meet his eyes. "Together," I confirm.

"I'm not scared, Dallas. I'll go in the dark with you. I'll go any-where with you. And I'll stay for as long as we need."

He looks at me, and for a second I think I see hope, even excitement, before it fades away.

I can't deny that I'm disappointed. He's afraid I can't handle what he needs. That I'm some fragile thing that will run scream-ing if I see the truth.

Secrets, I think. *All these damn secrets.*

It's stupid and frustrating, and I'm starting to think that I need to talk to Brody and get some tips on how to set up my room like a dungeon. Because other than going all-in with Dal-las, I'm not sure how else I can convince him that I will go with him wherever he leads.

But then he pulls me to him and kisses me, and it's so gentle and tender and filled with so much light, that it pushes every thought out of my head, so all that I am left with is warmth and love and Dallas.

I don't remember falling asleep, but I must have because when I wake the clock shows that it's already after three. I blink sleepily, secure in the circle of Dallas's arms.

I'm spooned against him, my back to his front and his cock nestled against my ass, and I like the way it feels. Intimate. Sweet. Sexual.

That's when I realize that he's naked against me. I don't know when he took off the suit—and I really would've liked to have seen that show—but honestly, I don't even care about that right now. Because he's hard. Seriously hard, the head of his cock teasing my rear, making my mind spin out all sorts of nasty, wonderful scenarios.

And then I think . . . *why not*?

Slowly, I pull out of his embrace. He stirs, but he doesn't wake, not even when I roll him over so that he is on his back, and I bite my lower lip because he hasn't lost his erection. If anything he's harder. And though I know that doesn't mean anything—he told me he loses it when he tries to penetrate—I can't help but wonder if maybe, just maybe . . .

I straddle him, moving slowly because I don't want to shift the bed and wake him. And, yeah, this feels kinky to me. And it feels a little like cheating. But I don't care, because if he can fuck me in his sleep, then he can fuck me awake—we just have to figure out the key to get us there.

But first things first.

I'm still wet, but I want to be more so, and so I touch myself as I straddle him, imagining how it will feel with him inside me. Pretending that it's his fingers playing with me, filling me, making me wet and so very ready.

And then I slowly lower myself, carefully positioning the tip and then slowly—so excruciatingly slowly, I start to thrust down. I bite my lip as I press against him, not wanting to hold his cock just in case that extra touch makes it all go away.

I can feel the pressure of entry, the way my body gives, and then he's inside me. Just the head, but he's inside me and it feels amazing and he's still asleep, and I'm thinking this may work.

I'm excited enough—optimistic enough—that I go faster than I should, taking him all in with one single, hard motion. I know it's a risk—I know he could go soft the moment I feel his balls against my rear—but even if it's just for a nanosecond, I want to feel him inside me again.

But he doesn't go soft—he's hard as a rock and he's filling me and I'm so incredibly turned on that I can't hold back and I ride him, pounding myself down on him, filling myself, and absolutely glorying in the fact that—oh, god, yes—this is possible.

I explode, bursting apart at the seams, and as I do, he loses it, and I barely notice because I can't do anything but break apart, and I can't feel anything but this insane pleasure wafting through me.

But as soon as I've come down and sanity returns, I realize what has happened. More than that, I realize he's awake, and I steel myself for his disappointment that he couldn't finish. But then I look down, and it's not frustration I see. Instead, there's a small, satisfied smile playing at his mouth.

"We're going to get there," he says, his eyes burning into mine. "And think how much fun we'll have trying."

25

Vanilla

I start to snuggle back against him, ready to fall off into sleep and the warmth of his arms, but Dallas is having none of it.

"No," he says. "I'm not through with you."

The command in his voice eviscerates my exhaustion and sends a trill of anticipation shooting straight through me, getting me excited all over again. "Oh?" I roll over and start to straddle him, but he holds me still.

"Oh, no, baby. For this, I want you dressed."

I frown—because "dressed" is not the direction in which my thoughts were going—but when I start to ask why, he gives just the slightest shake of his head and I keep my question to myself.

I go to my closet and start to pull on a pair of jeans, but once again he stops me. "Tank top, no bra. Skirt, no underwear. As short as you own."

"We're going out?"

"Did I say you could ask questions?"

Another tremor of excitement cuts through me in response to both his words and his tone, and I wonder what the hell he has in mind. This may be New York, but it's already after three, and even the late night clubs are shutting down and will be empty by four.

"Now," he says, and I start to rummage in my drawer for a tank top. I find a pink one, but then I remember the very thin, near transparent tank that I bought to go over a workout bra. It's not meant to be worn by itself, and I hesitate for a few minutes, but finally I put it on. I want to see the look on his face, yes, but more than that, I want him to realize that I'm willing to go with him. Wherever. However.

As for the skirt, I have a short leather skirt that I usually pair with leggings, since it barely hits the bottom of my ass. This one is a little more dicey, as I won't even be able to sit in a taxi without my bare rear touching the upholstery.

But same principle, right? He orders, I obey. He needs to know that I get that.

I turn to look at myself from all angles in the tri-fold mirror. I look hot, yes. But only if you define hot as the latest in street-walker fashion.

Still, I did as he said, and that should count for something.

He didn't tell me what to do about shoes, so I slip on my tallest stilettos in fire engine red, then strut out of the room. Or try to. With the heels and my own self-consciousness working against me, I can't say that I'm really rocking it.

He is standing as I enter and he's wearing his suit again, and with his hair mussed from sleep and sex, he looks all the hotter.

I look at him, trying to read his expression, but this is a man who knows how to hide his thoughts, and so I can only stand there nervously as he comes toward me, moving as smoothly and sensually as a panther on the prowl.

When he's less than a foot away, his eyes skim over me,

pausing at my hemline and again at my breasts before finally focusing on my face. "I can see your nipples, baby. Hell, I can practically see your cunt."

The words are raw, deliberately vulgar, and I can't help but think that he's testing me. I take a step toward him, then press my fingertip lightly against the indentation at the base of his neck, then trail it down his chest and abdomen to finally hook on the waist of his slacks. "And you like it," I say, trying to put a purr in my voice.

For a moment, his expression doesn't change and I think that I've misjudged him. Then I see the heat—and the amusement—flare in his eyes as an easy smile touches his kissable mouth. "Yes," he agrees. "I do."

He presses his hand to my back and steers me out of the room. "Are you going to tell me what we're doing?" I ask.

"What do you think?"

"No," I say, as we go down the stairs. "You're not going to tell me a thing."

"Does that turn you on? Knowing that everything is in my hands? Not having the slightest clue where I intend to take you or what I intend to do with you?"

We've reached the landing, and I'm breathing hard.

"Tell me, Jane," he orders. "I want to know if that makes you wet."

"Why don't you touch me and find out?" I pause as I say the words, then spread my legs just a little in invitation. My heart is pounding. My skin tingling from the electricity between us. There has always been heat between us, but there were always boundaries, too. We're unfettered now, and even though infinite possibilities lie between us, in this moment all I need is the slightest brush of his fingertip over my clit to make me completely explode.

He doesn't answer. He simply smiles and heads toward the door, then pauses before opening it. "With me, baby."

"Always," I say.

The night is warm, which is convenient since I'm practically naked. He leads the way to the subway station, and I can feel my anticipation grow, because I'm certain that he intends to finger me in the car, and I'm not certain how I feel about that, and when I realize how empty the car is, I start to think that train motion and Dallas and an explosive orgasm would be just fine by me.

But the bastard doesn't once touch me.

"Patience," he says, when we finally get off the train, and I'm so frustrated that I don't even know where we are because I haven't been paying attention to the signs or to my surroundings.

Which, frankly, is a big deal. I'm always aware of my surroundings and I never let down my guard.

Never, that is, until I had Dallas back in my bed.

"What?" he asks.

"You make me feel safe."

I understand from the way his expression goes sweetly tender that those weren't the words he was expecting. "I told you a long time ago that I'd always protect you."

"You did," I agree. "I believed you then, and I still believe you now."

He pauses at street level and kisses me gently. Then he waits a beat, smacks my ass, and orders me to walk ahead of him.

I grin and do, adding a little swing to my step just for the hell of it.

I can feel his eyes on me the entire time, and when I see a penny on the ground, I bend over at the waist to pick it up, just to give him an extremely naughty view. I hear his soft, "Christ, Jane," and smile with victory before I stand and continue walking without once turning around.

"Here," he finally says, stepping up beside me as I pass in front of a twenty-four-hour bodega located next to a poorly lit pay-to-park lot.

"Here?"

"Problem?" he asks innocently.

"We rode across the city to go to a market?"

"We did." He leaves it at that and goes inside.

I follow, both curious and amused.

The bodega serves ice cream, hand scooped into waffle cones, and Dallas orders a vanilla one. It costs less than two dollars, and we're on our way again.

"I come here at least once a week," he says. "Best ice cream in the city."

"Mmm." I don't know what he's up to, but I'm pretty sure it's not a snack break.

Instead of heading back the way we came, he leads me into the parking area, all the way into the back, past the last flickering yellow light, so that we are hidden in the shadows cast on the rough brick wall of the building that marks the back edge of this lot.

I look up at Dallas, intending to ask what happens now, but the words die on my tongue. All teasing has gone from his eyes, replaced by a burning desire so potent my knees go weak and my pussy clenches.

I watch as he licks the ice cream cone, and then have to stifle a moan when he brings the cone to my lips and orders me to taste it. I do. It's creamy and sweet and I want to lick it from his lips.

"Remember this, baby," he says, then taps the cone against my nose before licking the spot off. "This is as vanilla as I get."

I swallow. "Dallas." I don't say anything more. I'm not even sure what I was going to say.

"Lift your skirt."

I start to protest—we're outside, after all—but the truth is that his words have excited me. Both the idea and the no-nonsense command with which he's issued the order.

I raise the skirt until my sex is exposed.

"Oh, no, sweetheart. All the way."

I bite on my lower lip, but I do as he says, and as I do, I watch him. His eyes are on my pussy at first, but he lifts his head, then meets my eyes, and I want to cry out in victory at the look in his eyes. A look that says that I am his. And, yes, that he is mine.

"Tell me what you want," he says.

"You," I say simply. "Whatever you want me to do. Whatever you want to do to me."

"Whatever?" I notice the cone is starting to drip over his hand. "So if I told you to turn around and let me fuck that sweet ass right here, you'd be okay with that?"

"Yes." My nipples peak at the thought.

"If I told you to drop to your knees and suck my cock?"

"You know I would."

He leans closer and whispers in my ear. "And if I told you to move to the light and get yourself off in full sight of anyone walking by, simply because I want you to? Because you're mine now?"

I swallow, both aroused and repelled by the thought. But I don't tell him that. Instead I say, "Whatever you tell me, Dallas. I'm yours. I thought I made that clear."

My words are like an ignition switch, and he launches forward, his hands caging me, his mouth hungry on mine. I'm gasping, wildly aroused, my body on fire.

He closes his mouth over my breast, practically bare in the tank top. Then he moves lower still. I'm trembling against the brick, on fire from everything—his commands, his touch, the wild exhibitionism of this night.

Finally, he drops to his knees, and I have only a moment to be curious before he very gently strokes the melting cone over my hot, throbbing sex. I bite the inside of my cheek to keep from screaming from the wonderful, incredible, near-painful experience of the ice cream against my clit. And then his hot mouth is taking the edge off and taking me to a different edge altogether.

I grab his hair and hold him in place. I want his mouth on me. I want his tongue inside me.

I am so incredibly turned on that I pull the neck of my tank top down so that I can use one hand to tug at my nipple while I hold Dallas's mouth against my clit with the other.

He is laving me. Eating me. He's licking and sucking and making such wet, wonderful noises. And I'm close, but I want to be closer. I grind against him, desperate for release.

And then, finally, he thrusts two fingers inside me, then three. And as he sucks on my clit and fucks me hard with his fingers, I splay my arms out against the building, tilt my head back to the sky, and completely break apart.

My legs go weak and I collapse into his arms. He kisses me, a sticky vanilla kiss that I don't ever want to end. I'm wrapped up in him, exhausted from the hour, aroused by the man, and absolutely satisfied.

The King of Fuck, I think, as I hold him tight. He damn sure is.

And he belongs to me.

26

Last Door on the Right

"This is more than just fucking, isn't it?"

Dallas smiled as he remembered Jane's words that morning as she'd rolled over in bed to face him.

He'd known what she was asking. *Are we trying to make something here? Is it possible? Can I even dare to hope that we can have something real?*

They had some serious hurdles to face, god knew. And it would be hard. Just thinking about the issue of their parents made him cringe.

But none of that mattered, because there was only one answer that counted.

"Yes," he'd said. "Yes. It's a whole lot more."

They'd made love that morning—and as she'd reminded him, it didn't matter that he wasn't inside her, it was still making love—and then he'd made her breakfast. Thankfully Jane liked her privacy, and Ellen, her housekeeper, didn't live onsite, so he'd had time to run upstairs to get dressed when he heard the key in the front lock and the beep of Ellen disengaging the alarm system. The last thing they needed was for the help to start spreading rumors.

For a moment, he wondered what he would say to Archie, whom Dallas had always suspected knew of the attraction between the two Sykes children. That, however, was an issue he'd deal with later.

Right now, he was in his downtown office trying to catch up on both Sykes work and Deliverance work—and managing neither very efficiently since his thoughts kept returning to Jane.

He wished he was with her, and he hoped her taping was going well. He knew she was nervous—as far as he could tell, she'd tried on every single outfit she owned before settling on a simple but classic blue dress.

He'd offered to go with her, and though he could see the temptation in her eyes, she'd ultimately said no. "Colin said he wanted to come, too, and I told him what I'm telling you. I'd be too nervous with you right there."

He noted that neither Eli nor Lisa had offered to be there. Presumably because Eli—who had hired mercenaries—didn't agree with either Jane's or Bill's thesis any more than Dallas did.

"You don't need to be babysitting me, anyway," she continued, unaware of the turn his thoughts had taken. "You have work."

When he'd told her he could work from the townhouse and have dinner ready when she got back, she'd turned that offer down, too. "I have a surprise planned," she said with a grin. "But to do it, I have to have workmen in the house."

He lifted a brow. "A surprise? Involving workmen? Are you replacing your flatscreen TV and upgrading your game system?"

She cocked her head. "You're thinking along the right lines," she'd admitted, but refused to tell him anything more.

Finally, she'd told him to come back at nine, and not a minute before. Then she'd smacked him on the ass and told him it was her turn to give the orders.

Fair enough, but he'd have payback tonight.

The thought made him smile more.

"What the hell are you grinning about?" Liam quipped when Dallas answered the video call coming in over the secure channel on his laptop.

"Just having a good day," he said.

"Oh, really? I'm guessing that means you had a good night."

"That's one of the reasons you work for me," Dallas said. "You're so damn smart."

"I'm guessing Jane had a good night, too," Liam said, then laughed at the scowl Dallas shot him.

"Maybe too damn smart," Dallas said.

Liam chuckled. "I didn't call to talk about your torrid romance," he began, as Dallas shot him the bird. "Wanted to give you a heads-up that we may have caught another case."

Immediately, Dallas sobered. "Tell me."

Liam shook his head. "Let me do some follow-up. It's almost seven."

"Damn," Dallas said, realizing he'd lost track of time. He picked up the remote and clicked on his office television. *Evening Edge* was about to start, and Jane was in the first segment.

"She's going to kick ass," Liam said.

"She's nervous," Dallas said. "But she will. She grew up a Sykes, just like I did. She may hate media appearances, but she won't show it to the world."

What he was more interested in—other than simply watching her there on the screen—was what she had to say. They hadn't talked a lot about the book she was working on, but he knew enough to know that their views differed. The question was, how much?

Moments later, he had his answer.

She looked amazing on camera, just as he'd known she

would. And, yeah, he was so damn proud of how she presented herself with such strength and confidence.

But the words coming out of her mouth—and of her asshole ex-husband's—sat like heavy stones in his gut.

Names like *Benson* and *Deliverance*.

Adjectives like *dangerous* and *illegal*.

Ultimatums like *needs to be stopped*.

Sound bites like *dead children* and *serious injuries*.

And each one hit him like a blow.

"Vigilante rescuers," the host said, leaning forward in one of the casual chairs that made up the set. "It sounds like a Hollywood action movie."

"Except Hollywood has happy endings. In the real world, innocent people are injured and die in vigilante raids," Jane said.

"But is that necessarily the fault of these vigilantes?"

"Absolutely it is," Jane said. "They may look like they're dressed up in procedure. That they're investigating crimes and then moving in to catch the bad guys. But it isn't true."

She spoke with such passion that it seemed as if she was standing right next to Dallas, and every word twisted inside him.

"The people who run these groups are heartless, vicious monsters," she said. "The Benson group, Deliverance, and any others that may come to light—they're not focused on saving lives but on profit. On earning the fee paid by the parent of one specific child—and all the non-paying children are expendable."

"That's a strong accusation."

"It is," Bill agreed. "And while I'm not authorized to give details, I can say that there is evidence to support what Ms. Martin just said."

"They need to be stopped," Jane said, her eyes flashing with heat. "They break law after law in the course of their operations, which negatively impacts the ability of legitimate law enforcement to do their job. More than that, they extract their own justice. And that is simply not a role that civilians should be playing."

"Not only is it illegal," Bill said, "but there's no due process for those they punish."

"I can only document the facts in my books," Jane said. "But the work that WORR is doing is essential. People like William Martin and his team are the real heroes. Not these self-important, profiteering rogues."

"I understand that Benson's group is in custody?" the host asked.

"That's correct," Bill said. "And we're putting all our resources to locating and shutting down Deliverance."

"And the sooner the better," Jane added. "Before another child gets killed."

Dallas clicked the television off, and as he did, he realized that he'd left the connection to Liam open. He clicked the mouse to clear his screensaver, feeling raw. Feeling numb.

"You were watching, too?"

"Yeah," Liam said. "Bill's going to be a problem for us."

Dallas pressed his fingertips against his temple. As if his marriage to Jane wasn't enough, now Dallas had one more reason to put Bill Martin on his shit list. "I'm guessing that one of those resources he's mentioned will be Darcy. They're going to question him six ways from Sunday."

"Won't come back on us," Liam said.

"No, but I want to talk to him anyway," Dallas said. "I'm throwing a party next week. He's coming. We'll chat." He closed his eyes and sighed. "Right now, though, it's not Bill or Darcy that concerns me."

"I know."

"I have to tell her." He knew that—and at the same time, he was terrified that it would shatter everything between them. "I have to tell her about Deliverance. What I do. What we do. And I need her to understand that we're not like Benson. She'd never believe that either of us is only about chasing a dollar."

"Tell her even part of that, and you're putting us all at risk."

He ran his fingers through his hair. "Do you really think so?"

His friend sighed heavily. "Are we talking about what I believe? Or what I know? I believe that Jane would never put either of us in danger. But I don't know that for a fact. What I *do* know is that you're the one who put rules in place for Deliverance, and those rules were to protect all of us."

"I either tell her or I leave her. I can keep a secret from my sister. I can't keep it from my lover."

"So that really is where you two are."

"Yeah," Dallas said. "That's where we are." He tensed, unsure how Liam would react to that bit of news.

"'Bout damn time," Liam said, and Dallas relaxed. "Just think it through before you tell her. I'm not saying don't—I'm just saying think."

"I know," Dallas said. "I will." He'd also talk it over with the team. Liam was right—the rules were to protect all of them. He could put himself at risk. But he couldn't do that to the others.

Liam and Quince would understand and roll with whatever he decided, but Noah and Tony were different. They had their own reasons for being part of Deliverance, and Dallas could never break their trust or put them at risk. Not unless they gave the okay. Not unless they understood exactly what might happen if he breathed a word, even to Jane.

Fuck.

Just when he and Jane were finding their way and truly trying to work out this weird, fucked-up relationship, they had to deal with this. As if they didn't already have enough to deal with between family and secrets and the demons each of them lived with. Not to mention his own particular proclivities—and limitations—where sex was concerned. Now they had to toss social justice and criminology into the mix.

Not that he had expected their differing philosophies to be swept under the rug forever. Frankly, he hadn't thought much about it at all. But in the back of his mind he'd assumed it would only be an issue if WORR started to get close to Deliverance, something he hadn't believed was possible.

But this?

Christ, the timing just fucking sucked.

He spent the next half hour trying to take his mind off it. He couldn't talk with her about it tonight—he had to speak to the team first—which meant that he needed to genuinely congratulate her for doing a great job on television . . . and then casually shift the conversation away from conversation all together.

They'd deal with it—they had to deal with it. Just not tonight.

She'd ordered him back at nine—the memory of her smacking his ass still made him smile, and still conjured all sorts of glorious ideas for retaliation—and he left with five minutes to spare just in case he got held up.

He was turning the corner onto her block when he saw her on the front stoop. There was a man with her—tall, muscular, a little bit familiar—and when Jane raised her cheek to accept a kiss that was accompanied by a quick squeeze to her rear, Dallas just about lost his shit.

He picked up his pace, not sure what he intended to do except possibly smash the asshole's face in, when said asshole hopped on a Harley and roared past him, his head turning toward Dallas as he did, and his mouth curving into an easy smile.

What the fuck?

"Who the hell was that?" Dallas demanded as he sprinted up the steps to where Jane still stood, smiling as he approached.

Her eyes gleamed with mischief. "Him? Oh, he was just the workman I told you about." She took his hand. "Come inside. Out here, I have to kiss you like a brother, and that's really not how I want to kiss you right now."

Once they were inside, she pressed him against the wall and kissed him so hard and so deep that he almost—*almost*—forgot that he wanted to ask her why the workman was fondling her rear.

He managed to keep his wits though, and after he congratulated her on an excellent show, and she told him that she'd been nervous but had calmed once the taping started, he slid straight back to the topic of the asshole.

"He's a friend, and you're not allowed to be jealous." She hooked her arm through his. "Come on. I have something to show you."

"Not allowed to be jealous?"

"Not when it would take a supercomputer to calculate the number of women you've been with," she said, bypassing the main stairs and heading through the kitchen to the set of stairs that descended to the garden level.

"Women I've been with?" he repeated. "Are you telling me you've been with him?"

She stopped on the stairs. "You're jealous. I think I like this side of you."

"Jane."

"Fine." She rose up onto her toes and kissed him again. "He was here helping me with the project I told you about. And I promise you, no clothing was shed in the process. Now come on. I want you to see it."

The stairs opened onto the level where the servants' quarters used to be located. He hadn't been down there in years, and for the most part it looked about the same. A narrow hall painted white to make the space brighter despite the minimal natural light. And then rooms on either side, each one opening onto a small, dormitory-style room where the servants used to live back in the days when the house was first built.

His parents had used those rooms for storage.

He and Jane had used them for play.

Dallas had no idea what Jane used the rooms for these days, just as he had no idea why she'd brought him down here now. But they must have reached their destination, because she was standing in front of the very last door on the right, holding the key in her hand and bouncing a little nervously.

"Close your eyes," she insisted, after leading him right up to the door. "Don't peek until I say so."

He did as she said, amused, and then listened as she unlocked the room and pushed the door open. She took his hands and guided him in, and then moved to stand behind him so she could cover his eyes. "Okay, open," she said and then pulled her hands away with flourish.

Holy fuck.

It was a boudoir. Hell, it was a porn set.

It was a fantasy playroom with everything from leather to silk, chains and ropes, toys and video. And already his mind was going to just what he could do if he had her against that wall with her wrists in those cuffs and a flogger in his hand, her beautiful skin red for him, and her sweet moans making him hard as he took her over the edge, down into that sweet space where pain gave way to pleasure.

And that bed with the deep purple spread and the headboard with all sorts of handy hooks and leather straps. How many times could he make her come? How loud could he make her scream his name?

"Do you like?"

She was still behind him, her hands on his shoulders and her voice tentative.

He took one of her hands and lowered it, pressing against his rock hard erection. "What do you think?"

He could practically feel the worry draining away from her, and she moved around him to stand in the circle of his arms. "I know we've talked about it, but I wanted to make sure you know that I mean what I say. Wherever you need to go, I'm there with you. You don't have to be afraid you'll push me too far."

Her words ricocheted through him, humbling him and exciting him. He wanted to believe them. Wanted to believe this would work. That it could be real and true, and that somehow they'd surmount every obstacle.

With a gentle smile, she reached up and cupped his cheek. "You're thinking too hard. Don't think. Just know. That you want me. That I want you. And this is right, Dallas. Us. Together. That's a place we've been heading all our lives, and it took us too damn long to get here."

"When did you do this? How did you do it?"

"Brody—my friend from outside. He came in and worked all day." She looked down, shrugging a little. "He's a professional dom so he has the connections to make it happen fast."

"A professional dom?" A red streak of jealousy cut through him even as her words piqued his interest.

"Don't even go there," she said, rising up on her toes to kiss him. "After all the women you've been with? The few times I was with Brody—a long, long, long time ago—are not fair game."

"Fuck that," he said, and heard the growl in his voice as he grabbed her waist and pulled her close. "Anyone you've been with is fair game."

He could see the rise and fall of her chest as she breathed hard, as excited as he was.

"Don't you understand?" she whispered. "Don't you get it?

I've fucked a lot of men, Dallas. But I've never really been with anyone but you. I don't ever want to be."

Her words, so tender—so true—wrapped around him. He wanted to pull her close and cover her with kisses. He wanted to make her his in every way possible.

He wanted to touch her. To worship her.

He wanted to claim her.

"The bed," he said. "We start easy." He met her eyes. "We won't stay there."

She licked her lips, excitement flaring in her eyes. "Yes, sir." She started toward the bed, then looked back over her shoulder. "Dallas?" She swallowed. "I want you to tie me down. To the bed, I mean." She licked her lips, and he could practically see the nervous energy coming off her in waves. "Spread-eagled and naked."

His entire body was tense. He knew that being tied down had terrified her in captivity. "Baby, are you sure? Have you done that before?"

She shook her head. "No. I—no. But I want to." Her eyes burned into his. "Don't you see? With you, it's not fear, it's de-sire. It's trust, Dallas. Trust and love."

"Oh, baby." Christ, she melted him. How the hell could this woman melt him so damn easily?

"Dallas?"

"On the bed," he said. "In the dress." It was a V-neck style that buttoned up the front from hem to cleavage.

"Oh."

He almost laughed at her disappointment. "Don't worry. You'll be naked soon enough. But getting you there will be my pleasure. You just get on your back, hands above your head."

She did as told, and when she was stretched out, long and lean, he walked to the headboard and tugged on one of the two leather straps that her friend Brody had so conveniently placed at the top corners of the bed. "Arms above your head," he ordered, his cock stiffening when, once again, she complied without hesitation.

He bound her wrists, then moved to the foot of the bed and used the straps there to bind her ankles. "I like it," he said, letting his eyes roam over her, imagining each and every way he was going to touch her. But still, she was bound to a bed, and he couldn't shake his fear for her. "Are you okay? We need a safe word."

"No," she said. "We don't." She met his eyes. "You'll always protect me, remember?"

His cock strained against his jeans, the sweet, honest tenderness in her words doing him in. *Tonight,* he thought. *Surely he could manage to fuck her hard tonight.*

"All right," he said. "No safe word. But there's still something about this scene that's not quite how I want it . . ."

He trailed off as he got on the bed and straddled her, then very slowly undid the buttons on her dress. He couldn't get it off without releasing her, so he simply spread it open—then gasped when he saw the chain around her neck—and the small golden locket that he'd given her for her eleventh birthday.

He took a moment to let the fact that she'd not only kept the locket, but that she'd worn it tonight to sink in. Then he looked at her face—at the heat in her eyes—and returned to the task of undressing her.

The bra clasped in the front, and he opened it as well, spreading it as he had the dress. The panties were a different story, and he used the small knife he kept on his keychain to slice them at the hips, making her cry out with each motion of the blade. He pulled them off, and then cupped her bare pussy with his palm. She trembled beneath him, already swollen. Already wet.

She wanted him, no doubt about it.

More than that, she trusted him. Utterly and completely.

He slid off the bed and stood at the foot, looking down at the woman he adored. The woman he'd loved his entire life.

You'll always protect me, remember?

It's trust, Dallas. Trust and love.

She was giving herself to him so completely it humbled him—and if he took what she was offering without telling her the truth about Deliverance, then he really was a monster.

And he couldn't tell her now. Couldn't say one word without betraying his men.

Goddammit.

Goddammit all to hell.

Slowly, regretfully, he reached over and released her ankles. Then he walked to the head of the bed and uncuffed her wrists.

"Dallas? What's the matter?"

"I'm sorry," he said, because what else could he say? Nothing until he talked to the team.

"Sorry?" She sat up, pulling the bedspread up to cover her.

"I love you. Christ, Jane, I love you so much it hurts. But I can't do this to you. I have to go."

He didn't wait for her to answer. He couldn't even bear to look at her face.

He turned and he left.

And he hated himself every step of the way.

27

Secrets

What the hell?

I sit on the bed, a little confused, a little scared, a whole lot worried.

He said he can't do this to me—but do *what* to me?

Leave me? Apparently so, but I'm certain that's not all of it and I'm angry and hurt and frustrated.

More than that, I'm pissed and I'm embarrassed and I'm determined to figure out what the hell is going on.

I hurry back upstairs and get dressed, tossing on the first jeans and T-shirt I come across. I don't know for certain that he's going to the Hamptons house, but I figure it's a good bet. For one thing, he used to own an apartment in the city, but he sold it recently and hasn't bought a new one yet. For another, even if he's not there, Archie can tell me where he is. And at any rate, right now I'm too wired not to do something.

I consider calling his cellphone, but dismiss the idea. He

won't answer, and I'm not interested in playing phone tag. I just want answers.

I just want *him*.

So I drive too fast through the night, my head filled with worries and fears. I'd known that being with Dallas wouldn't be easy, but I'd really thought that we were communicating now, and this sudden and complete shut-down is truly freaking me out.

Was it me?

Was it seeing Brody? Realizing that I've slept with other men?

Was it the bondage? Because he knows that it scared me?

Why the hell isn't he just talking to me?

Questions run on an endless loop through my mind, but I still have no answers when I arrive at the house. I let myself in, thankful he didn't think to change the lock and alarm codes, then race upstairs to his bedroom.

It's empty, and for a second I think that he stayed in the city. That maybe he just went to his office. Or that he bought an apartment I don't know about.

Or that he's staying with a woman.

I swallow the bile that rises with that thought and start to press the intercom for Archie. But then I remember the security monitors and I push the button to acquire video for the garage. Dallas's car is there, which means that he's here, too. In the house or on the property, and I start scrolling through the screens to look for him.

By the time it cycles back to the garage, I'm baffled. He's nowhere to be found; either he's not here at all or he's in a room with no security monitor.

I remember what Brody said about his playroom, and my stomach twists again. Is that where he is? In a hidden hardcore dungeon with another woman? One he's comfortable taking to the edge because he's taken her there already?

One he's not afraid to *taint*?

I close my eyes in defense against the violent need to lash out. *Damn him.* I thought he understood. I thought he believed me when I told him that I would go there with him.

Bastard.

I don't even realize I've made a decision until I'm heading down to the basement. It's the best guess I have as to where the playroom is located, and since I don't remember seeing it on the security feed, I'm pretty certain I'm right.

It's accessed through stairs in both the kitchen and the garage, and I head to the kitchen, then descend to the next level, most of which is used for bulk pantry space and other storage. I walk down the narrow corridor that I remember so well from my childhood. There's a door at the end, and I pass through, then down another set of stairs that form a hard right angle before reaching the basement door.

I expect that door to be closed, but as I get closer, I realize that it isn't because I can hear voices, and I realize that my fears were justified, because the voice I hear is a woman's.

I can't make out words—honestly, I feel too sick to even concentrate—and I'm walking faster now, fueled by hurt and anger.

But when I get to the doorway, there's no toy-filled dungeon, but some sort of high-tech operations system that rivals what I've seen with Bill at WORR. Hell, it probably rivals the Pentagon.

I freeze just outside the door, my hand over my mouth as I look around and try to understand what I'm seeing. The video monitors. The maps. The various computers doing unknown tasks.

What the hell?

The woman's voice is coming from a video screen. It's on a loop, and she's running on a beach, urging whoever is holding the camera to "come on, handsome, don't make me wait."

I frown, confused. Is she talking to Dallas? I don't think so, because he's barely even looking at the video. Instead, he's angled to look at another monitor, this one showing a map of Mexico.

Then it fades, and I almost yelp when Liam's face pops onto the screen in its place.

Seriously. *What. The. Fuck*?

"She went missing yesterday," Liam says. "Her boyfriend reported it to local authorities. It's the case I mentioned, and she's skipped out on family and friends before, which is why we did a little more investigation before confirming the kidnapping."

"How did she end up on our radar?" Dallas asks.

"Her father is business partners with Mr. Liu, and was aware that Liu came to us instead of Chinese officials to get back his little boy. The burner phone we issued Liu is still active and linked to Tony's burner for another two days. Standard follow-up in case the boy needs special attention. He left a message. He wants to give Deliverance forty-eight hours, then pull in the feds."

Deliverance.

I start to sag, then reach for the doorframe to steady myself.

"What leads do we have?" Dallas asks.

"We've tracked her to Mexico City. I have Tony looking at—*behind you. Shit.*"

Dallas slams his palm down on a button on the console in front of him. Immediately, all the monitors in the room go dark.

He turns then, and when he sees me, his eyes go wide. "Jane."

"You're Deliverance?" My chest is so tight I can barely force out the words.

I watch as a flurry of emotion washes over his face. I'm holding my breath in defense against the truth that is coming. The truth that is so damn obvious there can be no other explanation even though I desperately hope I'm wrong.

"Tell me, dammit."

"Yes," he finally says. "I'm Deliverance."

28

Light and Shadows

He takes a step toward me, but I just shake my head. "Jane. Please. We have to talk."

I can't—I can't process it. I can't deal with it. Not the fact that he is at the heart of something I find so reprehensible. Not the fact that he kept it a secret. Not the fact that I thought I knew him better than anyone, and now my whole world is crashing down around me.

"Jane," he repeats. "Jane, please."

"No." It's the one word I can say. And when he takes another step toward me, I turn and race up the stairs.

I'm breathing hard when I get to my car, gulping in air as I struggle to get the key into the ignition. I shouldn't drive—I'm crying too hard—but I take off anyway and then park on the shoulder in front of a neighbor's house until I can get my shit together.

Or, at least, together enough so that I can drive without killing myself.

I don't know how long I sit there, half-expecting Dallas to

pull up behind me. He doesn't, and I can't help but laugh at the irony. He knows me well, after all. And that means he knows I need to be alone right now. Or, at least, I need to not be with him.

The truth is that I don't want to be alone, and as I head back to the city, I dial Brody. But I only get his voicemail, and the message I leave is garbled because the moment I try to speak I burst into tears again.

I'm such a fucking mess.

I'm exhausted by the time I reach the townhouse. Too little sleep, too much adrenaline, and now I've crashed and burned.

I stumble into the house, grateful for the exhaustion. Maybe I'll just pass out. Maybe I'll sleep without nightmares.

Maybe I'll wake up and the world will be sane again, and I'll realize that *this* is the nightmare.

I head into the kitchen to get a glass of wine to take to bed with me, and let out a shriek when I see both Brody and Stacey sitting at my breakfast table.

"What the hell?" I demand, as Brody leaps to his feet and comes to my side.

"Are you okay? I tried to call you back, but it just went to voicemail."

I shake my head, confused, and realize I must have turned my phone to silent. I glance at it quickly, half-expecting to see a missed call from Dallas. But there isn't one, and I'm not sure if I'm relieved or disappointed.

"Dammit, Jane, I was worried. What happened?"

"Dallas," I say. "I think—I think it may be over just when it's finally begun."

Just saying those words—those horrible words—makes me queasy. I slide into one of the chairs at the table as Stacey rises. There's an open bottle of wine on the counter—and they each already have a glass. She brings a fresh glass and pours it for me. "Do you want to talk about it?" she asks gently.

I shake my head. "Actually, yes. But I can't. It's—it's hard. It's personal." I can't tell them about Deliverance. Despite the fact that Deliverance represents something I abhor, I can't share that secret.

My eyes flick to Brody, who looks confused. He knows damn well that between the two of us, very little is too personal.

"Was it the room? Did it freak him out?"

"No. Yes. No," I decide. "That just triggered it. There are issues. Things in his past. Things that are his to share, you know. But—"

"But it's coming between you," Stacey says. "Fair enough."

I take a sip of wine, so grateful my friends are here even though I can't really tell them what's going on.

"Can you work through it?" Brody asks.

"I don't know," I say honestly. How the hell do you work through such a fundamental difference?

"Bullshit," Stacey says, her voice mild, but her expression fierce.

"Excuse me?" Despite everything, I'm amused. That is not a Stacey-like response.

"If Dallas were to die tomorrow, would you regret every single day that the two of you stayed apart for whatever the hell reason there is?"

I just gape at her.

"Dammit, I'm serious—maybe it really is over. But if it's surmountable, then for god's sake start climbing that mountain. Haven't you two lost enough time?"

We have, I think. We really have.

But I'm not sure how to get past this.

I'm still not sure when I wake up late in the morning, or when I go back to sleep, too sad and frustrated and lost to care about the fact that it's a gorgeous day and I'm missing all of it.

When I finally drag myself out of bed around eight Sunday evening, I'm still not sure what to do. I'm still numb. I'm still lost.

I haven't magically healed, and it's my life that is still a nightmare, but not the kind I can wake from. And the truth is, I'm starting to wonder if I truly understand what is at the core of my pain. Is it the difference in our beliefs? Or is it that he kept such a huge secret from me.

I don't know, and the question is still on my mind when Liam shows up at my doorstep Monday morning.

"You writing me off, too? Or can I come in?"

I frown, because I'm not. I hadn't even thought about calling Liam to chew him out. To tell him our friendship was on the outs. Honestly, except for the shock of seeing him on that video screen, I hadn't thought of him at all.

"It's different with Dallas," I say defensively as I let him in, then head to the living room.

"Because you're sleeping with him?"

I whip around to face him, surprised.

"Because you're in love with him?"

"I—he told you?"

"If he hadn't, you just did. Do you really think that matters to me? I've known you two should be together since you handed him that damn bunny."

I drop onto the couch and put my head in my hands, my elbows on my knees. "I'm all screwed up," I say to the floor. "And I'm so pissed off at Dallas."

"I get that," he says. "But you're not angry with him because of what he does. You know he's not like Benson. That Deliverance isn't like Benson."

I nod. I'd never believe that he or Liam would so callously put victims at risk in order to make a buck. "But that's not all of it. What you do—this vigilante bullshit—"

"You don't agree with it," he says. "Understood. But you don't agree with a lot of things people do and you don't write them off."

I lift my head to look at him, because his words are a mirror to my earlier thoughts. *What he did or what he kept secret? Which is really at the heart of my pain?*

"Take a hard look at Colin," Liam continues. "Tax fraud. Insider trading. And we both know he was into more dangerous stuff than that. Your arm didn't get broken back then because he fucked up his accounting. Smuggling, drugs, I don't know. But I do know he's done some messed up shit, and you know it, too."

I can only nod. He's right.

"Even your dad. He may not be part of Deliverance, but he did exactly what you say you're against. And yet here you are in this nice house from the family trust. And you love him and he's your father, and I don't think you've even thought to bring it up with him."

"No," I say. "I've thought about it. I just haven't said anything."

"Why not?"

I shrug. "Because he's my father. Because—because I love him and he did what he thought made sense and it's just easier to stay quiet and not tell him why I think he was so, so wrong."

"Funny, I was under the impression you loved Dallas, too."

I lick my lips. "I do," I whisper. But the truth is, Dallas matters more. It's not like it is with my father. I can't just stay quiet. Not if I want to be close. Not if I want there to be an *us*. And I do. God help me, I really do. But I don't know how to get past this wall.

I don't say that. I don't need to. I'm sure that Liam can see the answer on my face.

"That raid almost got him killed," I say. "Those damn mercenaries Daddy hired almost destroyed everything."

"Bullshit. Dallas was already transferred. Honestly, I think they set you up. I've thought about it a lot over the years, and I think they made sure you had clues. Made sure you had just enough evidence that the team could find where you'd been held. They wanted to blow up the building and take out a few of Eli's men. They wanted you all to think Dallas was dead. They were fucking with you. Because that's what evil does, and whoever snatched you two was pure fucking evil."

I frown. I'd never considered that. But the blindfold did slip. My clothes were covered with dirt that was easily traceable. I did hear those distinctive chimes, when a five minute difference would have meant I heard nothing. Could Liam be right?

I shake my head to clear my thoughts. "It's not just our kidnapping. What Deliverance does endangers the victims."

"We're saving victims," he counters.

He'd been sitting on the couch opposite me. Now he rises and walks to me, then squats so that he's right in front of me, his hands on my knees. "If it's any consolation, he decided after your TV gig that he had to tell you. But he couldn't do that without letting the others on the team know first. That call you walked in on? After we went through the new case specs, I was going to add the other guys to the feed. Let Dallas tell them he needed to let you in on the secret."

"Oh." I feel shaky. It hadn't occurred to me that he would ever want to tell me, or that he'd made the decision right before I took him to the playroom.

I only knew that he'd been hiding a huge piece of himself from me.

"Here's the bottom line, Jane. I believe in Deliverance. Dallas believes in Deliverance. We're not shutting it down. Probably not even when it's served its purpose."

"Purpose?"

"Why do you think he started it?"

"To find our kidnappers." Of course that's why. Of course he's been searching. Not only that, but I'm certain that he is searching mostly because of me. If he'd been held alone, I think he might have let it go.

I'll always protect you.

I close my eyes, feeling overwhelmed.

Liam doesn't relent. "It's grown beyond the original purpose because the entire team believes in the value—the necessity—of what we do. And the truth is, it doesn't matter if you believe it, too, Jane. All that matters is if you believe in Dallas. If you believe in the two of you."

I do, I think after Liam leaves and I am alone again. *I do believe in the two of us.*

Haven't I been the one all along telling Dallas that we can make it work? Despite family and society and secrets and sex? I've been like a broken record—and now I'm the one who's put on the brakes.

But I don't want it to end. So help me, I want this to be a beginning.

I'm still scared, though. Scared of secrets. Scared that he's angry about the way I left.

Scared that the reason he hasn't called since I walked out is because he thinks we were fools to try to make it work in the first place.

Most of all, though, I'm scared of losing him.

And that's the fear that drives me.

I force myself to shower for the first time since Saturday morning, then head back to the Hamptons. Once again, I'm not sure if he'll be there. Once again, I'm determined to wait.

Unfortunately, that's exactly what I have to do.

"I'm sorry, Miss Jane," Archie tells me. "Mr. Sykes had to go into the office this morning. I expect him back by dinner, though."

"Oh. Okay." I consider going back to the city and cornering him in his office. But I talk myself out of it. "Is it okay if I just hang out? Maybe spend the day by the pool?"

Archie's smile is both polite and gentle. "Of course. I'll go put together a light lunch. Would you care for wine?"

"I can't even begin to tell you how much I would like wine," I admit.

I head inside first to find a book, then return to the pool area. I'm wearing a light skirt with a thin sweater over a tank, so I take the sweater off, find a chaise in the shade, kick off my shoes, and settle in for the day.

I don't intend to fall asleep, but before I walked away from Dallas I wasn't getting much sleep because we'd filled the night with other, more interesting activities. After I walked away, I simply couldn't sleep. Or, rather, I couldn't sleep well. So after a few glasses of wine, exhaustion sucks me under, and I wake only when the mattress on the chaise shifts.

I blink, and find Dallas smiling down at me. "I talked with Liam. And then I went by the townhouse after work," he says. "You weren't there."

"I came here this morning," I counter. "You weren't here."

His mouth twitches with a tentative smile, but it never fully blooms. Instead, I watch as his brow furrows. And when he takes my hand, I hold tight, savoring the connection between us.

"Do you want to talk about it?" he asks. "About Deliverance. About what I do and how it works and why I started it?"

"Yes," I admit. "I want to know everything." I let go of his hand and push myself upright. "But not right now. Now, I just want to ask you one question."

"You can ask me anything," he says.

"Do you love me?"

I see the answer in his eyes before he says a word. "You know me better than anyone, Jane. Don't you know the answer is yes?"

His words fill me, leaving no room for lingering doubts or fears. I ease off the chaise and stand, then hold my hand out for him.

"Inside," he says. "My bedroom."

"Oh, no," I counter, leading him away from the house and to the cabana. "I want to finish what we started."

"Christ, I adore you," he says as he lifts me up. I cling to him as he hurries into the cabana, then tosses me back onto the bed before tying the curtains closed.

"We're going to make this work, aren't we?" I say, and I know that he understands I don't mean just sex. I mean everything. Family. Social taboos. Deliverance. Nightmares and secrets.

"We are," he promises. "But right now, I need you naked."

"Then I guess you're going to have to do something about that."

"Oh, I will."

He reaches for my tank top, but I smack his hand away. He raises his brows in warning.

"You first," I say. "I want to watch."

"Do you? Well, whatever the lady wants."

He strips, kicking off his shoes. Tugging off his socks. He unbuttons his white shirt and slides it off, revealing the sculpted abs I love so well.

Slowly, he takes off his belt, then tosses it aside. Then he unbuttons his pants, lowers his zipper, and eases out of his khaki slacks. He's wearing boxer briefs, and his erection is bulging against the material.

I actually lick my lips out of reflex, making him laugh. "No way, sweetheart. Not until I taste you."

"Finish the show," I insist, and then gasp when he lowers the briefs and his cock, huge and thick and perfect springs free.

The truth is that I do want to feel him inside me, so much that my muscles clench simply from the thought of it. But I am patient. I can wait.

And I will relish every moment of anticipation until we get there.

When he's naked, he moves to me. I'm so turned on that every brush of his skin against mine as he frees me from my skirt and tank makes me shiver. And when he tugs down my silk panties and then raises them to his nose, I writhe on the bed with pure, lustful need.

He tosses them aside, then eases onto the bed. He kisses my lips, then trails more kisses over my aching breasts, my belly, all the way down to just above my mound.

Then he raises his head and gives me a look that says he knows exactly where I want his mouth next, but that I am just going to have to wait.

"Bastard," I murmur.

"Sexy bastard to you," he counters, and I laugh despite him tormenting me.

Slowly, he tugs my legs apart, then cups my pussy, the pressure and the sensation of skin against skin making me even more crazed.

"One day," he says, "I'm going to fill you. I'm going to fuck you so hard you won't know if you want me to stop or to continue."

"Continue," I say as he thrusts three fingers inside, making me gasp. And then he pumps into me, hard and deep. I pound against him, fucking his hand shamelessly. And, yes, I want more. But this feels good. So damn good.

"Your mouth, your pussy, your ass. Every way I can be inside you, baby, I will be. Deep and hot and hard."

"Dallas. Oh, god, Dallas." He keeps his fingers inside me, thrusting hard, then lowers his mouth and sucks on my clit as waves of pleasure break over me, precursors to an explosive orgasm.

But it's when he lifts my rear and slides a finger into my ass that I really lose my mind. I want to writhe, but I can't. He's wholly in command of me. He owns me, and I am a slave to his touch, his tongue.

More and more, he teases, taking me close and pulling me back. Exhausting me. Thrilling me. I am screaming. Begging. I've never been particularly noisy in bed, but I am now. I want. I need. And I can't hold any of it inside.

And when my release finally comes, I arch up off the bed with such wild, wonderful violence I think that I might just reach the ceiling. When I'm spent and limp on the bed, he bends over and kisses me gently between my breasts. "I think someone liked that."

"Someone definitely did." I push myself up, then stroke the line of hair that arrows down his lower abs toward his cock. "And now I think it's your turn."

He's wonderfully hard, and I close my hand around his cock, then ease up onto my knees to be closer to where he's standing by the side of the bed. I stroke him, enjoying the velvety smoothness, and thinking that I just might want to taste him, too, when his hand closes over mine.

I look up and see that his green eyes are dark.

"What is it?"

"I can't come like that. Not from someone else stroking me, going down on me."

"Oh." I hadn't realized that, and for a moment I'm flummoxed. Then I shrug a little, and lie back on the bed, propped up on my elbows as I face him. "That's okay," I say. "I'll just stay right here and enjoy the view." I know, after all, that he's more than capable of jacking himself off, and I slide my own fingers between my legs in memory of that truly excellent moment on the beach.

"No," he says. "Come here. Behind me."

He sits on the edge of the bed, and I do as he says, my legs spread wide around him so that my thighs are against his hips, and my pussy is against his rear. "Give me your hand," he orders, and when I comply, he curls my fingers over his cock.

"But you said—"

"I said to give me your hand . . ." He trails off as he closes his hand over mine, and then he guides the action. My palm, but his motions, and it is crazy insane, this feeling of being there for him, for each other.

He grows stiffer under my hand. His cock twitches. His whole body contracts, and I can feel all of it because I'm pressed against him, legs to legs, back to chest. It's as intimate as intercourse, and I am wildly aroused. So much so that I feel his orgasm coming, and when he explodes, I cry out with him, and I swear that I have never felt more close to him than I do in that one, intimate moment.

His release seems to go on forever, and his body shudders in my arms, the pressure of his ass against my still-sensitive clit sending me over the edge again. I cling to him, our bodies shattering together, and then we collapse back on the bed.

"Wow," I say as I move to straddle him while he rolls onto his back. He holds me close, and I nuzzle against him, loving this feeling of skin against skin. "Wow," I say again, then relish the rumble of his laughter through me.

"Look at me," he says, when our laughter has faded. "I love you."

"I love you, too," I say. "So much." I shift so that I can stroke his face, his hair. "No more secrets," I say. "Not between us. Not again. Not ever."

"No more secrets," he agrees. And as he lifts his head and

captures me in the kind of kiss that claims my heart and my soul, I think that we have finally crossed a line. That we're going to be okay.

We're in love. We're moving forward.

And, somehow, someway, we're going to make this work.

29

New Secrets

The vibration of his phone woke Dallas and he reached down to the floor, fumbling for it from the pocket of his slacks. Groggy, he squinted at the screen, saw that it was Liam, and took the call. "What?"

"Are you alone?"

He frowned, confused. "What the hell?" he whispered, so as not to wake Jane, still sleeping peacefully. "She already knows."

"Not about this," Liam said, and the tightness in his voice had Dallas sliding out from under the covers and walking across the cabana to the curtain.

"Tell me."

"We've made progress on decrypting the hard drive we took from Ortega's property."

"You have a lead."

"Yeah," Liam said. "No confirmation yet—so keep that in mind. Maybe it's nothing at all, but . . ."

"Just spill it."

"Colin," Liam said. "He's all over Ortega's files."

Dallas clutched the phone tighter, not wanting to ask the question—not even wanting to consider the possibility—but knowing that he had to. "Are you saying he's involved with the kidnapping?"

"Hell, Dallas, I don't know," Liam said, sounding completely ripped apart. "Colin's been wrapped up in all sorts of bad shit since we were kids. Maybe he was into smuggling with Ortega. Or maybe they just had a standing poker night."

"Or maybe he's right in the thick of it," Dallas said, shutting his eyes and thinking of the man he'd come to think of as a friend. The man who was Jane's birth father.

"I hope to hell not. But we have to consider it. We have to look harder. Go deeper."

"I know." Dallas sighed, his heart raw. "Fuck."

"You can't tell her," Liam said. "Not yet. At the very least, not until we're sure."

"No," Dallas agreed, closing his eyes against this truth. This secret. "I can't tell her a goddamn thing."

The seductive S.I.N. series continues with

HOTTEST
Mess

Read on for a sneak peek . . .

Coming soon from Headline Eternal.

My earliest memories are of Dallas. Being with him. Laughing with him.

Loving him.

I don't remember when I realized that it was wrong, when I truly understood that we had to keep our growing desire secret. I only know that it glowed inside us, a spark just waiting to burn. And that when the worst happened—when we were captive together in the dark—we no longer cared about rules and expectations, taboos or punishments.

All we wanted then was to survive. All we cared about was finding comfort in each other's arms, the world outside be damned.

In some ways, those long, dark weeks were the best of my life. Terrifying and horrible, yes, but we belonged to each other. Fully. Completely.

After, in the real world, we were torn apart, everything we'd been to each other pushed aside. Buried.

A precious memory. A traumatic interlude.

A mistake.

Because we are brother and sister—bound as tightly by adoption as if we were tied by blood—and yet equally bound by need. By desire. By love.

For seventeen years, we fought a battle against our desire, but that is over now. Neither of us can fight any longer, and we have succumbed to heaven in each other's arms.

It's a forbidden love, a hidden passion.

It's a secret, and it has to stay that way.

But secrets scare me, because things hidden in the dark have power.

Dallas and I know that better than anyone.

So even though I am happier now than I have ever been, I am also more frightened than I can ever remember. Because I fully understand the stakes now.

I know the power of secrets.

And I'm terribly afraid that our secret is going to destroy us.

Pretty Little Liars

The universe is completely unfair.

For four long, luxurious days this Southampton mansion had been my personal paradise. Here my body had been adored. My skin stroked. My blood had burned with a passion that had been building over seventeen long years. I'd been touched and kissed and worshipped by the man I've loved my entire life, and I'd relished the freedom to explore every inch of him in return. My lips on his strong jaw, his tight abs. My tongue tasting the sweetness of his skin and the saltiness of his cock.

We made love tenderly, then violently, then tenderly once more. We curled together in each other's arms. We watched late-night television with our legs twined, until the sensation of skin against skin overwhelmed us and we muted the drone of talk show hosts, and explored each other again in the flickering light of the television.

We swam naked in the pool during the day, then walked along the beach in the moonlight.

Those days had been a gift. A reward.

A decadent, sensual heaven.

But all that changed this morning, and now this mansion that I love has transformed into hell. A luxurious hell with cool ocean breezes, a wet bar, liveried waiters offering sushi and canapés, and the man I love fondling the ass of a pert blonde with tits that are going to pop right out of that barely there dress if she so much as sneezes.

Bitch.

And I'm not the only one mentally plotting Blondie Bitch's demise. On the contrary, I'm certain that every female in the vicinity would take her down in a heartbeat in order to take the twit's place at his side. *Dallas Sykes.* The infamous billionaire bad boy. The man known publicly as one of the two heirs to the Sykes family fortune, and who women all over the country reverently refer to as the King of Fuck.

The man I love.

The man I can have in private, but never in public.

The man who is my brother.

Well, fuck.

The bitch leans closer to him, and as her teeth tug at his earlobe, I turn away—there's only so much torment I can take—and make a beeline for the bar.

"Woodford Reserve," I say to the bartender. "Two ice cubes." I recall the way his hand cupped her rear. "Actually, let's make that a double."

"Sure thing, miss."

Beside me, a runway-thin model-type with at least four inches on me takes a sip of red wine. "The hard stuff, huh? Guess you're singing the same song I am."

I glance at her, confused. "I'm sorry?"

Her mouth curves up in a way that makes her cheekbones even more prominent. She looks like a fairy with her pale skin and short dark hair. A devious fairy, I amend, seeing the glint in her pale blue eyes. "The Ode to Dallas," she clarifies. "The siren's song to make him ditch the bimbo and come straight to you. Or, in my case, me."

"*Oh.* Oh, no." My cheeks burn, and right then I'd totally welcome a natural disaster. A sinkhole, perhaps. Or a tsunami blowing in off Shinnecock Bay. "Me? With Dallas? That's not even—"

I clamp my mouth shut before I get in a serious *the lady doth protest too much* situation. How the hell could I have been so obvious? Could she really see the lust in my eyes? Surely not? Surely I was more careful. Because I *have* to be careful. I've been careful my whole damn life.

Yes, but before you two weren't together. Now you are. At least when you're alone. But not here. Not in the world. Not where it matters.

Her smile is knowing. "Oh, come on. Don't tell me that you don't—*wait.*" She tilts her head, studying me, and as I watch, her eyes go wide, and she presses four long fingers over her blood-red lips. "Oh, shit. I'm sorry. I didn't—"

"Didn't what?"

"Didn't recognize you. You're Jane, right? You're his sister. God, that was totally lame of me." She drags her perfectly manicured fingers through her pixie-style hair. "I just saw you looking at him, and I assumed that you—anyway, never mind." She draws a deep breath and extends her hand. "I'm Fiona. Did I mention I'm an idiot?"

I can't help but laugh. "Honest mistake. Really. I was looking at him. But that was irritation you were seeing. Not lust." That, at least, is half true, and I allow myself one deep breath in relief. Crisis averted. Bullet dodged.

But I'd be lying if I didn't admit that some tiny, screwed-up part of me wishes that she'd called my bluff. That she'd felt the heat that burns in my veins for him—and that she'd figured it out.

Because as much as I love Dallas, I hate that we have to hide.

And some rebellious, hidden, bold, *stupid* part of me wishes that we could be open and out there and real.

We can't, though. I know we can't. The law and our parents and the threat of public humiliation keep us trapped firmly in the shadows. And, honestly, I've never been too fond of the spotlight, so the idea of having tabloid attention focused on me because I'm sleeping with my brother really doesn't sit well.

But it's not just family and privacy and social mores that are keeping us apart. There's Deliverance, too. Because as long as Dallas is Top Secret Vigilante Guy, everything in his life is going to remain hidden, including the man he truly is. A man so very different from the one he shows the public. A man that even I don't fully know or understand, because we haven't yet talked about how Deliverance operates or about its core mission to track—and presumably kill—the miserable excuses for human beings who kidnapped us both seventeen years ago.

"Hey," Fiona says, her forehead creasing as she peers at me. "You okay?"

"Fine." I force a smile, even though I feel like crying. Because for the first time it's fully hit me. *He's mine.* Dallas Sykes is absolutely, one hundred percent, totally mine.

And yet I can never truly have him.

Not in the way that counts. Not in the way that matters.

We're living a lie that is shiny and perfect and wonderful in the shadows, but that shrivels and dies in the harsh light of day.

I love him. I do.

And even though we promised each other that we would make this work, I can't help but fear that's a promise we never should have made. Because it's a promise that is impossible to keep.

It began with an unforgettable indecent proposal from Damien Stark...

...But only his passion could set Nikki Fairchild free.

The irresistible, erotic, emotionally charged Stark series.

Available now from

headline
ETERNAL

A wedding, a honeymoon, a Valentine's Day,
a trip to Vegas and a Christmas
Damien Stark-style means one thing...

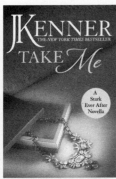
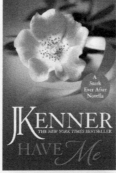

Happy Ever After is just the beginning...

The steamily seductive, dazzlingly romantic
Stark Ever After Novellas.

Available now from

Sylvia Brooks never lets anyone get too close.

 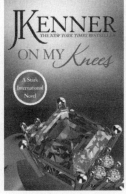 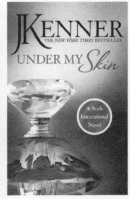

But Jackson Steele is the only man who's ever made her feel alive.

Return to the smoking hot Stark world with the explosive Stark International trilogy.

Available now from

headline
ETERNAL

headline
ETERNAL

FIND YOUR HEART'S DESIRE...

Three gorgeous, enigmatic and
powerful men...

...and the striking women who can bring
them to their knees.

Enthralling and sizzling hot, the Most Wanted series.

Available now from

headline
ETERNAL